Island in the Sea of Time

or,
Île dans la mer du temps
Остров в море времени

Ron Cogan

Note:
This is a novel and the events pertaining to characters are entirely fictional. However, the historical events of 2020-2022 taking place in the background are all real and depicted as accurately as possible.

Copyright © 2023 Ron Cogan
All rights reserved.
ISBN-13: 979-8396366022

Contents

I.	Pure Heroine	9
II.	"Wear a Mask"	17
III.	2020	21
IV.	Savannah	45
V.	Pandemia	59
VI.	Sweden	71
VII.	The Direction of Prayer	85
VIII.	Türkiye	93
IX.	South Beach	109
X.	Nadia	137
XI.	*Vita Nuova*	151
XII.	New York	171
XIII.	Time Does not Exist	185
XIV.	Zermatt	191
XV.	Δ	213
XVI.	Seven Seas	231
XVII.	Rome	245
XVIII.	Saint-Tropez to Baghdad	257
XIX.	Omicron	291
XX.	Nymphetamine	305

Appendix
- Map of Manhattan — 326
- Map of Miami — 327
- About the author — 328

4

"The epidemic of *cholera morbus*, whose first victims were struck down in the standing water of the market, had, in eleven weeks, been responsible for the greatest death toll in our history. Until that time the eminent dead were interred under the flagstones in the churches, in the exclusive vicinity of archbishops and capitulars, while the less wealthy were buried in the patios of convents. The poor were sent to the colonial cemetery, located on a windy hill that was separated from the city by a canal. After the first two weeks of the cholera epidemic, the cemetery was overflowing and there was no room left in the churches.

"By official decree Dr. M. A. Urbino personally designed and directed public health measures, but on his own initiative he intervened to such an extent in every social question that during the most critical moments of the plague no higher authority seemed to exist. Years later, reviewing the chronicle of those days, Dr. Juvenal Urbino confirmed that his father's methodology had been less than scientific and, in many ways contrary to reason, so that in large measure it has fostered the proliferation of the plague."

Gabriel García Márquez – *Love in the Time of Cholera*

I
PURE HEROINE

8

Chapter I – Pure Heroine

It was the happiest moment of my life. She turned to me on the bed, smiling, and opened her eyes. Nadia's blue eyes never ceased to amaze; they seemed to hold the promise of a world's possibilities. Her eyes were like a horizon of infinite thought responding to every vague and eternal dream in my soul. She wrapped her legs around mine – so that we lay more comfortably and intimately – purring with contented anticipation.

A breeze moving the balcony curtains signaled an impending rain front, which should cool down a bit the tropical heat, but the music faintly heard from the beach bar downstairs continued uninterrupted. The fluffy clouds, which had hung motionless in the azure the entire day, now appeared to be moving around and assembling, as if gearing up for battle. A warm rain began, which probably interrupted the people sitting outdoors at the beach bar, but these afternoon downpours never lasted long.

It was February 14, 2021, Miami Beach. We were unaware of this, but at this exact time savage blizzards of snow and ice were devastating the rest of the country. Cities from Seattle to Dallas were setting records for snowfall and cold. The deep freeze overwhelmed the Texas power grid, leaving five million people without electricity. In New York, where two feet of snow accumulated, people were sheltering inside, practically imprisoned, since even if they wanted to go somewhere, they couldn't – there was nowhere to go.

The leaders of the northeastern states once again prohibited restaurants, bars, and other venues from opening. It was the same in much of Europe, a winter of plague, fear, and lonely isolation. In Florida it was different. Originally I'm from Geneva, and I had been living in New York for 10 years, until the start of this winter, when I realized that it would be essential to escape to Miami to avoid the disaster in the north.

Distracted, we failed to notice at which point the rain stopped. The setting sun was already illuminating the palm trees visible on the 1 Hotel rooftop directly opposite the balcony, and encrimsoning the clouds as they sounded their retreat eastward away from the sun. Most days in the winter though, the sun prevailed entirely, and scorched the sky unobstructed by clouds.

Consciousness of place came ebbing back to me slowly. Contemplating things at a later time, my feeling persisted in how surreal everything with Nadia is, impossible to believe because it is too good. In this actual moment however, the feeling is much stronger than that – it can only be described as transcendentalism, which means being totally removed from the world, from space, from time, and from identity, dissolved in the infinite, together with her. The feeling was that nothing else existed, or could possibly exist, except our connection.

When one feels a connection such as this, different from any other one has ever experienced, the degree of unreality is such that it actually leaves one stunned that such experiences are possible in life – how abruptly it startles us out of rudimentary existence and causes us to view with apathy all those other sensations and emotions of a lifetime, all those other passions and feelings throughout our past illusory life, in short everything from before this moment, that we, in our ignorance and our naïvety, have previously thought exceptional.

For the first time I understood the writings of Auguste Villiers de l'Isle-Adam, who reasoned that the best time to end one's life is not at life's lowest point, but at it's highest. Because after living through life's highest point, everything else will be lesser in comparison. The difficulty is that nobody ever knows that this has been the highest point and nothing in the rest of one's life will be as good. Something made me feel that this was that moment and that is the only rationale I can come up with as to why I suddenly began to feel a pleasant and carefree indifference to dying.

When does one *not* want to die? One clings to and struggles to prolong one's life at the times when one has hopes, goals, and plans. But what goals or plans could I have?? – Everything has happened just now... It was liberating.

*   *   *

I traced my hand along her soft, darkly tanned, tattooed skin, moist from the heat, and we continued to kiss. At any moment Chiara, the other girl who lived with us, might come in. All three of us were refugees here in Miami.

We were refugees from the destructive and bizarre restrictions imposed in New York that made the city into a veritable warzone under siege, locked down and frozen, practically impossible to survive in. We were similar to the refugees from the Nazi occupation of Paris in 1940 who hurriedly threw together the most essential belongings in one suitcase and fled south to the Côte d'Azur, not knowing when they would return to the city. However, Otto von Stülpnagel, Hitler's viceroy in Paris, did not shut down nightlife to the degree that Governor Cuomo did in New York. Here in Miami, in stark contrast, there was freedom. Nightclubs like Mynt were packed so full of revelers it would have been a hazard even in normal times.

At the start of the winter whenever I looked at BBC or Al Jazeera, they revealed a fresh set of restrictions being imposed somewhere, in London or Madrid or Los Angeles. At this point I would only turn on the news out of *schadenfreude*. Normally this is not a wholesome feeling – to get enjoyment from others' suffering – but I felt it was justified in this case because these people brought it upon themselves. Why did they submit? Why didn't they rebel? Did they forget the Beastie Boys' song "Fight for your right"?

Apparently these people actually believed the propaganda. I have to admit I also felt *schadenfreude* when I looked at the weather report for New York. This was because the worse the weather and conditions there became, the higher the relative value of my relocation was. (New York also has constant wind in the winter, a wind so poisonously cold it defies belief). Being able to work remotely on my computer, I had started planning an escape from New York as early as September 2020. By the time it was December and the anticipated Winter Shutdown was imposed, anyone who wanted to get to South Beach was unable to find apartments.

This was the case with Chiara, an Italian girl with beautiful long blonde hair that contrasted elegantly with dark eyebrows. I met her in July 2020 in New York. She came to Miami briefly, with only a small suitcase, and stayed at a hotel. While she was down here the shutdown was imposed. She felt such distaste to go back into a city of Arctic cold, where every person you saw around you was bizarrely muzzled with a face covering (and prodded you to muzzle yourself as well) – even if going back just briefly to collect more clothes – that she kept prolonging her return until she ended up remaining in Miami 4 months.

After the initial hotel, she stayed with her friend Nadia, who was an even more beautiful Syrian girl. I exaggerate when I say we were 'refugees' from New York. I shouldn't forget that she was an actual refugee from the Syrian Civil War.

Nadia did not have her own apartment yet in Miami. She had come from New York to South Beach in October to stay at someone's place that was vacant only until the end of January. She and Chiara couldn't stay there past that time. Meanwhile, prices for hotels or short-term rentals in South Beach were astronomical, and going back to New York was not a viable option because of the ongoing disaster there. Both girls were going to be homeless once they lost that apartment.

At this point I had briefly met Nadia only twice at some gatherings in South Beach, stunned by her beauty as soon as I saw her the first time. Then in the middle of January I got a call from her asking if she and Chiara could temporarily stay with me. Chiara knew that I had a good apartment in a good location, and suggested to Nadia that she ask me.

It was supposed to be, she said, for 4 days or so. It ended up being a month. When people asked me later how the two of us met, I said, "We met in my apartment in Miami. She and another girl ended up staying there, and that's where we became acquainted."

At the time I was happy as everything was so new and surreal, and I wasn't even sure what to expect. It was only later, as time passed and I foolishly started having greater expectations in this relationship, that misfortune occurred.

II
"WEAR A MASK"

II – "Wear a Mask"

Not since Muhammad emerged from the Cave of Hira with the divine revelation of the Quran was there such a massive spread of a new religious movement across the world. Adherence to corona belief had characteristics similar to the dogma of a religion, with all its idealistic ritual. Faster than the spread of the virus itself was the contagious spread of this mental affliction, as a result of which people who were totally normal before, began practicing religious beliefs and rituals that had no practical meaning whatsoever. Such as wearing facemasks outdoors.

A friend in Tehran, Niloofar, sadly reported to me, "Now we have to wear *double hijab*. We have to cover both our hair and our mouth."

Like the Persian hijab, the facemask became an essential garb for the new corona religion: a piece of cloth whose only purpose was that it was mandated by religion. A lack of adequate maskage brought about public consternation like an improper hijab in Iran.

Sometimes the hijab slips, uncovering more than 4 inches of hair: it's *improper hijab*. Sometimes the facemask slips down, uncovering someone's nose: improper hijab. A loosely-tied bandana around one's neck and chin? The person is obviously a scoundrel making no effort to maintain proper hijab.

Like a religion, it is impossible to use arguments, statistics, or logic to convince a believer the other way. The world became divided into corona believers and unbelievers.

In the same way as believers in Muhammad were shocked that some people stubbornly refused the believe the new faith, many corona believers were incredulous and even enraged that anyone would question elements of their faith and disrespect public opinion. They even called their irrational faith "science".

The unbelievers didn't deny the existence of the virus SARS CoV-2 of course. But they denied that the measures taken against it were necessary or beneficial.

III
2020

III – 2020

After that last chapter, I lost half of my readers. So if (and I'm being optimistic here) there were a total of maybe twenty who picked up this book, there must be only perhaps ten left. But of course, indifference to what may or may not appeal to the general public is essential for an author, since writers write for themselves and not for their readers.

As when other years begin, at the start of 2020 I had no idea what the year would bring, aside from the trips I had already planned for January and February. I liked the symmetry and æsthetics of the numbers 2020 and I resolved to take initiative do more interesting things so that the year would be memorable.

But I could not anticipate the many ways in which the corona pandemic would radically improve my life. Never before had I traveled so much, and met so many people, as in 2020. For some people, whose travel and socializing happened to be reduced in the year, this may seem counterintuitive, but actually the reasons why this happened are logical.

I have heard many people reminisce about "quarantines", staying inside for long periods, a lack of travel, "social distancing", "Zoom calls", and lots of long-term mask wearing, even into late 2021. I was lucky never to have experienced any of these things. Part of the luck is being a citizen of two (relatively) free countries: United States and Switzerland. If I had the misfortune of living in say, Melbourne, under the dictatorship of medical fascists, it would have been quite difficult to escape and to live a normal life in these times.

I never took any vaccines, and never took a corona PCR test. Despite this I crossed international borders dozens of times. Every single time these documents were required to cross a border I showed tests or vaccines that I fabricated myself. It simplified life a great deal to do it this way. I never wore a mask, except on extremely rare occasions. Most (but not all) airplanes required it, and occasionally at certain periods of time a store, museum, or some place did as well. Sometimes a bandana around my neck and chin sufficed. I was very lucky that "mask Nazis", the enforcers of mask requirements, were not more ubiquitous around me in life, because I can barely overcome the discomfort of having a muzzle on my face for more than five minutes.

In January and February 2020 I had time to achieve two trips: one was to Medellín, where I rented a BMW motorcycle and explored the Andes mountains and the favellas around the city. The other was to India, Nepal, Oman, and Saudi Arabia. Word was already out about a major epidemic of a new type of SARS in China. In Indian and Nepalese airports, travelers from China and a few countries adjacent to it were being funneled into separate queues, where they would undergo some kind of screening.

In India I started with the legendary nightlife of Delhi and the refined architecture of Jaipur. Whenever I saw a tour group of Chinese appearance, such as the many walking around the Taj Mahal in Agra, I would wonder to myself, "Are they from China and might be spreading the virus? Or just from Singapore or Taiwan?" In any Chinatown I felt uncomfortable, as in the one in

Kathmandu, since anyone there might have recently come from China.

Kathmandu was a city of surprising density and size – pleasantly chaotic. I made a pilgrimage to the colossal Buddha Stupa, with the eyes of Buddha painted on the stupa's tower. From Kathmandu I flew to Lukla, the so-called 'most dangerous airport in the world', due to the runway's location on a short, inclined slope on the edge of a cliff in the Himalayas, and the always unpredictable weather. From there I took a helicopter higher still into the snowy Himalayas, above 5000 meters, to do some hiking in the vicinity of Everest.

I next flew to Muscat – a change of scenery from the highest mountains to the coast of the Arabian Sea. It was the only direct connection from Nepal on the way to Jeddah, further west across the desert. By the time I was in Saudia, the virus had spread to Iran and Italy. An Italian epidemiologist was being interviewed on BBC: "We are not concerned about this outbreak. It is being contained in several small communes in northern Italy and we have established a *cordon sanitaire* around them. As of now there have been only 7 fatalities. We believe this will be kept under control."

* * *

When I got back to New York in early March 2020, I happened to meet a Turkish girl, Zeynep, a girl with considerable personal attractions and a very hourglass figure. We had a few dates and kissed. In the meantime, Italy saw that things were not under control at all. Italy took the unprecedented step of a nationwide lockdown on March 9. The New York Stock Exchange crashed. Things happened fast from here on. Due to the large amount of daily travel between Milan and every city in Europe and New York, the virus was obviously now worldwide.

I met Zeynep on March 12 and everything was fine. She looked alluring in a fur coat and high-heel tall gray suede boots. She came to my office which was full of people, business as usual, and we went for lunch. We did not mention one word about the spreading epidemic in our conversation. I was really looking forward to the next day, Friday, March 13, when we were supposed to have another date, going to the new Edge observation deck on the 100th floor at Hudson Yards and then a restaurant. But on the morning of March 13 the Governor of New York decided that all public spaces need to be closed, which included the Hudson Yards tower. I told Zeynep we could skip the tower and instead just go to the restaurant. She said no.

I asked, "Why not?"

"I'm scared."

"Of what? This is nothing. It's not worse than a flu."

It happened to be fantastic weather for March and it was a Friday and I wanted to go out. I asked many of my friends if they wanted to go to a rooftop bar or something. I still had not had the chance to see anyone and tell them stories from my trip to India. But everyone said no.

I told them, "There are 25 cases of this flu in Manhattan out of a population of 2 million. Even if the actual number is more, it's not like the plague but a flu."

They were afraid.

I went back to Zeynep, "I'm trying to go out and take advantage of this beautiful weather. I asked some friends – nobody wants to go. Can you come and we'll go to a rooftop bar in LES?"

She refused – even though she saw me yesterday. "I really can't. This is a serious thing."

"But what changed since yesterday? What do you know now that you didn't?" For some reason today everything was different.

I felt betrayed. I felt that out of all the people I knew in New York, she was the one who really shouldn't have left me. If I hadn't been nonsensically abandoned at this point, maybe I wouldn't have needed to travel around America and Europe all the coming months, looking for places where there were people to escape the solitude.

I went to the CitizenM hotel rooftop bar. Oddly, they said they were closed due to safety concerns. Why? Next I tried Mr. Purple, the rooftop bar at Indigo Hotel in the Lower East Side. This is one of the best rooftops in New York and they earned my respect as being the last to close and the first to reopen. They had an active scene there tonight. I met a few young college age people who, like me, were relishing their wisdom of going out and partying while others were being cowards.

A spirit of contradiction has always, in some sense, guided my thoughts.

Not trusting the media, I did my own analysis of the data, as well as studying virology, epidemiology, and the history of pandemics. It became immediately obvious that a true case fatality rate cannot be determined. (The percentage of cases who do not recover). The data coming in from different places pointed to entirely different rates. Differing demographics was one factor. Even more important was the inability to determine the true number of cases. This was due to the mildness of the virus. It was known that the virus was *so mild*, huge numbers of asymptomatic or unreported cases were out there. This would obviously have a significant impact on the case fatality rate.

China reported a very high rate, apparently reporting the percentage of deaths among a small number of severe cases, not among *all* infections. I decided that, logically, the lowest case fatality rate of all the sample places should be used, since (adjusted for demographics) the lowest rate is probably lower for the reason that it is counting the true number of cases most accurately.

The WHO and the rest of the world went the opposite way, using the very high Chinese rate in their models and projections, rendering their models meaningless. The panic and demand for lockdowns came from these numbers, even after these numbers came to be proven incorrect later.

(For the sake of simplicity, when I mention China in this book I am referring to the People's Republic of China, i.e. the statist dictatorship. For the island, the Republic of China, I use the name Taiwan).

I decided at the time that corona would probably just be in a similar ballpark as bad flu pandemics like the 1958 Asian flu and 1968 Hong Kong flu. 1969, if you recall, was when Woodstock took place in upstate New York, and nobody thought to cancel it due to the Hong Kong flu going around.

Can you imagine, when asking one's grandparents whether they too saw Hendrix or Jefferson Airplane at Woodstock that they would say, "No, I made sure not to go to that, I didn't even leave the house."

"Why?"

"Because of germs. There was something going around that year!"

Coronavirus had one major advantage over influenza: it was already clearly established that children were completely unaffected by it. And that *almost all* deaths involved old age or underlying factors like heart disease, diabetes, obesity, and immune problems. The data from Italy and New York showed that the chance of a young person without underlying health factors to not recover from corona was less than one in a million. One in a million means, if this book was three times as long, and out of all that text one letter or symbol was selected at random, the chance that it would be this particular omega: Ω

So as long as you weren't ill and didn't live at home with very old people, why would you care about corona?

Any more than you cared about other risks like the flu, or a train derailment, or a *wild boar* attack in the forest?

Whenever I mentioned this to a corona believer, the response was invariably that they knew about one instance, an acquaintance of an acquaintance, or someone they read about in the news, who was young and in great health, and died. That is unfortunate, but it is also known that, according to Alexander Dumas in *La Reine Margot*, a wild boar almost killed King Charles IX of France in 1574. Even great kings are at risk of boar attacks, so why aren't we concerned about boars as well?

Greek mythology is full of dangerous boars. Ovid writes of a great boar sent by Artemis to ravage the region of Calydon in Aetolia. The rampage of the boar ended up destroying vineyards, killing many people, and forcing villagers to take refuge inside the city walls of Calydon.

Terrible as this story is, to me corona was not a whole lot more dangerous of a threat than the return of the Calydonian boar.

I was working in risk management in an insurance company, where I picked up some basic knowledge of econometrics. Earlier, I authored a paper comparing cat bonds vs reinsurance in dealing with Florida hurricane risk. (A cat bond is not a bond that pays interest in cats, but is short for catastrophe bond). And another paper suggesting that pension funds hedge their longevity risk by selling life insurance policies and offset their interest rate risk by acquiring more high-duration assets in their investments.

A spirit of contradiction is consistent with a job in risk. People are always coming to you with proposals for business ventures that seem to be extremely lucrative and worth doing. It's necessary to question everything they say, be skeptical about every assumption, and start by disagreeing. Likewise I was skeptical about everything the media and politicians said about corona. Much of it didn't make sense.

At that time, my best friend in the New York area was a Russian, called Vadim Mikhailovich. The interesting thing about this new corona belief religion was that it was impossible to tell from a person's past that they would succumb to the faith. Extremely like-minded on politics before, on this issue, he came to acquire views diametrically opposed to mine. Upon learning of the spread of coronavirus in the US, he secluded himself in his New Jersey apartment and did not emerge outdoors for 3 months.

He was inside for 3 months.

His belief in the danger of the virus was so extreme, he stayed inside for so long despite not having a washing machine. He would fill his bathtub with detergent and wash his clothes and bedsheets there, stirring them with a stick. I don't know how he achieved drying the wet laundry after this.

Vadim believed in the necessity of a lockdown here similar to Italy. He would prod me, "It's going to happen soon. You won't be allowed to go outside."

The thought filled him with glee. He wanted everyone to be confined in the same way that he was confining himself. I, on the other hand, was in terror from the thought of an Italian-style lockdown. I said, "There's no way that will happen here."

In case things did get bad, I made sure to go out extra hard on the weekend. Maybe it would be my last time. I ended up at Flying Cock, a crowded college bar in Murray Hill not far from me. (I live on 21st and Park). I stayed there drinking and dancing with people till it closed.

On the morning of March 16 came the announcement that all restaurants and bars would have to close in New York. This was a shock. Even Vadim was predicting that this wouldn't happen for another week maybe. I came to the office that day, seeing fewer people than usual. The St. Patrick's Day parade on March 17 was canceled. I came that day to the office as well and there was almost no one. I complained to the remaining people, "If the economy shuts down like this for two months it will be destroyed. There will be a spiraling debt crisis, or massive inflation. The consequences of a shutdown like this will be worse than the virus itself." They agreed with me.

At the time everyone thought these measures would only need to persist for around two months, after which everything will be over. I have many acquaintances worldwide, from Oaxaca to Osaka, and I got the situation directly from many of them: in Western Europe, Colombia, Mexico, South Africa, Qatar, Beirut, Delhi, and Sydney everything was closed. For now, Jakarta, Kathmandu, Istanbul, Tehran, Riga, Russia, and Brazil were still holding on, but they would shut down very soon. The exception to the rule were Tokyo, Taipei, Stockholm, and Minsk. They were resisting the trend and would remain mostly open.

David Lin, the Taiwanese ambassador in London, warned that the Chinese communist propaganda machine is trying to convince the world that its draconian response to corona is the only possible way. He was ignored, as more and more countries in Europe enforced a lockdown.

But there were extremely important differences between the lockdowns in all these places and the shutdown in New York. In New York, restaurants, bars, and other public places were not allowed to function. Otherwise there were no rules being imposed on individuals. The tradition of individual rights and framework of laws in the US does not allow for this. The US is (at least in theory) a rule of law, not a rule of the democratic mob and their whims.

It was the same in Japan and Switzerland, whose constitutions are based on the American one. A professor of Japanese constitutional law stated in April, "Only requests and instructions can be issued to citizens, not orders; they can't be forced to comply."

But most countries' governments, from tyrannical democracies to sultanates and monarchies, did whatever they wanted, without the slightest regard for things like individual rights, constitutions, and process of law.

As a result, one heard about frightful things happening worldwide, the biggest global event of misery since World War II. And all self-imposed.

South Africa banned alcohol, apparently in an effort to get people to have less fun. The president, Cyril Ramaphosa, was shocked that anyone would want to have fun in the throes of such a grave threat to the country: "In the midst of our national effort to fight against this virus there are unfortunately a number of people who have taken to organizing parties, who have drinking sprees..."

Colombia had a more creative strategy to get people to stop socializing: in the capital Bogotá only women were allowed outside on odd numbered days and only men allowed on even numbered days. The same idea was also enforced in Panama. Naturally since the main reason people wanted to go outside was to see someone of the opposite gender, this effectively stopped most of the fun. However, lesbians and gays were unaffected by this and couples could continue to meet up. There was a rise in the number of men dressing as women in order to be able to go out on a women's day.

Some countries enforced a nighttime curfew. Some chose a weekend curfew, meaning you couldn't even go to buy food if you ran out over the weekend. Some, like Jordan and Lebanon went all-in and copied the China template of a 24hr curfew every day. Nobody allowed outside at any time, even to buy food. The Jordanian army was mobilized to enforce the ban of people leaving their home. But this quickly failed as, unlike in China with its armies of hazmat-suited workers, there were not enough people to supply everyone with food. These kind of imprisonment-lockdowns continued in many Chinese cities at various times for years ahead.

In India the police came armed with heavy sticks to beat down crowds that were not "social distancing". In South America and Europe thousands of heavy fines were given out to people for a variety of reasons, such as shopping in a grocery store that was not actually the closest one to one's home.

In London gatherings of more than two people were forbidden.

In Spain people would "rent" a dog for a short while because they wanted to be outside in the fresh air and dog-walking was an allowable reason. But children were not allowed outside at all in Spain for months. In some countries, dog-walking wasn't allowed and people were forced to have their dog perform its business inside.

There was no limit to the absurdity. (And some of these measures came back with every subsequent wave, even late into 2021).

In New York one had freedom of movement. You could go to a friend's house, walk in Central Park, take the subway, go to the company office if you wanted, or drive or fly to another city.

I was bristling just at the loss of restaurants; I don't know what I would have done if I was living at this time in Paris (where I had lived before about ten years ago). Maybe I would be going out protesting, building barricades on the streets, getting arrested. Unfortunately I would be the only one protesting. Everyone was believing in the propaganda and meekly complying by sitting at home. This is odd, since Parisians have a rich history of revolts and insurrections – every few years during the 19th century they were building barricades on the streets and demanding change in the government. From monarchy to republic to empire to monarchy to republic, etc.

In 2018 and 2019 there were enormous *Gilets jaunes* (yellow vest) protests in Paris, with hundreds of thousands of people causing chaos and burning cars. A group barricaded themselves around the Arc de Triomphe, met by police with water cannon trucks and tear gas grenades.

Then, instead of continuing into 2020, they obeyed the health restrictions and went home.

In Beirut in late 2019 and early 2020 there were even more serious protests against the government. Half the city was out on the streets, refusing to back down unless the government resigned. Lebanese protestors are truly tough and stubborn fighters, having lived through 3 decades of civil wars. All it took to disperse these protesters was one word: *corona*. Everyone believed and meekly went home without the slightest disagreement. The streets became empty.

In late March only the weather determined if I would stay inside or not. Rain or excessive cold would make me stay in. Any day of decent weather I was exploring the island, seeing what was going on. Manhattan was a great place to be during this epidemic. It was only islanders on the island, only people who lived there. No tourists or commuters from the metro area.

I got around by biking or walking, rarely taking the subway because at this point it was operating on a limited schedule, with only half or less of the number of trains. But when I did, on two occasions I saw a person in a full hazmat suit riding the train. A hazmat suit! What did they think this was – Chernobyl? I never even once wore a facemask on the subway throughout the entire pandemic.

Taking over after Milan, New York was the world's biggest epicenter of coronavirus at this time. The global media portrayed the situation in the city as dire. Apparently people were dying so fast there was no room for the bodies. Relatives in Geneva asked me, "Is it true there are body bags on the streets? The news said that Central Park was transformed into a morgue?"

"No, nothing like that is happening. I was in Central Park today. The park is 800 meters across and 4 kilometers long. There's nothing you can see that's different. I think there might be a small tent in one corner of the park that is being used as a temporary hospital or something."

What the media portrayed to them, as well as to all the friends who couldn't meet me the weekend of March 13, I do not know. But they all seemed to think that Manhattan was in a medieval plague as in a Hermann Hesse novel, with piles of the deceased being thrown on horse carts parked at every door.

The actual data, assuming it was accurate, was that 500 people died every day in New York at the peak of the epidemic here. This was a greater excess than anywhere else in the world, since it was 3 times higher than the normal amount of deaths per day in the city, which is 170. But not an overwhelming amount for a city of 9 million. (19 million in the metro area). And 99.2% of the New York corona deaths had an underlying health condition.

Acquaintances worldwide were surprised at the level of freedom in New York (the world's biggest epicenter). They were all in a place that was not even close to being such a center of contagion – some cities had only a dozen cases so far – and yet they had far less freedom.

By the end of March, almost everyone now worldwide (except Japan, Taiwan, Sweden, and Belarus) was sitting at home. And many of them were incessantly complaining about how bored they were. I thought: even if you are unfortunately confined at home by medical fascists, where are your books? Why don't you read and write?

I quickly discovered Shake Shack in Madison Park. It's hard to believe but in late March 2020 the epicenter of nightlife in Manhattan was this burger shack in Madison Park. They had beer and wine and burgers. You could stand near the shack drinking or sit at one of the numerous benches in the park. By mid-April, when magnolias and sakuras were blooming, the weather was getting warmer, and it was becoming pleasant to sit in Washington Park as well. This became another epicenter of gatherings. People brought their own alcohol to Washington Park, or it was possible to buy cocktails in Tio Pepe, a Mexican taco stand a few blocks west in the West Village. It was mostly NYU students in the park. Why should they care about corona? The worst that could happen to them was a mild cold. For their demographic, the CDC calculated their recovery rate, upon catching corona, to be 99.997%. Skateboarders were still sitting around the fountain passing around marijuana joints. Other groups were sitting on the grass drinking beer or champagne, shooting corks up in the air as they opened a bottle. (One sensible change that occurred in 2020 was that for the first time drinking alcohol outdoors was allowed in New York. Before, it was prohibited).

As far as I know from my observations, on the island of Manhattan with a population of 2 million, there were only two outdoor bars open for business: Madison Park Shake Shack and Tio Pepe.

That's 1 million people per bar. (A million people would exceed the capacity of 21 Yankee stadiums). If there's only one bar for a million people one would think it would be overwhelmed by customers. If only a tenth of 1% of that million came at a given time, that would a thousand people.

It was never even close to that. The biggest queue I ever saw was around 10 people for each place, but not more. What this means is that the vast majority of those 2 million people stayed home. For what reason, how and by whom they were convinced to do this – I do not know.

Getting a cocktail at Tio Pepe reminded me of the Florentine wine windows that functioned during the Renaissance. Wine merchants in Florence continued doing business during plague epidemics by selling out of small windows while avoiding physical contact with customers.

My apartment building has a rooftop with tables and chairs and during warm weather it would have been a fantastic place to have gatherings, if people were willing to come. But Zeynep, Vadim, and other friends – I lost all of them in this pandemic. They drank the kool-aid and vanished. I needed them more than they needed me. Some of them were recently married couples, happy to be left isolated by themselves, with no desire to see anyone else. They told me to bother off and deal with it. "Find a hobby." Some friends I lost permanently because they couldn't cope with me being outside the faith.

The predominance of desolation in nearly all periods of my life has been traumatic, from my youth in Switzerland to the current day. I have never lived with anyone besides family, and very rarely was able to travel or ski with a friend. I love exploring mountains and forests but actually there were a total of zero occasions when I was able to go hiking with a friend, other than just walking in the immediate vicinity of the Alpine village where my summer house was.

It is in the deepness of nature, when removed miles from the nearest person, surrounded by sublimity of cliffs, waterfalls, and noble ancient trees, that the sad oppression and desolation is most felt. Despite this, I have to go – the forest draws me in and I have to see and experience these sights and environments even though I go alone.

I prefer hiking in mountains within the range of a city, like Innsbruck, Hong Kong, or Cape Town, where one can descend to the presence of crowds of people that same evening, or maybe even meet someone interesting on the trail.

Traveling alone, I try to only go to cities. My biggest fear when traveling is to end up in a remote place without people where total quiet and darkness falls after 10:00PM. This happened, for instance, when I took a side trip from Buenos Aires to Punta del Este in Uruguay. I heard it was a fashionable, very lively coastal resort town. But it is only crowded at certain specific periods and was deserted now. I couldn't wait to get back to the city.

Sometimes, when the weather is bad and I am working on something, like a book or travel plans, I could be content to stay at home for three days straight and talk to no one. But not any more days than that. When the shutdown of life in New York began, the sudden desolation was perturbing. I would go to Shake Shack in Madison Park, not only for fresh air outdoors, but also to satisfy my need to visually see people. I would get comfort just from seeing crowds around me, standing drinking cups of beer and wine, even if I didn't talk with anyone.

Despite the lack of people, it was overall a pleasant time to be on Manhattan Island. The streets were free of cars and it was fun to take an electric Citibike and ride around. I would often ride down to Washington Park, drink there, then walk up to Madison Park, drink more or have a shack burger. The Shack was one of the only places to go out for food.

Meanwhile, I read comments of people lashing out angrily against people not "quarantining" for extensive periods. According to them, people like me were "selfishly endangering society" while staying home is "sacrificing for the collective good". Actually the contagious nature of corona makes it impossible to contain so the most effective and prudent thing to do would have been to isolate and protect old people, especially in nursing homes, while promoting contagion and herd immunity among young people. In my many arguments with Vadim, I wrote that the hardships of quarantining everyone is actually the more dangerous option in the long-term, as people would remain without exposure to the new virus and waves would continue for years later.

Vadim disagreed. He wanted the harshest Chinese measures to be introduced here and worldwide. "If the whole world just stopped being selfish and stayed home for 3 weeks this would be over at once." Actually this was a completely false assumption. In fact, 3 years after corona first occurred, draconian measures to contain it were still continuing in China.

* * *

In the middle of May, people discovered masks.

Apparently based on the instruction of some medical fascists in the government, people in New York became convinced that masks will save the world and they immediately adopted the practice, like a herd of conformists. Many people are always looking for some cult of conformity. During the peak of the epidemic in mid-April, and into the first days of May, there were practically zero masks on the streets of New York. Then by May 10, suddenly, around 95% of people were wearing a mask outdoors.

Anyone with a basic understanding of contagious respiratory diseases will know that the slightest breeze immediately dissipates viral material from a person's breath. A person's immune system functions to eliminate viruses and bacteria, unless there are so many of them that the immune system is overwhelmed. The only way there can be many of them is from prolonged exposure. A person has to sit next to a person indoors, in still air, for 15-20 minutes, to gain enough exposure to viral matter to risk infection. In the case of corona, it was a novel virus which few people have natural immunity to. So the ease of an infection is much greater than with common cold or other existing viruses, but still, there must be prolonged exposure, and that exposure is practically impossible outdoors, inhaling a single particle of corona.

So why masks outdoors? It was not enforced; it was voluntary. How did 95% of people suddenly start doing the same thing voluntarily?

Some people were riding a bike wearing one. Some were driving a car, alone, wearing one. Was this for æsthetic purposes or did they also keep it on while they were alone at home?

I don't watch American news and didn't get the memo that everyone apparently received. But not all of them watch the news either. How did this religious belief spread so rapidly? The missionaries spreading belief in Jesus or Muhammad never in their wildest successes had such an instant conversion rate as this. Was the word spread through friends and acquaintances? How exactly did it happen? Perhaps they would encounter someone and ask, "Why are you wearing a facemask now? Does it help?"

The other would mumble through the mask, "Yes, *gesundheitführer* #1 said we should all do it."

"Oh, *gesundheitführer* #1 said that?... That's very significant, that it came from him. Well, I'll do it too. I'll keep it on forever, until I get the word from him that I can take it off."

It reminded me of *Rhinocéros*, Eugène Ionesco's 1959 allegory of conformity, where every character turns into a rhinoceros by the end of the play. Over time, even the individualists who initially resisted, couldn't bear anymore the fact that they, still looking like human beings, were becoming more and more in the minority, in the abnormal fringe, and finally they too turned into rhinoceroses.

The motivations of mask-lovers, as I learned later, were complex. It did not have to do with safety only. They put up with the massive discomfort for months and years also for symbolic reasons, to show that they are loyal members of the faith. Many religions have unique clothing to demonstrate one's belief, from yarmulkas to turbans, and this was no different.

Some stores were already beginning to demand masks for everyone. I was avoiding those stores of course. Viruses like flu and corona are spread by aerosols, which are not filtered by a facemask. They can only be filtered by an air filtration system. Dr. Anthony Fauci, director of the National Institute of Allergy and Infectious Diseases, explained this in February 2020, "The typical mask is not really effective in keeping out a virus, which is small enough to pass through the material. It might, however, provide some slight benefit in keeping out gross droplets if someone coughs or sneezes on you."

So the alternative to a masks, was just to not cough or sneeze on people. The demands of the goons in the stores was additionally insulting to me because it felt like they were saying they don't believe that I am capable of keeping myself from coughing and sneezing on everyone – therefore I need to be muzzled like a camel to ensure that. I know that some people do, but I've never coughed or sneezed on anyone, not just in 2020 but all the years before that. So I don't want to be treated like a camel.

Furthermore, I knew that the mask was detrimental to one's own health. Being touched and adjusted all day, the mask immediately became unhygienic. Rather than breathing fresh air, one has to press this bacteria-filled object against one's mouth and try to breathe through it instead. And the reason for the mask Nazis enforcing something detrimental to your own health? Just to muzzle you against coughing and sneezing on other people. In addition to the physical discomfort, it was also degrading to have to comply with the goons' demands.

In Scotland, police were ordered to shave their beards so that facemasks could lie more closely on their face, reminiscent of Tsar Peter of Russia ordering the boyars to shave their beards or pay a beard tax of 100 rubles. This actually made some sense, since if you have to wear a mask, to do it with a full, voluminous beard looks truly ridiculous.

While people in most parts of the world started, from around this point, to be subjected to onerous maskage requirements, in some countries just indoors, in some countries outdoors as well, I was lucky to be relatively free of this atrocious obligation. My company is in a large office building, but on the occasional times I went there, neither the staff in the lobby nor my fellow colleagues on my floor sought to ask for masks. I live in a doorman building on Park Avenue, but the doormen were all sensible guys from Serbia who hated the masks that they were forced to wear so there was no problem there either. New York never enforced masks on the subway or other public places, so I was free to be the one person out of a hundred walking around normally.

IV
SAVANNAH

IV – Savannah

It was becoming evident that a reopening of restaurants and bars would take much longer than anticipated. At first I thought April 30, then perhaps May 15, which would be the two month mark. Or end of May, by the time of the Memorial Day long weekend. But no.

Bill de Blasio, the mayor of New York, said that a true reopening remains "a few months away at minimum." I reasoned that De Blasio, a communist, would naturally be more reluctant to reopen, but Governor Cuomo, who is slightly less radical, might permit it earlier. In any case, now it became completely *unknown and interminable*. It was only subject to the uncontested will of the medical fascists in charge, not to anything else. I was getting bored of Madison, Washington, and Central parks already. I started becoming agitated to try to escape the city.

But where? Most of the world was in the same predicament. I did not want to go to a remote location like a forest somewhere. I already had that in Central Park if I wanted nature. I wanted to go somewhere I could find myself immersed in the greatest number of people and to be able to socialize and enjoy nightlife. The benefit from this, in my estimation, was far greater than the drawback of potentially catching corona. A beacon of light this whole time was Sweden. I became absorbed in plans to try to get there.

Although most of the world canceled all their flights, there were still exceptions and important business made it necessary for New York to continue daily flights this whole time to several cities in Europe, viz. London, Paris,

Frankfurt, Zürich. Unfortunately, a flight to Stockholm connecting through one of these cities was, at this time, astronomically expensive. There were inexpensive flights seemingly available through Reykjavik. However, when I called Icelandair, I found out that although they are still on the schedule, each flight is being canceled one week in advance and likely all the flights in the near future will also be canceled.

For the time being I abandoned schemes to get to Stockholm but I looked around at the rest of the 50 states. Not all states were being run by socialists or fascists. I soon learned that Georgia became the most progressive state at reopening. South Carolina was not far behind.

Over the next year I would continuously be seeking out the most free and open places worldwide that I could get to. April and October were the only months in 2020 I did not travel. (And 2021 was similar).

As soon as I found out that Georgia has reopened restaurants and bars in mid-May I bought a ticket to Savannah.

The bridges and tunnels, and the multilane highways throughout the metropolis and on the way to the airport were empty. One could speed to JFK in a record 20 minutes from midtown, regardless if it was during peak rush hour or not. Almost nobody was driving across town.

I took a picture at the airport, surrounded by people, with planes visible in the background and, since I had heard from some friends that all air traffic entirely in their particular countries was suspended, sent them this evidence of the freedom that existed in the States.

Interestingly, this was so early that mask mandates had not made their way to the airlines yet. On the flight from New York to Savannah, no masks were required. This would be the last time until April 2022. The people I talked to on the plane were all traveling for important business that can't be delayed. Nobody was traveling for fun. However, once in Savannah I saw that there were a lot of tourists who arrived there by car from nearby states.

The freedom of reopened Savannah was a breath of fresh air compared to New York. There were no masks concealing the faces of the pretty girls on the streets. Savannah, being in the deep south, is sultry. With its antebellum and Victorian houses and mammoth oaks drenched with Spanish moss, it is one of the most gracious and elegant American cities. If the character of a town can be feminine, this is it.

I got a haircut for the first time since March. More importantly, I was able to have dinner at a restaurant for the first time since then. I could choose indoor or outdoor. At this point, it was still a month before outdoor restaurants were opened in New York, and more than 4 months before indoor restaurants were opened there. Why the difference? Politics.

I went to Belford's and had scallops, among the best I ever had. Maybe my perception was favorably biased because it had been so long that I had been denied the ability to sit in a proper restaurant.

After dinner I went to a rooftop bar, and then a busy indoor bar, where one could actually stand at the bar and order drinks. This was extremely progressive, as most other cities, even when they re-opened indoor bars later, made people sit down and didn't allow drinking while standing.

I talked with people at the bar, "Where are you from? This is great, that we can actually go to a bar."

"Yeah, I'm from Kentucky! Not the same there."

"I'm from New York."

"Oh, I heard it was really bad up there!"

"Yeah, it's really bad. They want to keep it shut down forever."

"It's ridiculous."

"It's the government. The most harm in all of this has been from them."

"Yeah. You're absolutely right."

I wondered, why do people from the hick states understand these basic things that few in New York and Europe do?

In Savannah I rented a fast Dodge Challenger and, turning on the radio to old rock music, drove north two hours to Charleston, South Carolina. Occasionally metal came on, like Megadeth or Judas Priest.

Charleston was another beautiful town with Southern charm and delectable seafood. During this trip, it was uncomfortable touching the doors of taxis, light switches in hotels, and everything in the car I rented. But I got over it. I washed my hands a bit more frequently, and I used antiseptic wipes to clean my phone.

I'm actually a germophobe, and can't stand touching things touched by a lot of people, like door handles. I try to touch as little as possible when leaving home. But almost every place in New York has irritatingly-heavy doors that need to be pulled to enter. I would always try to open them with my sleeve. But what if I'm wearing short-sleeves? It's absurdly primitive and uncivilized compared to Zürich, where many doors are automatic and swiftly open by themselves when you want to enter. In Tokyo you don't even have to open the door of a taxi – it opens automatically for you. How crude to have to fumble with a door handle oneself.

Americans have relatively dirty standards for a 1st world country. They have always been indifferent to touching things and acquiring germs on their hands. They inexplicably love wearing shoes indoors and soiling their homes. So their sudden pathological germophobia, as soon as they became aware of corona, surprised me. I remained on the same level of reasonable germophobia as before, but they really changed.

Charleston was a bit less progressive in bar re-openings than Savannah. They had capacity limits and various rules which made it less than fun. However, there was one particular bar there that was the best of the trip. It was extremely loud and crowded, it was barely possible to push through to the barkeeps to order a drink. A band was playing country music accompanied by a musician singing. This bar was definitely violating South Carolina's capacity limits, but apparently it was because they didn't care about violating rules – they just let people do what they wanted.

This was in the American spirit of resistance so little found elsewhere. Throughout the pandemic there were pockets of resistance at certain times, in Europe too where people were beaten down with water cannons in Berlin and Amsterdam at anti-lockdown protests. But nothing substantial ever materialized. No politician was overthrown or held accountable for the suffering they caused. It was shameful how easily the majority submitted to tyranny. It will happen again, whenever governments choose to fabricate a crisis. The ultimate resource of oppression is the cooperation of the oppressed.

There was a strong correlation, of course, between socialists and corona believers. This can be explained by the socialists' affinity towards larger government. Naturally, a crisis like this increases the size and scope of government, especially when people are not working and receiving money from the government instead. People in California didn't care about being prevented from working since they got benefits which exceeded their regular wages. When jobs returned they didn't want to go back to work, where they would make less. Meanwhile the US federal budget deficit has averaged $2.7 trillion in the 4 years after 2019. Where does this come from? It can only come from increasing debt and inflating the monetary supply. Few people care, since the effects on economic stagnation and inflation are not visible immediately.

A crisis also gives governments legitimacy to become veritable dictatorships, and exercise control on minute aspects of people's day to day lives, like how often and at what times of day they can walk their dog, whether they can buy alcohol, and the specific number of guests they are permitted to have in their home.

Before, differences in politics between people were not felt that much. Nobody that I know argued about politics and even socialists and capitalists could be friends. Not so about corona politics. It was always an emotional matter for everyone. It was like two people in 1940 Berlin or Paris disagreeing about whether the Nazi party was good or bad for Europe. For the corona believers, anyone not believing was a dangerous enemy of the people who is helping to spread the virus. "If you just obey and behave, this will all be over already! It's only because of people like you that we need to continue restrictions!"

In this book, for simplicity, I use the terms socialist and fascist interchangeably, as they are both just different flavors of the same thing, government control, and the differences between them are insignificant to me compared to their mutual opposition to individual freedom.

*   *   *

When I got back to New York it was the end of May 2020. I met a girl on instagram and told her about my trip.

"Why did you go there?" she asked, thinking that I must have had some emergency reason to risk such a dangerous trip during a pandemic.

"Oh, just to go to restaurants and bars."

She was shocked. She sent me a 'gif', an animated image, of Bernie Sanders shaking his head at me. (Sanders is a well-known socialist and former candidate for president).

When I questioned her reasoning, she blocked me, preventing further communication.

I saw a girl on tinder whose caption on her profile read, "If you're not taking social distancing in this crisis seriously you are stupid and I hate you." I don't know why she was on tinder if she loves social distancing so much.

There was another girl who I knew on instagram for a while, although we had never met. She was a hardcore corona believer. I wrote her, "I just got back from Charleston and everything is fine there. When do you think New York will realize this epidemic is over?"

This alerted her to the fact that I was not a member of the faith, much like a jocular mention of all the lunches at noon that I had with ample servings of wine and pork during Ramadan would have alerted someone that I am not a true believer in Islam. She asked, "Are you serious?"

"Yes. And next I plan to visit Sweden to investigate how things are going there."

"Er In Sweden cases are on the rise."

I wondered – could that be true? Could Sweden have failed in its no-lockdown strategy and is the epidemic accelerating there? On the other hand, I knew that Sweden was being demonized and vilified by the global media and they were constantly reporting lies about it.

It took me only a few seconds to find out. I searched on Google for coronavirus cases in Sweden and a chart came up showing a sharp spike in the beginning of April followed by a slow but steady decline. The final number on the chart was zero. The cases had continued to decline and now on most days the number of new cases was zero.

I sent her this chart. Even before, when I made it known to her I wasn't a believer she had begun to hate me. But this persistence in contradicting her faith made her enraged. "Oh, you know how to use Google. Congrats." She then launched on a long tirade of personal insults too loathsome to reproduce here. She did not know me very well so her insults were not even pertinent. She insulted my status as an immigrant. She insulted Geneva, where I'm from, as a boring and useless city. Her insults ranged from the size of a part of my anatomy to the low salary I probably have, to the fact that I used to live in a poor part of Brooklyn. Then she blocked me.

It is a trait of many political zealots and radicals, that when they discover one's politics to be different, they begin on a course of personal insults, anything they can think of. Most Marxists and Leninists are like this, and now also the corona movement acquired believers of similar fervor. A good thing about the pandemic was that naturally people like that were also the same people who were staying home the most, so one didn't encounter them in actual life. The people one encountered the most were also the most interesting and like-minded people, since they are also going out and traveling. One certainly wouldn't run into a girl like that in a bar in Charleston.

In the meantime, Zeynep finally got bored of staying home in Brooklyn. She apologized for not seeing me for so long and offered to meet up in Madison Park. We picked a day and I looked forward to it with eagerness. Unfortunately that day happened to be June 1st. Large groups of "BLM" along with plain old-fashioned communist protestors came marching onto the island. During the day they walked around, armed with sticks and bats and chanting slogans against President Trump. At night, they broke into stores to loot. This chaos was a natural result of large amounts of people with no jobs or school, no money, and nothing to do, and the island of Manhattan being relatively empty and unguarded. The mayor, a self-described communist, was partially on their side and did not protect the island. Manhattan, the wealthy island from whose tall citadels one may look with disdain at the mainland, was being raided by anyone who wanted to join the mob. Most stores took no measures except covering their windows – Dolce & Gabbana covered the lower 4 meters of their glass façade with wooden boards. Saks on Fifth Avenue didn't want to risk an incursion. They reinforced their boards with a layer of barbed wire, and manned the entire perimeter of the store with scores of guards standing at one meter intervals, many of whom held the leash of an attack dog (Alsatian hounds). They also had generators to provide electricity for flood lights.

Eventually, the NYPD started shutting down entrances to the bridges, which helped. One interesting thing they did was shut both entrances to the Manhattan Bridge at the same time as a large mob of protestors was already on the bridge. This effectively trapped them there for several unpleasant hours, a piece of revenge which may have deterred other groups from trying to enter the island on later days.

On June 1st I was waiting for Zeynep but once again she didn't come because she was scared to leave home – this time for a new reason. I went to Madison Park and took pictures, showing her everything is calm, but she persisted in her refusal. I went to Washington Park as well where it was an ordinary day. People were sitting on the grass and on benches, gathering with beer and wine. What people don't realize is that the island is very big. A disturbance in one part of the island is completely unnoticeable everywhere else on the island.

Soon after this Zeynep went back to her hometown of Izmir, Türkiye, and I wouldn't see her again until January 2022 in Miami. More on that later.

My next trip was to Dallas, since I learned that Texas reopened. But Dallas is one of those places that has an evocative name; unappealing reality. Like Baghdad and Casablanca, it's a place where the historical allure of the name alone is reason enough to go there, but once you're there you realize it falls far short of expectations. Dallas, although it has a population of 7 million, is very provincial and boring. It was fun going out again, meeting people in Deep Ellum bars, shooting revolvers and rifles at a range, but that was it. I was going in the direction of wanting to explore more of middle-America, the fly-over states, but it was so bad it made me stop entirely and cross off a bunch of other cities in the interior of the country from my list.

I met a group of college guys from Arlington who were very happy that bars had reopened. Unfortunately for them, two weeks after my visit the Governor of Texas decided to shut them down again, due to rising "cases".

Since I knew these flights to Dallas would require masks, I took the initiative of creating my own, with a very lightweight fabric, which would be the least uncomfortable and the easiest to breathe in. It rested on my nose, but the lower part was completely open and did not touch my chin, enabling me to breathe normally. It was a huge improvement in comfort over a "real" mask.

V
PANDEMIA

V – Pandemia

When I got back to New York the scene had improved dramatically. Bars all over the island were now permitted to sell drinks "to-go". It was a major turning point and a significant change from the time when Shake Shack and Tio Pepe where the only bars in all of Manhattan. It was from this point on that life during the pandemic in New York became enjoyable – actually it became more enjoyable than at any time before the pandemic.

Suddenly, immense crowds gathered on the street near bars that were supplying drinks, primarily in the West Village but also in the East Village. For instance at the intersection of W4^{th} and W10^{th} (the West Village is a world in which two parallel streets can intersect). It was reminiscent of Piazza Colonne di San Lorenzo in Milan or Baixo Gávea in Rio de Janeiro. Something like this was not seen in the past in New York because, like in the rest of America, drinking outdoors on a public street was not allowed. There were occasional masks visible in the crowds, but not too many, since the people who came to socialize were not radical believers.

I was drinking a cup of wine and talking with a group of random people. Having finished the cup, and wanting another, I went with one of the girls to the nearest bar to order more. She, upon lining up at the queue, put on a mask, and soon thereafter asked, "Why don't you wear a mask?"

I was surprised – although on the queue most people did indeed have masks, if we looked around we could see scores of people without them. I replied, "Cause it doesn't do anything… And also I'm not sick."

She was actually curious about my reasons, "Aren't you concerned about asymptomatic spread?"

I laughed and told her I wasn't. "Imagine – a disease so dangerous sometimes you need to test for it to even know you have it!"

Seeing the number of people in these crowds in the Village, and also how many people there now were in the parks (maybe thousands of people in Central Park), I decided to try my old friends one more time. I thought that by now they would have loosened up from their terror of corona. It was mid-June; the weather was warm. One of my friends, Paul, consented for me to visit his apartment. He was an athlete during college and worked in banking. However, in subsequent communication I let it known that I had been in Dallas recently.

"Oh, you just came back from Dallas?"

"Yeah."

"When were you there?"

"I got back on Sunday."

There was a long delay. Eventually he wrote back, "I'm sorry, but I can't have you over. You just got back, and cases there are on the rise."

It was generally the same with everyone else. I tried another friend, Georges, one of my closest. He was also from Geneva like me, but he was Americanized and had become a *yupster*, a blend of hipster and yuppie, spending a lot of time grooming his perfectly trimmed beard and moustache. He owned retro technologies ironically, like a VCR, record player, and typewriter. In his pursuit of originality, in Switzerland he called himself 'George', the English pronunciation, while in America he used the French way, *Zhorzh*. He was one of those people who claimed that

Bushwick, a ghetto-looking neighborhood of squalor and low-rise unsightly square buildings, was better than West Village because the Village was too mainstream. With his natural aversion against the mainstream, I had hopes that he would take an independent view about the corona propaganda. I asked if he would visit my rooftop.

He said he was still uncomfortable taking subways and taxis. Since he wouldn't come to the island I offered to visit him in Brooklyn. He wrote, "No, that wouldn't work for us. We're taking quarantine seriously here."

I was speechless. What can one say to that?

Just to put this into context, all the corona mayhem was because of the potential of catching something similar to a cold or flu. Despite his hipsterism, when it came to corona he lost his flair for individualism and merged with the herd.

Georges was supposed to have a wedding in Saint-Tropez in September 2020. That was postponed one year to 2021 (which enabled me to go there with Nadia, who I hadn't met yet). More on that later.

At this time I met a girl on tinder, Tahira from Afghanistan. There is no Afghan ethnicity – the country is a mix of primarily Pashtuns, Persians, Uzbeks, and some others. She was one of the others, a Hazara. Besides Kabul she also lived in Quetta, Pakistan and Bishkek, Kyrgyzstan. She studied fashion design at Parsons and was working to start a clothing company. In short, an extremely interesting and exotic background, precisely the type of girl I'm most interested in.

We agreed to split a bottle of wine in Central Park. I thought a convenient place to meet would be the benches by the Group of Bears sculpture on 79th street. As I sat on one of the benches I saw an extremely beautiful and well-dressed girl passing in the distance, but apparently it wasn't her because she kept going. Then, a minute later, I saw her walking back and I saw that it was her. We kissed on both cheeks.

I said, "I saw you walking past over there and you looked so amazing I was hoping that would be you. And it actually was."

We went to my favorite spot in the park, a pretty shaded hilltop with lush grass overlooking the field adjacent to 5th avenue. Although it is called Cedar Hill, it appeared that it was pine trees providing the shade. I had a bottle of rosé and two transparent plastic cups.

This was the best date I ever had in New York. I didn't know how a girl would dress for a date involving sitting in the park. I assumed sneakers, or in the best case, wedge-heel shoes. But it was even better than that – she had black stacked heel shoes with a tall heel. Together with a black short skirt it made her legs appear very long and thin. We drank the whole bottle and bonded over our common dislike of masks and travel uncertainty.

I walked her home to Upper East Side and we kissed at her door. Until it happened, I still had no idea what her penchant for kissing would be during a pandemic. At this time old friends didn't even want to be in the same room with me, some people didn't want to shake hands, replacing that with a brief touching of elbows, yet we had just met and she was fine with exchanging saliva.

I laughed, "I didn't know whether you'd be fine with kissing."

"Sure. Why not?"

I finally found someone else who didn't care about all this.

The next day we went to bars in the East Village, which had small make-shift seating areas outdoors. We drank another bottle of wine in my apartment, where she was very interested by my numerous fashion books and a pair of Prada shoes with 145mm heels that I used as a bookend in my library.

I have three rooms – living room, bedroom, and an office, which has so many bookshelves it is like a library. I would read either in a snug armchair or in an oriel niche in the living room, unless it was a warm sunny day, in which case I would read on the rooftop. Many other apartments in Manhattan that I have seen are so small it is ludicrous. Some, having a room even smaller than my library, call it a bedroom, but the door barely opens into their so-called room and a tiny bed fills up the entire surface area.

When Tahira and I met the next time, it was a very exciting moment in New York because outdoor restaurants were finally allowed to open for the first time. Some streets were closed to cars to allow for greater space to put tables. The weather in Summer 2020 was very good and all summer it was possible to enjoy dining out and drinking in restaurants till midnight.

The end of June also saw a massive street party take place for Gay Day weekend. Music played from a bus in the West Village, on top of which and around people were dancing – it reminded me of a bloco during Rio Carnaval. At one point a brief thunderstorm passed, leaving everyone wet. People simply took off their shirts and remained on the street. It was mad and marvelous chaos. After the rainshower passed a rainbow formed in the eastern sky.

The romance with Tahira was not to last though. Just when I thought the prospects were extremely good, she told me she met someone else, and it was over. She didn't even remain in communication.

This was heartbreaking, as I had suddenly gone from having zero friends in New York, to having the best friend imaginable, and back to nothing. But this book is not about her and I won't spend any more time on it.

With the opening of restaurants, the online dating scene in New York became like it never was before and never will be again. Many people were tired of the lack of interaction, and wanted to meet people. But offices, schools, bars, and clubs were still closed, so there were no places one could meet anyone. Except online. In the past, I had gotten on average one date from tinder every three or four months. It was clearly ineffective. Now, so many girls wanted to meet it created scheduling problems. This was a really unprecedented time in New York.

There was Veronika from St. Petersburg, a nurse who had to wear a mask for work and hated it. When we went to Café Select, a Swiss restaurant, she explained a whole range of reasons why masks are foolish, useless, and counterproductive.

Another girl I met was Vivie Octavia from Jakarta. Most Indonesians do not have family names. Some have just one single name (like Suharto, the former president). In Vivie's case, she has two given names, the second standing for the month she was born, October.

Later this year, for her birthday in the beginning of October, Vivie decided to go with her friends on a last minute trip to Hawaii. Unfortunately, none of them did the proper research. After an 11 hour flight, she was able to get into Hawaii, but was informed when she got there that she will have to quarantine for many days. They were taken to the hotel and the hotel cooperated with the medical fascists by strictly monitoring their movements. They were not even allowed to walk around the hotel property, which included pools and a beach. Faced with this intolerable fascism, they left the next day on a flight to California. These years were perilous for travel without checking and verifying half a dozen different things. And even when everything seems fine, some place might suddenly change the requirements without notice, making a trip impossible. The IATA website was accurate with regard to each country's entry requirements: which passports, visas, tests, and vaccines were needed. I relied on it heavily in my planning. The possibilities of quarantines though, were not covered there. Also one had to do separate research to determine what is open and what is not, whether there were any onerous restrictions, and to what degree were mask rules enforced. It was not enough to research the rules themselves. For instance, Istanbul officially had a 900 lira fine for not wearing a mask on the street but this was never enforced. On the other hand, Qatar did enforce its mask rules and people on the street without a mask were fined. The amount of due diligence research, for even simple trips, had radically increased.

I had already resumed my attempts to get to Sweden. I bought tickets on Lufthansa transferring through Frankfurt. But for some reason Lufthansa later canceled those flights and refunded the money. Next I got flights on my home airline, Swiss Air, via Zürich.

On July 7 news came out that the citizens of Melbourne, who were temporarily released from captivity after a strict 2½ month lockdown, were again going back into a lockdown. (Expected to last 2 months but who knows how long?)

This was exactly what I said would happen. Australia isolated itself and had no exposure to the virus, leaving it vulnerable to future waves. Although happening on the opposite side of the world, this news was very ill-boding and darkened my mood. It showed that the corona insanity will continue for a very long time, as "cases" rise and fall in different parts of the world, leaving complete uncertainty in travel and nightlife. I wanted to go to Bali and Cape Town this year – that's off the table. I realized that even Carnaval in Rio in February 2021 is uncertain. (It even didn't happen in February 2022! I finally went in April 2022. They held it after Lent instead of before it).

The most dire uncertainty though, is what a disaster it would be in New York in the winter if things aren't fully reopened then. This was the moment, although it was still the scorching heat of midsummer, when I started thinking about relocating for the winter. But Miami was not initially my first choice. I was considering Nice, Malta, Tel-Aviv, Cartagena, Medellín, and Hawaii. Miami eventually became the only choice because it was the only place that had freedom.

July 2020 was when I met Chiara, and we immediately got along based on our shared desire to resume traveling internationally. I told her I was going to Sweden and she joked about getting married so that she can then benefit from my passport and the ability to go to Europe.

"Or maybe I can hide in a suitcase and you can take me," she said.

"You don't have Italian citizenship?"

"No – I was thinking of applying for it, since my grandparents were Italian citizens, but didn't really need it so kept putting it off. But now I really need it, and it's too late!"

We were on the same page regarding hatred of masks and all the other nonsense. We went to Saint-Tropez Soho, a fashionable restaurant with good French food that expanded outdoors over half of Spring street. The whole street was closed to cars. While we were there, a summer thunderstorm started, a mass of violently descending water all around us, a monsoon. Bolts of lightning shot horizontally across the sky, resulting in a monstrous rockslide of thunder that activated car alarms everywhere. Although we were under a tent, the wind was so strong this didn't matter and we became wet. I was sitting closer to the edge and my shirt was completely soaked. The food was almost done anyway but the wine glasses became a mix of wine and rainwater.

The rain stopped but another incident soon followed to add color to the evening. Turning on the corner of 6th avenue, a large mob of "BLM" protestors came marching down Spring street. They too, were drenched from the rain. Chiara was filming them and this caught their attention.

"Stop filming us, yo, this is how we get caught for shit."

"Get caught for what; I'm just interested in what you're doing," she responded.

Another of them was becoming enraged, "Look at y'all, sitting here, eating, drinking wine, while we marching for our rights." (The fact that the wine was now mixed with rainwater and undrinkable was not noticed by them).

One of them climbed over the barrier separating the tables from the street and was yelling something incomprehensible. I stood up, but remained silent, since there's no telling what could provoke them. It required the attention of the waiters to come out and push these people back onto the street.

VI
SWEDEN

VI – Sweden

The next day I was finally flying to Switzerland, my home country, but there were uncertainties. I was supposed to land in the morning and then board an evening flight to Sweden, leaving me half a day in Zürich. But Switzerland recently announced a quarantine for anyone coming from America. I didn't know if they would make me stay in the airport or allow me into the city.

At least, this was in the days before test and vaccine requirements, because back in July 2020 there was no vaccine, and PCR tests were not readily available and would take about 5 days, making them of no value anyway.

JFK Terminal 1 was completely empty, since this terminal is only used by foreign airlines making transatlantic or transpacific flights (my favorite terminal). It was bizarre seeing the rows and rows of parallel ribbon barriers usually used to funnel people into a queue, all neat and empty. Seeing the eerie emptiness of the large halls of the airport terminal felt good, since it demonstrated to me what a privilege it was to be one of the only people who can take a transatlantic flight right now. Both continents were only allowing their own citizens to come. So one needed to be a European citizen to go to Europe and a US citizen or resident to go to US. Every European country had its own specific requirements, and some even suspended domestic travel within the Schengen area, but both Sweden and Switzerland admitted anyone European.

There was only one agent at the check-in counter and only one person in front of me. It was taking a while. He had a valid visa to Portugal, but was being denied boarding on the flight via Zürich because he wasn't European, and therefore couldn't even transfer there since that would mean going through Swiss passport control for the Schengen area. They said they would rebook him on a direct flight to Lisbon with a partner airline on another day.

When I approached the agent I proudly exhibited my bright red Swiss passport and everything was fine.

The lounges in the airport were closed but I had wine at a bar. Here in the airport an indoor bar was open, but in the city, not yet. There were almost no people around.

And the plane was empty. It was a giant Airbus A330 with two aisles and 45 rows, and there were only 7 passengers, including myself. I took an entire row. I used the window seat when we were taking off and landing, and all the 4 middle seats for sleeping at night. The food service was normal, with standard food and wine. A great thing about the amount of space was that there was no need or requirement for masks, since social distancing of much greater than 3 meters was maintained between every passenger. I was grateful to Swiss Air for continuing to run empty planes on a daily basis. I'm not sure why they did it.

My earlier concern for strictness at the border was misguided. There was the same double-door glass booth as in the past. I scanned my passport, walked in, the computer took a picture, and the doors opened. I was in Europe.

There was no need to talk to anyone or fill out any forms. Nobody asked, "Where are you from?", "Where are you going?", or whether I will quarantine.

Talks about travel quarantine seem so out of place in the current century. They reminded me of the travels of Mark Twain in 1867, a time when there were actually dangerous cholera epidemics, not just a cold. Twain went on a steamer from America to a diverse number of places in the Mediterranean and Black Seas, one of the first "cruise ships". But many of the ports did not allow a ship to disembark foreign passengers without first quarantining for 10 days. Twain being Twain, he would not sit still on a ship watching an interesting city right in front of him, so close, but maddeningly inaccessible. He famously evaded quarantine in Athens by sneaking off the ship in a rowboat at night, seeing all the city's monuments during the night, and returning before dawn.

Similar to the current day, sometimes the quarantine requirements were absurd and a preemptive evasion was necessary to get around them. For instance, there was no quarantine at the seaport near Rome but there was one at Naples. Twain learned this, and simply stayed onshore in Rome and took the train to Naples. There he reunited with the ship, and while the rest of the passengers were being quarantined on the ship for 10 days he was at liberty in the city.

I had half a day in Zürich before my evening flight so I went to all the spots long-time familiar to me, including climbing to the top of the Grossmünster church. At the cliff overlooking the city I talked to a couple of girls traveling from Spain. We took pictures for each other. The atmosphere was very relaxed and pleasant and the level of maskage was much lower than in New York.

What Geneva and Zürich lack in size they make up for in wealth. Even across Western Europe, from Stockholm to Milan to Madrid, people are impressed with you if you say you're from Zürich or Geneva.

By nighttime I was in Stockholm. Despite the rumors, Sweden was not actually so free in terms of corona restrictions. Yes, they never had a shutdown or lockdown at any point, but dance clubs were closed, and people were only allowed in bars if they had a seat. People did get up from their seats and mingle, but obviously the rules were designed to limit the amount of random socializing that make bars fun. I met a few Swedes, but overall I found Swedes to be relatively cold and unwelcoming to foreigners, unlike say, Bavarians, Austrians, or Persians.

The biggest advantage of Sweden, I felt, was the general hatred of masks there. I carried out an experiment in which I would count the total number of masks I would see in my time there. I only counted 8 over the course of 4 full days. That's only an average of 2 per day. This included riding on the subway.

Just the presence of one country that can manage without masks is enough to demonstrate that full faith in masks is misguided. At the moment I was in Stockholm, news came out that Barcelona was back under a new lockdown. But mask usage in Spain was one of the highest in the world! Nearly 100% of people wore a mask there. Why didn't they work? Meanwhile Sweden was fine.

Georges told me earlier, "If everyone just wore a mask we could reopen faster in New York."

I responded, "Everyone already wears a mask!"

"You don't! And you think more people shouldn't."

"I seriously don't think that a handful of people without a mask are what's driving all the infections worldwide. I think it's the people with a mask. It doesn't do anything!"

Anders Tegnell, the chief epidemiologist of Sweden, made clear the Swedish position on maskage. Like the famous doctor from Henrik Ibsen's play *Enemy of the*

People, he stood alone against the entire world of conformity and spoke the truth. Ibsen's main premise in the play was that numbers of people do not make truth. The tendency throughout history has been to accept that *collective* thinking has more validity than an individual's. But numbers of believers, even if they are millions, do not give validity to an idea.

Tegnell not only explained that masks are practically useless in this pandemic, but that they are harmful: They are unhygienic in the way people are using them, limit intake of oxygen and fresh air, and create a false sense of security while not actually helping.

Also, what he didn't mention is that they are extremely uncomfortable and they are an eyesore – they look bad.

On other topics, Tegnell concisely and truthfully said, "Closing borders is ridiculous because Covid-19 is in every country now," and "Closing schools is meaningless, and terrible for the psychiatric and physical health of children." Common sense, but practically no other government official was saying this. And most were ardently working in the opposite direction: to keep borders and schools closed as much as possible.

In the Fotografiska Museum in Stockholm I made the acquaintance of Sara, a young Tunisian-Swedish doctor. She grew up in Luleå, a town in northern Sweden near the Arctic Circle, which was a big contrast to the deserts of Kairouan.

We had coffee in the museum café. She and all her family had already recently had coronavirus and were fine.

She asked me, "How many deaths in children do you think occurred in Sweden during the peak of the epidemic, while we had all of our schools open, without masks or any restrictions?"

"I don't know – five?"

"Less."

"One or two?"

"No, even less. Zero."

"Oh, that's very little."

"Yes, out of 2 million children."

"Is there any data you can actually trust and use to compare things at this point?" I asked.

"You have to understand that none of the numbers on corona deaths per capita can be compared among countries because you don't know how everyone calculates those numbers."

"Do you know how they're calculated in Sweden?"

"Yes – in Sweden, anyone who dies having had corona is counted as a corona death. This overstates the numbers, you see? Now take Germany. There, only deaths that have been proven to be directly caused by corona are counted as corona deaths. This understates the numbers."

Months later, I found out how the UK calculates. A headline on BBC highlighted the current count of the total number of fatalities in the UK. In small print at the bottom of the screen, it said, "Refers to number of deaths within 30 days of a positive test." So anything, including heart disease, old age, and car crashes, were counted as a corona death if there was a positive corona test in the last 30 days.

I asked Sara, "What about excess deaths? Is that a valid measurement for evaluating the effects of the virus?"

"No," she said. "Because even the excess deaths, you don't know if they were caused by coronavirus, or by something else, such as the lockdowns themselves. People have been getting less medical care for everything –

delaying operations, not screening for illnesses, not getting treatment. Also, there have been suicides. The lockdowns in other countries have caused many deaths."

"Is there any actual data on that?"

"It's too early to tell, but it's known that in the first two months of the pandemic in the US, 33% of excess deaths were not corona related. And it's worse for younger people. For people under 45 years, 77% of their excess deaths were due to factors other than corona. It could get even worse in developing countries. Tuberculosis, for instance, kills more than a million people a year, mostly in South and Southeast Asia. It will undoubtedly get less treatment and prevention this year and lead to a lot more deaths. Malaria too."

To find the truth about things, especially during a global upheaval, it's necessary to travel, to observe, and to interview people. Although we have internet and 24 hour news broadcasts, there was so much misinformation and omission of information in all the major sources that it was in some ways just as obscure as to what was really going on in the world as it was in World War II, when channels of communication and transportation were almost nonexistent, and no information at all was available from within the occupied territories of the USSR, Nazi Germany, and Japan. But not too many people were traveling and observing right now, and even worse, they were sitting inside and relying on only one unchanging source of news propaganda that coincided with their predetermined and biased beliefs.

A typical example: In Summer 2020, at the same time that Sweden was being vilified by the media for not having a lockdown and not wearing masks, Czechia was praised for its measures, "There is no question that Czechia's remarkable progress on Covid-19 was the result of requiring an entire society to wear face masks." (*USA Today*). Then, when the fall and winter came and Czechia had one of the world's highest rates of death per capita, much higher than Sweden, the media ignored Czechia's failure to contain the new wave and did not retract its earlier praise. Nobody asked why the masks did not work.

The same misleading propaganda repeated again and again, fooling people who did not look at the world for themselves or do their own analysis.

Observations and gaining information were an added bonus, but my primary goal in Sweden had been to drink and meet people.

* * *

I flew back to Zürich for the New York transfer. Nobody checked any ID documents at all, except for my boarding pass, as this was a flight within the Schengen area and between two free countries. Having afternoon tea on the other side of the fluffy clouds, I reflected on the amazing privilege of flying.

I thought that while it is indeed true that travelling through an airport entails a great deal of inconvenience and potential problems, on the other hand you're experiencing something miraculous: you're in a giant metal container suspended 6 miles above the ground, by the energy given off by some flammable liquids in the engines. This whole structure, *the size of a building*, smoothly powering your journey to an unthinkably distant land.

While working in my office, I see jets, helis, and propellered seaplanes from my window, wondering when I will be on one again. An aircraft was in Switzerland this morning; it's circling New York today, its eternal mobility an imaginative counterpoint to the confinement and stagnation of home. The airplane is the only thing that can truly un-tether us from the concept of location.

I'm fascinated by those television screens at airports, casually showing the list of the day's departures, like some fantastical menu of exotic options. Now there are not as many. But in the past you could see next to each other Tokyo, Buenos Aires, Cairo. Then Lisbon, Vancouver, New Orléans. This cosmopolitan vignette delivered in such a humble, matter-of-fact way on that simple screen.

Two doors side by side, Gate 1 and Gate 2 – passengers 5 *meters* apart now will in several hours be on *opposite sides of the earth from each other.*

When I returned to New York the passport control procedures were the same. Like always, I used the mobile passport app which let me use the queue that diplomats and pilots use. Now it didn't matter, but when there are hundreds of people waiting, it skips that. Barely a question was asked. There was one difference in that a form with contact information had to be filled in. Starting from now, New York was requiring a quarantine at home of two weeks for anyone coming from Europe, or from a number of other US states.

But this quarantine was not enforced. So effectively, it became merely a suggestion. Which I ignored of course, going out every day.

This was another advantage of America. Not only in China, but in many other Asian countries, like South Korea and Taiwan, people's exact locations were being tracked via one's phone. And no, one couldn't just leave the phone at home – that wasn't allowed. Quarantine there was actually enforced, unlike in New York.

I had some dreams about quarantine though. In one, I was being quarantined in a trailer house in upstate New York. The weather was fantastic, a bright azure sky, green fields and trees around me, but I was being forcibly confined in this small, narrow house for an undetermined amount of time. Some friends and acquaintances, like Paul, came by to tauntingly shoot water guns at me through the wire screens of the windows.

In another dream, a whole terminal of an airport in China was being quarantined because of corona. Anyone suspected of having corona was being forcibly detained there. A train would continue to run between terminals but its doors would not open when it got to this one. Along with a few other people, I climbed onto the top of the train and, hanging on as it went to another terminal, was able to escape.

In August 2020 some rooftop bars had reopened, only their outdoor sections, like Indigo Hotel and 230 Fifth. Of course they required a mask or bandana to go through the elevator and indoor parts.

Seeing masks again everywhere was a shock. Occasionally someone would refuse to get on the same elevator as me, seeing I wasn't wearing a mask. Or even worse, some people would not get on it even after I had left, as if merely by not wearing a mask I had somehow contaminated the air in the elevator!

There were a few groceries stores around me that required masks and one Japanese store that didn't care. I boycotted the other stores and only went to the Japanese one. Once I tried to get coffee in a Starbucks and the clerk was mumbling something. I couldn't understand what he was saying since his mouth was blocked by a facemask. I realized he was inquiring why I don't have a mask.

"I don't have one," I said.

"In case you haven't noticed," he elucidated, putting his hands on his hips, "we're in a pandemic."

"Oh, is that right?," I laughed. "I haven't watched the news!"

What I told him was true. I occasionally got news from BBC and France24, but I never watch or read American news. The global media was, it is true, overwhelmingly pessimistic and often misleading. But then I found out that only 54% of international news stories about corona were negative in tone, whereas a massive 91% of American ones were. I can't imagine what kind of propaganda American media was force-feeding the people. It must have been just as biased as the Russian media propaganda about the war in Ukraine in 2022 (in which an evil war of aggression is somehow transformed into a peacekeeping activity of self-defense).

For instance, stories about cases going up were 450% more common than stories about cases going down, regardless of whether the actual cases were going up or down in a certain place.

Interestingly, the CDC recognized how abhorrently negative American news sources were, and for the benefit of mental health, in January 2021 they made a statement advising people to, "Take breaks from watching, reading, or listening to news stories."

I was very lucky that masks weren't enforced on the subway, since I used it to get around the island very often, and never once wore a mask. The signs were there but that was it. Sometimes even the police themselves were without a mask.

Among the passengers, extremely rarely did anyone make a comment. People usually mind their own business on the NYC subway. Once, though, a woman sitting in the same subway car angrily demanded why I wasn't wearing a mask.

One never knows what to say to such people. It's because there are just so many reasons for not wearing a mask, such a diverse array of rational reasons not to want to do it, that it's hard to decide on just one of them to reply to this person.

I could have said, "Cause I want to breathe clean air," or explained that corona isn't dangerous but even if it was, the masks don't do anything. Or I might have said, "I just came from Sweden, where nobody wears masks on the subway and everything is fine."

I said – probably making her think, according to her religion, that I was some kind of wild scoundrel – "If I didn't wear a mask on the plane from Europe coming here yesterday, I'm surely not going to put one on now on this empty train."

VII
THE DIRECTION OF PRAYER

84

VII – The Direction of Prayer

When you look at a map of the world, it is a surface of symbols. One flag is the symbol for an entire state; one name the symbol for the complexity of a city, the culture, customs, cuisines, and architecture that have developed there over centuries. The map is criss-crossed by a myriad of roads, borders, rivers, and place names – cataloguing everything and yet showing nothing. In and of itself, the map is meaningless. It can also be misleading, showing irrational or superfluous borders that do not correspond to societal realities. How can one look at all these opaque symbols and not want to go see for oneself what is behind them?

A desire to see and know what is actually going on in the places visible on the world map has always motivated me to undertake the difficult journey to get there. One can't learn anything from just reading about it. You have to be there.

*   *   *

Mecca was always an important place for me to see, and I had exceptional timing, as I got in there in late February 2020 just 3 days before they closed it to foreigners on account of the corona pandemic. Saudia Arabia had only started letting in purposeless visitors for the first time in late 2019. Prior to that only people on a business visa or hajj/umrah pilgrimage visa could get in. As a result I was one of the first people in the world to come to Jeddah for no reason other than chilling, seeing the city, and going on tinder dates with Saudi girls. From Jeddah, I also had a chance to make the pilgrimage to Mecca, without applying through the official channels.

There was a time when traveling brought the traveler into contact with civilizations which were radically different from his own. One traveled somewhere with little to no expectation of what would happen. During the last few centuries such instances have become increasingly rare, but still possible. This was one of those instances.

While I was in Sweden, Chiara was in Tulum. When we were both back in New York in August 2020, she came to my apartment to smoke shisha. I opened a box of Japanese flash-dried strawberries encased in dark chocolate.

She talked about misadventures in Tulum – she had met up with a former *petit ami* there who said he would spend time with her but kept leaving her at night to chase girls, and didn't want to pay for her expenses. She met other guys there who were even worse. She declared that she is permanently disillusioned with dating guys.

"Maybe you should try girls," I said.

I showed her a new picture frame I had recently placed on my wall, a photo of myself standing next to the Kaaba in Mecca, surrounded by pilgrims most of whom were garbed in the traditional toga composed of two white sheets. Below the picture I hung up a curved Damascus steel blade in a sheath that I got in Damascus during a separate trip.

Impressed by the photo, she asked, "When did you go to Mecca?"

"February of this year."

"They let you in?"

"Yeah, why not?" I said this casually, knowing now how easy it was to get into Mecca. But before I went, I didn't know what exactly would happen when I traveled to the city.

"Non-Muslims aren't allowed there, I thought."

"That's true, but how do they know?"

I pulled out a book from one of the shelves in my library room: *1000 Roads to Mecca*. This contained excerpts from the writings of people who made the pilgrimage over the course of 10 centuries, ranging from ancient travelers like Ibn Batutta, to Christian impostors like Sir Richard Burton, to 20th century Islamic converts such as Malcolm X and Lady Evelyn Cobbold.

As she looked at it, I said, "According to this book, the last time a non-Muslim traveled to Mecca and wrote an account about it was Arthur Wavell in 1908. So if I were to write about my pilgrimage there, it would be the first one in 112 years."

"Why don't you write it?"

"Not enough time. I've had so many travels I don't have time to write about them. I also have to work."

"So how did you get there?"

"I took an Uber from Jeddah. It's about an hour."

"And nobody asked you anything?"

I laughed, "Only one time. When we were approaching the city, the driver said, 'You know you have to be Muslim to enter Mecca. Are you Muslim?' I said, 'Yeah, of course.' That was it."

"And how was it?"

"It was incredible, to approach the Kaaba for the first time – the place people have been making a pilgrimage to for a thousand years... It is the direction of prayer of Muslims throughout the world, and here it is, right next to me. There were people there from all over the world – Indonesians, Arabs, Africans. There's something to be said for a religion that forces people to travel. One of the five pillars of Islam is to make the journey to Mecca. You have a chance to see things along the way; meet with people from all over the world. On the other hand, I've been to Melbourne and I saw people who never in their lives have been to Sydney! I traveled to the opposite side of the Earth to visit Sydney and they don't even care to go there even though it is right next door!"

"Idiots. I've seen worse – people in some village in Illinois who have never even been to Chicago. Not to mention New York."

"Ha. So, in Mecca I was perhaps the only European-looking person, but nobody paid any attention. There were 2 or 3 others but they may have been Turkish. Just in case actually, I had in my pocket a letter from an imam in New York saying that I converted to Islam. I did some research online before going to Saudia, but I couldn't get any information about whether anyone actually checked people coming into Mecca or not. There was a checkpoint on the highway approaching the city that looked like a toll booth, and cars slowed down when they went through it, but the people were not stopping anyone or looking carefully into the cars. I had no idea before going, so just in case I got this letter. I studied Islam, read some of the Quran, and developed a detailed cover story about how and why I converted to Islam a year ago in Casablanca. Then I went to the NYU Islamic Center and attended a seminar where I spoke about my journey to spirituality, etc. I borrowed some ideas from Tolstoy's religious books and I mentioned a girl I liked in Casablanca as one of the reasons for my conversion. That I think was the most believable thing. I felt a bit like George from *Seinfeld* when he went to the Latvian Orthodox priests and said he wanted to convert because of a girl. So the imam wrote me a letter explaining I converted...

"The only adventure was when I was leaving the city. At first I tried to get an Uber again, but they have these gigantic buildings like the Fairmont Hotel and complicated series of tunnels under them. I couldn't find the area where the Uber driver could go. Eventually I gave up and just took a regular taxi to Jeddah. The driver was from Sudan; he barely spoke any English. He also asked me if I was Muslim, but without waiting for my reply he waved his hands dismissively, saying, 'It all the same.' We started going towards Jeddah, but for some reason he didn't realize he needed to fill up on gas before we left Mecca. We ended up in the middle of the desert, and he suddenly saw he's running out of gas. He started searching for a gas station; it was difficult to find. I didn't imagine it would be hard to find gas in Saudi Arabia. Then when he finally found one, at that moment the prayer time began. They really take these prayers seriously in Saudia. It happens 5 times a day and sometimes it could last half an hour. Everywhere becomes deserted. We waited in the car until the prayer ended, then finally got gas. I was worried cause I wanted to make it in time for sunset at one rooftop bar in Jeddah."

"Ha. And how was Jeddah?"

"It was okay, except for the fact there was no alcohol. They're very strict on bringing in alcohol. That said, there've been a lot of reforms under the crown prince, Mohammed bin Salman, and it has become much more progressive. There is no more hijab requirement – woman can wear whatever they want. You can go on dates freely with someone you're not married to. It's different than before. It's a lot more freedom."

"Did you go on dates?"

"Of course. I met a very interesting girl working for the Islamic Development Bank, Aisha. I wish that I lived there; being there 3 days of course is not enough time."

"You don't want to live there! They don't have alcohol."

I laughed, "Yes, that's true actually. Oh, and I met a girl on Oman Air from Muscat to Jeddah. She was sitting next to me reading a very interesting little book."

I went over to a bookshelf and pulled out Alfred de Musset's *Gamiani*. "It was this book. Take a look at it," I said, opening a random page.

Chiara looked through some paragraphs, "Wow this is hardcore."

De Musset, the French poet, anonymously published an extremely explicit, lascivious story of debauchery in 1833. It is rumored that his affair with George Sand was an inspiration and that she helped him write it. Its indelicacy prevents me from summarizing it further. I was impressed that this young, virginal-looking Saudi girl was reading this in public. Although it was concealed sufficiently well, anyway, by the relative lack of knowledge of the works of de Musset by the general public.

"Did you talk to her?" Chiara asked.

"Yeah, we talked about literature. She was studying European literature in university. Eventually, she even let me borrow her book for the rest of the flight!"

"And why were you in Oman?"

"Oh, this was actually just the last portion of a much longer trip, did I tell you? I started in India, went around Rajasthan by train, then went to Nepal. I had much more interesting adventures in India."

"It's good you got that in in February! Now we can't travel wherever we want anymore!"

VIII
TÜRKIYE

VIII – Türkiye

In addition to a short train trip to Boston in August, I wanted to take another big trip in September. The range of options was limited due to all the corona issues. I decided on Türkiye and Polska.

I stayed some days in Warsaw, attending a Chopin concert, and took the high-speed train to Krakow and back. It was a new line and very fast. I could hear the familiar sweet murmuring of the wheels against the rail as the train took a curve. The sound brought back memories of my youth – many summers traveling all over Western Europe by train. Navigating through the aisles to find my way back to my seat, I crossed paths with an animated group of Polish student girls, laughing as the swaying and tilting train was making them and me almost fall on the people sitting by the aisle.

In Krakow and Warsaw there are a number of beautiful Catholic churches, and I would enter into each one I saw, to contemplate the architecture, sit and rest.

Churches should always be open, never closed. In many cities they are the one and only interior space available for the public, regardless of one's class or faith, to meditate and rest while contemplating magnificent æsthetics. This gift of æsthetics that the builders of the church gave to the world should not be denied to people; it should be accessible to all, on every day. If one were to choose a religion based on the beauty of its temples, one would probably pick Catholicism.

It was in Krakow that I saw, for the first time since the pandemic began, a real full-scale dance club, with no restrictions whatsoever. People were going wild; they probably wanted to make up for lost time. I saw one teenage guy walking around with a 1.5 liter Grey Goose bottle pouring large amounts of it into peoples' mouths. It was refreshing to see. New York was still several months away from achieving this. Like it was during olden times, traveling during corona frequently meant arriving somewhere with no idea what you would find. Unfortunately for Poland, this was just an interlude. When the fall and winter came, all of Europe would go back again to lockdowns and corona troubles.

On the plane I was re-reading Thomas Mann's *Death in Venice*, literally about a death in the labyrinths of Venice during a cholera epidemic; allegorically about pursuing a forever-elusive goal through the labyrinths of life. Interestingly, in that period of time, the Venetian authorities tried as much as possible to downplay and even conceal the growing epidemic, whereas now it is the opposite – governments try to exaggerate an epidemic beyond the actual risks.

At this moment, at a coronavirus task force meeting in Washington D.C., Dr. Fauci was saying that Americans were not yet afraid enough. "They need to be more afraid," he said. (I learned this from Dr. Scott Atlas, also on the task force, who I met some time later in New York). Was Fauci talking about me? Perhaps he was imagining that people like me were traveling around and spreading the virus and that we would all be better off if we were sitting at home for months like my friend Vadim Mikhailovich.

From Warsaw I went to Bodrum. I knew a Turkish girl, Büşra, who was spending the summer there. We went to Buddhabar, Zuma, and Gümüşlük, drank lots of Turkish *rakı* (the alcohol that tastes like anise and changes from clear to white when you put ice in it), and had fun swimming in the Aegean Sea. As soon as I got there, Türkiye instituted a new rule that bars had to stop playing music after 12 midnight. Why? Is that really going to defeat the pandemic? A lack of music to make people dance a few hours less than they might have?

Or did epidemiologists discover that corona only attacks after midnight?

Büşra introduced me to Bouchra, her friend from Algeria who was also there for the summer but would probably stay longer. It was a novel situation because they had an identical name, but one used the Turkish spelling while the other the French Algerian spelling. Also interesting was that I could only speak to one of them at a time. Büşra knew Turkish and English, Bouchra knew Turkish, Arabic, and French, while I knew English and French. When they spoke to each other I couldn't understand, and likewise when I spoke with one of them, the other couldn't understand. But it was lovely spending time drinking *rakı* with them in Gümüşlük.

After that I went to Istanbul, a city I was very well acquainted with, where I had numerous friends. Istanbul is the world's meeting place, as it lets in practically every nationality without a visa. People from all over the world who can't go to Europe or America on account of visa requirements, can always meet in Istanbul. Also, Türkiye decided to not limit its borders during the pandemic either. At the current time, it was one of the only places that everyone was free to travel to.

I would always remember how welcoming it was when so many other countries were turning people away. That was September 2020. Even two years later, some countries were still not letting people in. Needless to say, I don't understand this. Naturally, I'm in favor of less borders, not more.

Istanbul is gradually becoming more diverse and cosmopolitan again, like it was in the 19th century as an imperial capital Constantinople. Edmondo De Amicis, who traveled here from Italy in 1874, devoted six pages of his travel memoirs to his amazement at the diversity of people he encountered on the Galata Bridge. And now as well, you can stand by the railing of the bridge, and, against the backdrop of ferries criss-crossing the Golden Horn and minarets in the distance, watch every nationality in the world crossing the bridge.

Many acquaintances living here were not Turkish, like Zhanna from Kazakhstan and Lara from Jordan. I also heard that ever-increasing numbers of Russians and Ukrainians were relocating to the city.

Like always, I stayed at the Soho House in Pera and spent my days walking up and down İstiklal, the pedestrian street with red trams. I crossed the Galata Bridge to revisit the familiar mosques and bazaars of the old town. In the congested alleys of the Spice Bazaar, exotic scents of spice reminded me that I was in the Orient.

To put this in context, I had friends in Brooklyn who were still too afraid at this point to cross the bridge to Manhattan Island, lest they catch a cold or something.

I sat and meditated in the middle of the Süleymaniye mosque's abundant carpeting. The best part of the floor space of the mosque is reserved for Muslims and not permitted to tourists – of course I was entitled to go there (having touched the Kaaba in Mecca confers on me very high status in Islam). It reminded me of my favorite temples in Bangkok, such as Wat Suthat Thepwararam, which is also in a beautifully ornate, carpeted chamber and a nice place to meditate. However, here the Buddha was missing; I had to pretend there was a Buddha sculpture. The only Buddhas in Türkiye are in Buddhabar.

Somehow I found one of the cavernous tunnels serving as an entrance to the labyrinths of the Grand Bazaar. A Turkish merchant brought me coffee, and I sat on a tiny stool drinking from a tiny cup surrounded on all sides by oriental rugs – hanging on the walls, stacked on the floor, and arrayed in rows of rolled-up cylinders. Then I paid a visit to the Sophia church, which President Erdoğan believes can be a mosque even though it was the worldwide center of Christianity for a thousand years.

I took a ferry across the water to check out Kadıköy, my first time on the Asian side, a much more bohemian neighborhood than Nişantaşı and Beşiktaş, with lots of young people drinking on the streets. There I discovered one of the best cocktail bars I've seen worldwide. The bar was L-shaped, and a portion of it faced the street, as the entire wall could be opened up. I could sit at the bar and look out over the street, where people were also congregated at outdoor tables. On the bar stool next to me two girls were beautifully kissing each other. One had teal highlights in her black hair; the other had tattoos all over her arms depicting damsels and tigers. They were so close to me it was impossible not to observe them, as I casually sipped my cocktail, and I even noticed that the one with the tattoos had a piercing on her tongue. These are things you won't see if you only remain within Nişantaşı and Pera. And in some surrounding countries it would even be illegal.

In Istanbul I met one new girl, Gökçen, with whom I had drinks at the rooftop bar at Soho House. Sunsets here were exquisite every day, an explosion of orange and yellow, the same color as the aperol spritz in my hand, over the endless expanse of the city, strewn with minarets.

She had light brown hair and, although her heels were moderately low, she was still slightly taller than me. She had surreally-long and thin legs. When she crossed her legs, she was able to go further and double-cross them, such that the upper leg twisted under and again slightly over the other one.

After the rooftop she suggested we go to Mikla, not far from there, one of the best restaurants in the city. She was the daughter of a Turkish diplomat, and at only 24, she owned her own casting/modeling agency, while herself being more attractive than most of the models there. She talked nonstop, which I loved, since I can relax and not have the pressure of needing to talk and can just listen to her. Even more amazingly, she wanted to split the bill. I thought this might be something like the Persian custom *taarof*, but she insisted.

I couldn't imagine that a girl would ever be so generous and willing to pass on an opportunity not to pay somewhere. I tried to convince Gökçen to let me pay, but it wasn't *taarof*. She actually wanted to, because it would be embarrassing for her not to. Her resolve to show she's an independent and self-reliant person, and her belief that with that being true, not contributing would be impolite, made her extremely attractive for me.

The Soho House, a members' club, was lodged in an old mansion whose architecture was a perfection of chic elegance, and the environment made it enjoyable to do some work there on a laptop if one wanted. I encountered people from London who were living in the house long-term, tired of the uncertainty of changing restrictions in England, especially the travel rules. They hadn't been back to London since corona began. In England and many other countries of Europe, travel (if it was possible at all) was strictly governed by a color coded map: green through red. Even coming back home from a green country was onerous, with convoluted requirements and procedures concerning tests, re-tests, and quarantines. Forget about attempting to came back after daring to visit a red country! Sometimes, a country shifted from green to red in the middle of a trip, leaving people either stranded away from home indefinitely, or scrambling to change their flight and return to England right away in the one or two days before implementation of the color shift!

I only had to consult the IATA website about which countries will let me in – never any concerns about getting back to the US. The British had the additional problem about getting back. Some people just didn't travel for two years. Australians had it even worse. If they left the country they effectively could not come back. Anyone coming back to Australia, or even going from one state to another, like Victoria to New South Wales, had to complete a term of imprisonment in a government-run quarantine facility, and pay $3000 Australian dollars for it.

It seems in the Soho House I had found one of those pockets of corona resistance in the world. A place where people came to live a normal life and escape the persecution and meddling of medical fascists. In England, meanwhile, the government started telling people what is the maximum number of friends and family who can gather outdoors or in someone's home. There were debates about whether children under 12 should be counted as part of that maximum number of people or not. In what kind of a world do people submit to a government that dictates the conditions under which people can or can't visit your home, and whether or not young children should be granted an exception?

That said, Istanbul had problems too of course. 'Mask theatre' was abundant here. Although the alleged 900 lira fine for no mask was not enforced and was being ignored by many people, most businesses would prod you for a mask. I carried around a bandana in my pocket and would tie it around my mouth and neck. It was easy to drop down and lift back up as needed. For instance, to buy baklava at Hafiz Mustafa in Taksim, it was necessary to lift the bandana over my mouth.

The most absurd were the restaurants and bars that required mask theatre at the door. A meaningless ritual of showing you had a mask, and using it to cover your mouth while walking 10 meters to the table or the bar. Then, apparently, when standing around the bar and talking with people, coronavirus does not exist. But when walking the 10 meters to get in, it does.

The staff here, at least, were not hostile about the mask reminders. One didn't see the type of zealous mask Nazis that one sometimes encountered in New York, who fervently latched on to their duty of enforcing masks as a holy jihad.

By sheer coincidence, I found out via instagram that a girl I met two years ago in Casablanca, Noor, was in town. In Casablanca, we shared a very pleasant smoke in a shisha lounge. Since then I had been trying to see her without success. She could only go to a few countries, as she could not get either a US or an EU visa. We narrowly missed each other by a few days when I was in Kuala Lumpur in 2019.

Now finally we were in the same place. For two years we've been corresponding. I was extremely happy to be seeing her at last. We met again, and nothing happened. There was no chemistry.

This was a lesson – it is not possible to expect anything based on a brief encounter in the past. For two years I had hope in something that didn't exist. We never know what will happen – you could long for something for two years only to discover it was a mistaken expectation. At the same time, a new encounter one never expected could suddenly happen and within a day become the best thing in one's life.

Turkish Airlines to New York was problematic. The plane was completely full, not like the transatlantic flights to Europe. For some reason they decided to remove wine from the flight, as if being sober would lessen the spread of corona. And they decided that the mask I made myself which allowed me to actually breathe was not acceptable. All these ridiculous rules vary according to the personality of the crew you happen to encounter that day. What benefit do they get from harassing me, and pointing out a non-compliance with some fascist regulation? Why is it so important to them? The only argument I ever heard was, "It's a rule." They insisted that I wear a cloth mask that fully covered my chin and didn't allow me to breathe. On a 10 hour flight. Since it is known that coronavirus is irrelevant when eating and drinking, I had to milk that activity for all it was worth. In order to "buy time" without a mask, I went about eating extremely slowly. I ate and drank so slowly that the food remained on my table for several hours. All this time I was entitled to sit in comfort without a mask and with freedom to breathe.

*   *   *

In October, New York reopened indoor restaurants, but I doubted it would last. Bars were not fully open and there were capacity restrictions and various rules. I started working to secure an apartment in Miami. The melancholy chill of fall was in the air. Winter was coming. I was still considering going to the Mediterranean in November, to work remotely from perhaps Nice or Malta for three weeks before going to Miami. But the news out of Europe was getting worse and worse. The corona enthusiasts were using rising case numbers to justify more and more restrictions. Europe this winter would turn out to be a disaster of depressing lockdowns.

During this time I invited an old friend, Alex, to have dinner at Llama-san, a Nikkei (Peruvian/Japanese) restaurant in the West Village. We hadn't spoken since the beginning of the pandemic.

He asked, "Is it an outdoor place?"

"No," I replied, "It's too cold to eat outside. It's indoor."

"Oh. I won't be able to make it then. I'm not doing indoor activities."

I was surprised. By this point I had been going to indoor restaurants for 5 *months*, since Savannah. And I had just come back from a trip to 4 cities in 2 countries, where everyone was spending time indoors, including at packed clubs in Poland. I asked him why.

"With this virus, if there's one person infected in a given room, everyone in that room can get infected. And cases are on the rise in New York."

Without mentioning that what he said was hogwash, I said, "Okay, so given that, what's the worst that could happen to you? You're young, healthy..."

"The thing is, it's not like I work for a company and can get paid time off. I run my own business; I can't afford to take any time off. If I get sick and have to go to the hospital, the business won't function. There's nobody who can take over for me..."

The thing that amused me most about this was that his business was a boutique mechanic shop for high performance motorcycles. His hobby was to race motorcycles – I saw him take turns at such a fast speed that his knee would scrape the pavement from the extreme tilt of the bike. He had another hobby which was arguably even more dangerous than this – mountain biking down a steep forest path that included ramps for jumping over obstacles.

He was not a frail person, and he indulged in activities of such a crazy risk level, yet the thing he was afraid of being hospitalized for, was inhaling a molecule of corona in a restaurant!

Thanksgiving was coming up soon. This is an American holiday that involves having a large family feast. For several years, my Polish friend, Pan Denis, and his Persian wife Ghazal hosted a supper on this day, inviting people who didn't have family in New York. Pan Denis resembled Conor McGregor except that he was bald. Otherwise, he was almost as athletic as McGregor and had the same beard. When I inquired, I found out that this year, they canceled the Thanksgiving soirée. Apparently they decided that the risk of corona was too great. Even though everyone who would have come was young and fit.

Was Pan Denis getting fed propaganda from the news? Curious, I looked up what CNN was saying at this time and was amazed at what I found. Dr. Leana Wen, Baltimore health commissioner and CNN's medical expert, wrote:

> We are facing a *firestorm of coronavirus* around the US that's much worse than we've seen at any time during the

> pandemic. There are more than 100,000 people being infected every single day... People's behaviors unfortunately don't reflect this. We need to keep in mind that we have an extremely contagious virus with us... It's critical that we wear masks. We also need to avoid crowds and keep up social distancing.

She gave commentary on some commonly asked questions, such as what to do about Thanksgiving. Of course, the recommendation was to skip holiday gatherings in favor of virtual events. But she noted that if one must gather in person, the ideal way was to meet with people outdoors, with everyone wearing face coverings and keeping more than 6 feet apart. She also suggested a questionnaire for invited family members – asking them things like, "How frequently have you come into close contact with people outside of your household?" and "Where outside your immediate neighborhood have you traveled in the last month?"

And what if you fail the test? Are you disinvited, like Paul disinvited me when he learned about my trip to Dallas in June?

Seeing interesting articles like this gave me some insight into the corona believers' religion. I couldn't wait to get to Miami and "come into close contact" with people who didn't have these grave and serious concerns – the closer the better.

Dr. Wen answered another question, this time a very provocative and risqué one: it was about the prudence of actual physical contact with friends and family, such as hugging. Her reply was strict: the direction given was that to do this safely, people should first "quarantine for 14 days, then get tested." I'm not making this up.

There is a Starbucks coffee museum on 9th avenue and 15th street, which is also a store and a café. I was passing by and walked in to take a look, interested in the coffee-roasting machinery on display. I was not in the store for two minutes before a clerk confronted me about my lack of mask. I had a bandana in my pocket, and tied it over my mouth, thinking that would suffice. I continued to walk around but before long, another clerk ran up to me, urgently remonstrating that my nose wasn't covered. Shocked at this lunacy I brushed him away and walked to another section of the store. I already complied with the bandana – what more did they want?

The clerks gathered in number and confronted me again, saying that they must demand that I leave if I don't comply.

I asked, "Why?"

"We have this policy."

"But I have this," I pointed to the bandana.

"It doesn't fully comply with our policy."

"I see," I said, taking it off entirely and putting it back in my pocket. "But I was recently in Poland and Sweden and nobody wears any masks at all indoors."

"But you're not there. This is America."

"What's the difference?"

They were exasperated with my noncompliance, "You have to leave."

I was already on my way out, but I called them Nazis before exiting.

I needed to get out of this city, to go below the Dixie line. Through extraordinary luck, the real estate agent who sold my last apartment in New York had an acquaintance in Miami who was also an agent. He was an Italian called

Andrea. One of the apartments he was marketing was a fantastic property in the condominium building attached to the 1 Hotel South Beach, but he only liked to do business with reliable people that he knew or were recommended to him, which greatly limited his client base. All of his regular clients were Italians, none of whom could make it to the US this year because the US was banning Europeans. As a result, the owner was facing the possibility of a vacant apartment for the peak season. I was able to negotiate a rental price about half the prior year's market value.

IX
SOUTH BEACH

IX – South Beach

I have been guilty of omitting the heroine of this book for too long, like Henry Fielding also did in *Tom Jones*. The only reason one would ever read *Tom Jones* is to relish the most interesting character in there, Sophia, but there is one part of the book where 145 pages are completely Sophy-less: entirely lacking in any mention of Sophia. Nevertheless, the reader can derive comfort from the fact that since this chapter is finally about Miami, Nadia should be due to appear shortly.

November 28 I arrived in Miami, even the airport already feeling more free and relaxed than up north. The weather was fantastic compared to the poisonous Arctic chill that had already begun in New York. Political differences aside, the improved almost-tropical weather alone creates a totally different feeling to everything. When it is actually sunny and warm and walking outdoors is a pleasure rather than a chore, the perception of life is changed. Everything is tinged, not with melancholy and gloom, but with sultriness and optimism.

I had my very first indication of what awaited me here when I stepped into the sleeve connecting the plane to the terminal, feeling a sensation of warmth I had not felt for a long time. Leaving the terminal, going outside, I was hit by a breeze and I did not even mind the wind; sweet currents of air compared to the vicious currents in New York.

The first person I talked to was the affable Cuban taxi driver, not wearing a mask, who took me to South Beach. He was talking about how, as a Cuban whose family escaped the tyranny of the Castro regime, he understands the importance of freedom. I immediately felt I was in the right place.

(Miami also had a lot of Venezuelans, people even more conscious of the need for freedom, as their once-prosperous country was very recently destroyed by a cruel ideology. Seven million left Venezuela, almost a quarter of the country's population).

Andrea met me at the apartment building on 23rd and Collins. It was a one-bedroom furnished apartment, with keycard access to the 3 pools and beach bar of the 1 Hotel. It had a balcony from which one could look from above at the pools, beach bar, and ocean.

Furnished apartments in different places could vary quite widely in their quality, but this one was so good it was better than a hotel. There was every type of kitchen appliance possible, including a good espresso machine, a cappuccino foam maker, dishwasher, and horizontal toaster. The curved television had every possible functionality. There was a washer and dryer, a Japanese toilet, and supplies of everything: soap, shampoo, and a hundred towels of different sizes. It had recently been stylishly remodeled with granite countertops and brand new furniture.

The negotiated price was $15,000 for 3 months. This was a lot more than an apartment in downtown Miami would have cost, but a very good value for its location on the beach, especially considering it was connected to the 1 Hotel. For comparison, one night at the hotel was typically $1000. Around Christmas and New Years, it was $2000 a night. In the end of December, only one week staying at the 1 Hotel would have cost the same as my entire 3 months!

It was only recently, that fall, that I discovered the Cercle project on YouTube. All my time in Miami, Cercle formed the perfect background music on the TV, particularly the DJ sets of Zhu in Japan, Sébastien Léger in Egypt, Lee Burridge in Savaya in Bali, Mathame in Mexico City, Einmusik/Jonas Saalbach in Norway, and Acid Pauli in Armenia.

I was working every day – I didn't take any vacation days to be here. I did not work very intensively though. My routine was as follows. I would wake up at 9 and start working, but would not schedule any conference calls before 10. Around noon, no matter how busy I was, if the weather was sunny I would go read at the pool for 30-45 minutes and swim. Then I would work till 5, and go biking down further south in South Beach to have dinner, and come back on bike. I wanted to get such an early dinner in order to have the pleasure of riding while the sun was still out. There were shared Citibikes similar to those in New York.

It was not an ordinary bike ride – starting at 23rd street it was a ride down the beach path with the glittering sea to my left, various bars playing music on my right. Then after 15th street the path reached Ocean Drive – one would ride past beautiful girls on bikes or roller blades, people in swimwear playing volleyball, and muscular athletes doing pull-ups in outdoor gyms, all while facing the bright and warm sun shining through palm trees.

It was not an ordinary pool either. The caliber of people at the 1 Hotel was such that sometimes focusing on the words in the book was difficult because the numerous girls tanning all around were bewildering.

I worked on the balcony, with the ocean waves as my background. The sea was sometimes a beautiful keppel color, a greenish-blue, not as azure as the sky. The pool was below the balcony, then past it was the 1 Hotel Beach Bar in the midst of trees, then the beach bike path, then a line of green shrubbery before the beach began. I had a mouse, an extension cord providing electricity, and there was shade the whole day since the balcony faced north. Occasionally, a day might have been too cold to sit outside, and in that case I worked on a table inside.

Working in æsthetic and comfortable surroundings was essential for me. It is theoretically possible to work in a windowless cubicle somewhere in the bowels of an office building, never seeing the sun, and many people work there, but for me, that kind of environment would be hateful to work in and would have very negative effects on productivity. In the New York office I had an equally good view as in Miami, with my desk in front of a window directly overlooking Bryant Park – lush greenery in the summer, an ice skating rink and Christmas tree in the winter, a century of architectural styles on display, including the 1924 gothic black Art Deco Radiator Building.

The beach bar was, at the time, one of the best bars to go in all of Miami, and it was so close I could see it from my balcony, as well as hear the music from there in the evening. Another option was the rooftop bar at 1 Hotel. And finally, if the weather was too cold, there was also the lobby bar. Being nearest to the street, the comfortable, huge white divans in the lobby bar were the best place to meet someone coming to visit.

Every weekend, I had an obligation, perhaps a holy mission, to go clubbing. This was an obligation because of how things had changed in the world.

In December 2020, the entire world was shuttered. New York was closed again. Europe was under even grimmer lockdowns. Everyone was suffering, even worse than in the spring of 2020.

Due to this, I felt the need to go out as much as possible, more often than I normally would. I needed to take advantage of this freedom, to relish it, since others couldn't. It was all the more enjoyable when I knew that we in Miami were among the only people worldwide with this possibility. I would take videos and taunt friends in London and Milan, partly out of *schadenfreude*, boasting of the freedom in Florida.

A few months later, when corona vaccines became available, Vadim from New Jersey asked if I was getting one. I sent a picture from Mynt, crowded with hundreds of people, hands in the air when a popular song came on, some getting up on tables to dance because there was no room to stand elsewhere. I said, "This is my vaccine."

Indeed, an alternative to the vaccines was to acquire immunity the old-fashioned way, through exposure.

Since February, aside from a handful of places, I had not seen a proper club until now. The quantity of people packed inside clubs like Mynt was something to savor. It was giving me energy, just to be there, to bask and immerse in the general gaiety and *joie de vivre*. The more tightly it was filled with people the more happy I was.

On one of the days during Art Basel weekend, I went to Mynt, where I had a reservation at the restaurant part next door to the club. After I ate, the hostess was supposed to get me through to the club bypassing the crowd at the door, but the crowd was so massive we couldn't get through. The club was already full inside and there were the same number of people outside still trying to get in. She led me through the kitchen of the restaurant, and then through a back door that led directly into the club. Once I got in I realized there were so many people it was nearly impossible to even move in any direction without forcibly pushing through.

I had gone from one island to another – Manhattan to Miami Beach – but the differences were astounding. I recalled Leana Wen and her directions: "Only meet with people outdoors, with everyone wearing face coverings and keeping more than 6 feet apart." No physical contact unless you've been in isolation for 2 weeks and have tested negative.

It was such a relief, such a joy, to be in a place like this compared to the corona-fearing rest of the world.

And the crowd was all of the same mindset as me – otherwise they wouldn't have been here, savoring their escape from corona Nazism and partying. That girl who sent me a 'gif' of Bernie Sanders shaking his head at me obviously wasn't one of the people drinking at Mynt. She wouldn't be in a place like this; she was sitting at home. As a result, the type of people in Miami at this time was different than it ever was before and after.

One of my friends in New York, Anna, saw my instagram post showing the crowds at Mynt and severely criticized me for going out and having a good time, on the basis that her grandpa had died recently. He was 91 years old. What surprised me about the current times was that all of a sudden, people started imagining that death doesn't exist and that people naturally live forever. Her loss would have happened, with 100% certainty, regardless of the level of partying in Miami and the quantity of masks in restaurants and parks. And did closing offices and schools have any positives for people who are retired and don't go to them anyway?

It is noteworthy that the freedom in Florida did not produce a worse epidemic than in New York. In fact, out of the 10 largest states in the country, Florida had the best outcome in terms of least increase in excess deaths. In New York excess mortality increased 20% from 2020 to 2022, in California 18%, and in Florida 16%, even with its older average age of population.

So Florida was dealing with its epidemic better *and* maintaining freedom, while New York and California were having a worse epidemic, and having no freedom.

This was mostly thanks to the leadership of Florida's governor, Ron DeSantis. Unlike other governors, he was on top of all the data and the medical research. He followed the actual science, not what the media pushed. Accordingly, he made the right conclusions, which were to focus efforts on protecting older folks, especially in nursing homes, and leave the rest of us alone. Florida prioritized the vaccine for old people; New York mandated it for everyone. New York forced businesses to verify that each person had a vaccine. Florida did the opposite, forbidding businesses from checking.

Florida was done with the onerous restrictions in October 2020. None of that worked or had any benefit. There would be no more shutdowns from then on, regardless of what the rest of the world believed. Schools were reopened that fall and children were fine. (California didn't reopen most schools until a year later). The governor used his executive power to overrule any local municipalities trying to enforce mask mandates or other restrictions. Later, reflecting on this time, DeSantis wrote of his success, "People across the globe looked to Florida as a citadel of freedom in a world gone mad."

Achieving a relocation here for the whole winter, with the ability to work remotely, was like hitting a jackpot. And, just like Summer 2020 was the best time ever in New York, this Winter 2020-21 was the best period of time in Miami, a unique period of history that had no precedent.

"It was the best of times, it was the worst of times, it was the age of wisdom, it was the age of foolishness, it was the epoch of belief, it was the epoch of incredulity, it was the spring of hope, it was the winter of despair." These words of Dickens, written about the French Revolution, could have accurately been written about the disparities of experience during the corona pandemic.

Another advantage of Florida is that it has no state income tax. One could save 13% of one's income if living there instead of New York. This added to the long list of reasons Florida was having the greatest population growth of any state. If Ron DeSantis runs for president, a good slogan would be 'Make America Florida'.

* * *

The second weekend of December, I was walking back home on Collins Avenue after a night out, and I decided to have one last drink at Mynt. Mynt was not the best club, but it was the one that I had gone to more than any other club in my life, due to its convenient location, and typically no entry fee. It has been around for decades.

This night at Mynt I met Steven and Helen from New York. During the winter in Miami, I would meet many people from New York, since Miami is New York's backyard. But this winter in particular, the people who were traveling to Miami from the rest of America were the category of independent-thinking, party-loving, rational, and mostly young people. Miami was like a magnet for everyone in America who wanted to have fun.

As a result, when I eventually returned to New York, my best friends changed to the new ones from New York who I met while in Miami.

Several days after that night in Mynt, Helen and Steven invited me to *Mila*, at the time the most fashionable restaurant in South Beach. They were there with Alexys, a Floridian girl, and Lucrezia, a Venezuelan girl from New York.

Lucrezia happened to know Chiara, who was in Miami by this point, and was also at Mila at another table. She found out Lucrezia was here, came over and recognized me.

I knew Helen, who knew Lucrezia, who was friends with Chiara, who knew me. It was like in Turgenev or Henry James novels where a small set of fashionable people runs into each other in foreign places like Rome and Baden-Baden.

But it was only due to the corona pandemic that I fell into this fashionable circle, which I was never previously a part of in New York. I was like Dan Humphrey from *Gossip Girl*, a poor outsider from Brooklyn who only recently had been fortunate enough to make the move from there to Park Avenue.

Coming to see where Chiara went, a surreally beautiful girl came to our table and sat next to me. This was Nadia.

It was bewildering. I lost sense of my surroundings. I don't know what was said at the table. I don't know how much time went by. She was wearing a short black leather skirt with a wide belt and a black blouse with a plunging neckline. She had brown hair and was extremely tanned. I couldn't place where she might be from – from the side her nose looked cute and vaguely Middle Eastern; she had blue eyes. She could have been Levantine, or perhaps from somewhere else in the Mediterranean. I asked, and she said Syria.

I was glad it was a place I could talk about, having been there. One of the advantages of having traveled everywhere is not being ignorant about the places people are from. And when it's a place like Syria, I'm sure that 99.9% of people she meets have never been there. I said, "Oh, I've been to Damascus last year."

"You've been to Damascus? Wait, why?"

"I was doing a road trip – Amman, Petra, Damascus, Beirut."

"That's very cool. I can't believe they let you in. I'm from Aleppo. It's ruins now though…"

Soon after she vanished, leaving only the vape smoke exhaled into her wine glass which gradually dissipated after she was gone.

The evening, with the others, went on and ended with an afterparty at my place. I talked with Lucrezia on my balcony, drinking a glass of sake with her. She was wearing a black crêpe dress, quite alluringly décolleté, with some gold cross-hatch embroidery over the full skirt and Manolo black stiletto sandals. The view from my balcony was magical at night as well – when the moon was full it illuminated the waves of the ocean, an avenue of molten silver wavering between the beach and the horizon. Meanwhile lines of red lanterns hung in zigzags across the palm trees illuminated the beach bar below, this sandy forested area, all the foliage and greenery lit red and orange a contrast to the sharp and orderly rectangular outlines of the blue pools in an adjacent area. Alexys stepped out onto the balcony to take a look. She had a Dolce & Gabbana metallic ribbon/flower headband, tight black jeans with heels, and a black t-shirt with the words "french kiss" on it in gold cursive. I had learned by this point that I actually had quite a prestigious address, and many people wanted to come over. Collins Avenue was better than Park Avenue in New York.

Like New York in Summer 2020, the dating scene in Miami in Winter 20-21 was unlike ever before or after. Again, there were some weeks where I had scheduling problems. There were instances when I had to plan a lunch date because every evening of the week was already taken.

It was an anomaly, a deviation in the course of time, a strange and abnormal historical period where society worldwide was temporarily altered in ways both predictable and unpredictable.

We were still in the midst of a pandemic, even though things were fine in Florida. People wanted to date again, to catch up on what was missed during the shutdown. Another factor was that there were fewer visitors to Miami than in a typical winter. International people couldn't come to the US, and throughout the US lots of people were still afraid to fly somewhere. The reduced numbers did not make it feel empty though, since it was balanced by a reduced amount of venues that were open (for instance Delano was closed). The places that were open were all crowded, and the attractiveness of girls did not change, as both the local girls who live there, and the ones who visit tend to be far better than in the average city worldwide.

There was some danger though, in that some of the Miami girls were only interested in meeting for the sake of materialism and profit. One girl, a Russian, managed to gain a few dinners before I realized that she was completely disinterested in me from the start. I told her I wouldn't see her again. Another one, a Chilean who was a bottle girl at E11even, although a lot more warm and flirtatious, openly admitted that she is seeking someone to pay for her apartment and other things. This was very distasteful, and made me skeptical of girls working in nightlife, but at least she was honest about it.

In South Beach I could get around everywhere on the island by bike or walking. Even when going biking, I always wore light summer pants. Unless going to the pool or beach, I never left the apartment without changing shorts to pants. In my culture, when in a metropolitan environment (no matter if it's a hot city like Miami or Abu Dhabi), wearing shorts is only appropriate for boys under a certain age, like 18. (And the older a man gets, the more bizarre it looks for him to wear shorts, especially the unsightly ones that extend below the knee – when an elderly person does it, it looks outright clownish).

At night in Miami, if it was warm I typically wore black pants and a black or dark long-sleeved shirt hanging out of the pants. If it was colder, I added a slim black blazer.

Occasionally I would rent a convertible and explore farther areas of South Florida. A convertible was the best thing to drive in this warm weather. There was a rental service in South Beach that delivered a car to my driveway whenever I wanted.

I became acquainted with everything in the area – Brickell, Wynwood, Design District, Sunny Isles, Coral Gables, the Everglades, Key Largo, Fort Lauderdale, and Villa Vizcaya. I liked stopping at the seafood restaurants overlooking the Miami River – Garcia's and Casablanca. I had a problem at Komodo though, a restaurant in Brickell. The part of Miami on the mainland was a separate municipality than the island of Miami Beach. On the mainland, they still clung to nonsensical mask ideas. They instructed me that whenever I get up from the table, I need to wear a mask. Fine. I tied a bandana around my neck when I got up. Several waiters started to run in my direction, with great urgency demanding that I also cover my nose. Why? "It's a rule." I could not handle the ridiculousness of this absurdity. None of this theatre was required in Miami Beach, on the island. One never saw any masks there. So I stayed on the island and didn't go to restaurants on the mainland the rest of the winter.

New Years Eve, the last day of 2020, was a particularly warm night, and I biked to Ocean Drive where large crowds had gathered to watch the midnight countdown and to light fireworks. Hundreds of people were drinking in the bars along Ocean Drive and outdoors in the park next to it. In contrast, cities in Europe effectively canceled New Years Eve, telling people to stay home. Some cities showed fireworks on television, but there were no crowds watching them. It was done just for the recording.

In South Africa, on December 28, 2020, the authorities decided that coronavirus cases were too high and the country went back into a partial lockdown with compulsory mask wearing. There was also a curfew at 9:00 PM, and alcohol was once again prohibited. This being just 3 days before New Years Eve, some people were desperate to get alcohol for the holiday and broke into stores to get it. A friend in Johannesburg described to me the chaos happening there. Zach was an Afrikaner DJ and his whole career was upended by the South African corona restrictions. And to make things worse, there was not enough alcohol now to even have clandestine private parties. By a lucky coincidence, I was chatting at the same time with Keliya, a friend in Mozambique (formerly Portuguese East Africa). She mentioned going to South Africa (it is a 6 hour drive from Maputo to Joburg), "I was actually thinking about loading the car up with alcohol and selling it there haha. But I don't know anyone who could buy so much."

I wrote, "I might actually know someone who could take it off you and distribute it. Let me check."

Contacting Zach, I found out he would be more than pleased to purchase and unload any amount of smuggled alcohol, "even if the car was filled to the top."

So I introduced the two of them and facilitated a mutually beneficial trade.

Walking back along Collins in the first hours of 2021, intoxicated people were stumbling out of every bar and hotel that lined the street. Beautiful girls I didn't know smiled at me and wished me a happy new year. The smiles of beautiful demoiselles are the adornment of life; one remembers an evening or a room because girls were smiling in it. Would this be possible to see if they were wearing masks like in Paris and Barcelona right now??

No – nobody was smiling on the street there and if they were, you wouldn't be able to see it.

I saw a good scene at Setai and walked in to have some final drinks. Bars and restaurants were supposed to close at 12:00 in Miami (now increased to 1:00). It was silly and nonsensical, but personally I didn't mind this restriction, as I was going out every Friday and Saturday, and it was enough. I didn't need to stay out till 5:00 and ruin the next day. Also, it meant everything started earlier (clubs were already full by 10).

Today was New Years Eve though and Setai wasn't following the 1:00 closing guideline. I had a drink and happened to meet Laura and Isabela, Colombian girls. Laura had a sapphire ferronnière hanging on her forehead, long gloves, and a 20cm cigarette holder, evidently having come from a 1920s-themed party. We found out that we were both intending to go to the Soho House tomorrow so exchanged numbers and agreed to meet there.

Having drinks the next day at the Soho House on 1/1, Laura continued to flirt with me but eventually made it known that she has a fiancé.

"Oh, I thought you were single," I said.

"No," she laughed, while pressed up against me on the divan and touching my arm. Sometimes South American girls are so warm one can mistake it for flirtation.

"So where is he?" I asked.

"He's in Spain. He can't get here yet, for a few months probably."

"Okay, so I see we can continue seeing each other."

Laughing, she said, "If you want, I can set you up with my little cousin, Sara, or Sarita. Here, let me show you her picture."

She showed me pictures on her phone, but they were vague and poor quality. I said yes mostly out of politeness, thinking it would be worth a shot but wasn't entirely convinced.

The beach bar at 1 Hotel was best in the hour before sunset and the two hours after it got dark. This winter, when not all venues were open, people were more concentrated in a smaller list of places, and the beach bar was one of them, especially on New Years weekend, which also had perfect weather for being outdoors. On Saturday, January 2nd, I could hear the music from my apartment even with the balcony door closed. I stepped outside to see how it looked from above and, seeing a lot of people, I went down. Since the beach bar is mostly covered in sand, I'm always impressed how girls navigate it in high heels, especially stilettos, but I'm very glad they decide to wear them. This day there was a DJ playing some good beats that sounded a bit like Brazilian samba, but I could make out that the words were French Creole. He was set up next to one of the circular wooden platforms which serves as a dance floor. The crowd was beautiful and the vibe reminded me of Tulum. I could see some people openly taking cocaine at a table, not bothering to conceal it. I thought that this should definitely be the place I invite Sarita to.

A few days later, I met Sarita in the lobby of 1 Hotel, a convenient place to meet because one required a key card in order to get from the lobby to the beach bar. There were orchids and azaleas around. I enjoyed the fact that anyone could come and sit on the divans near the lobby bar without any questions asked or needing to order anything. This is unlike some snooty hotel lobbies in New York, typically the smaller sized hotels, where they require you to buy something if you want to enjoy the opulence of their seating area.

This casualness did not diminish the quality of people one saw in the 1 Hotel lobby though. Many were well dressed and very frequently I even saw girls with the Yves-Saint-Laurent shoes where the heel consists of a metal figure of the letters YSL. Seeing this exquisite shoe anywhere made me very glad.

This can be explained mostly by the hotel's location, on a more upscale part of Collins – 24th street. (The riffraff were nearer to 11th street). North of the hotel it was quiet and there wasn't much until you got to the Faena District in Mid-Beach, and immediately south were the W and Setai, also good hotels. However, a better location to live, in my opinion, is Sofi (South of Fifth), since there are more restaurants and places within walking distance without needing a bike.

As I sat on one of the divans, still not knowing what to expect with Sarita, I saw her walk in and got up to meet her.

It is amazing how bad some people are at taking pictures, because none of the photos Laura showed me came even close to representing how good she looked. She had a coquettish black lace décolleté crop top, a white skirt and Chanel sandals, high-heel and with the interlocking CC symbol on the vamps. Everything was black and white – I liked the contrast between her pure black hair and crisp white skirt. Her hair was similar to that of Bely's Sofia Petrovna in *Peterburg*, who was also distinguished by the extraordinary luxuriance of her straight black hair. But one could tell Sarita was Colombian at first glance. The most striking feature of her figure was that, although slender, it had dangerous curves that seemed like they should be impossible.

The only problem was that she was living in Miami just a short time and her English was not good. We went to the beach bar, and I helped her walk across the sand to the barstools at the central bar. Her shoes were slipping off on the high chair so she dropped them down side by side on the floor.

The barkeep knew me, and also I had a discount at the bar because I was living in the apartments attached to the hotel. We got several drinks and I liked the way she always maintained some form of physical contact – either our legs were touching as we sat on the adjacent barstools, or perhaps her hand was on my arm. She had cat-eye eyeliner.

When we went to leave, I picked up her shoes and handed them to her. She put them on before stepping off the chair. She gave her valet ticket to the hotel's staff outside the lobby, since she came by car. I thought it was a bit difficult finding things to talk about since she wasn't extremely fluent in English, so I suggested we go to Treehouse, a dance club, next weekend.

While we waited for her car to come, standing outside by the wall of the hotel building, I embraced her; the little Spanish vixen pressed herself closely against me, and we kissed. All the while until her car arrived and the valets were trying to get her attention to signal that it is here.

Not long after this, I met up with Chiara at Setai, whose pure blonde hair was a contrast at the exact opposite end of the color spectrum, but equally striking in its blondeness as Sarita's blackness. It happened to be January 13, the Russian New Year, which I always try to celebrate, since having another reason for drinking is a good thing, but can rarely find anyone willing to join. (It is also hard to convince people to gather for marking the occasion of the Chinese and Persian New Years that follow after). Chiara was living with Nadia at this point and she brought her along. Nadia was wearing a motorcycle jacket, a short one that showed her waist. I was very glad to see her again. Chiara disappeared because she saw some acquaintance she knew and the two of us talked at the bar.

"I came here in the end of November," I said. "Where do you live?"

"Just down the street, 19th and Washington. I got here end of October."

"What do you do here?"

"Nothing," she laughed. "I'm looking for a job, but there's not much right now."

"I see. I'm working for the same company in New York but I can work remotely." While saying this I was touching the softness of the leather of her motorcycle jacket and enjoying the texture of it – the soft lapels; the sleeves. I zipped and unzipped the small decorative zipper at the end of her sleeve.

"So you've benefited from the pandemic."

"Yes, you could say that. There is a lot of travel uncertainty though."

"Yes! I just got back from Saint-Thomas, but there are so many places I couldn't go, like Portugal. And did you know the US is going to start requiring tests to come back?"

"Yeah, I heard about that today."

It was actually a crazy and unexpected piece of news, that after a long time not requiring anything from US citizens, the US would now require a negative test from everyone to come back to the country. This would cause extreme hardships, since nobody wants to seek out and pay for some medical exam while traveling, and also to face the risk of perhaps getting a positive test result. A positive test would leave one stranded for an unknown length of time in a foreign city, with your flight tickets lost. Some countries might even make you quarantine in isolation until you get a negative test result.

It turned out to be a negligible concern, because the CDC's fine print said that there is an exception to the negative test requirement: instead of showing a negative test you could show a positive test within the last 3 months along with a letter from a doctor saying you recovered from corona. Both documents were extremely easy to falsify and traveling back to the US (for me and Nadia) continued without any inconvenience. More on that later.

Soon I met Sarita again in the 1 Hotel lobby and we went to Treehouse, a club two blocks away. Although small, this is one of the legendary clubs in South Beach. I had been going there since 2013. They sometimes had good DJs, as well as some kind of plant-like decoration hanging from the ceiling that looks good when lasers illuminate it.

This time she wore tight jeans. She also had a short, white shirt so tight it seemed like it was barely being held together by the middle 2 or 3 buttons that were fastened. Being Colombian, the dance floor was her natural element, and she was so good at it, so sultry and intimate. When we went to the outdoor bar to take a break, Nadia called me. I told her I couldn't talk now.

She texted me asking if she and Chiara could stay with me last weekend of January. I was fine with that.

"For how long?" I asked.

"Like Friday to Monday."

"Okay, but I have to work on the weekdays, 9-5. I have conference calls. So you can't make noise."

"Yeah of course."

After a pause, there was another message from her, "There's one more thing, I have a dog, but I promise he's literally the best, most well behaved dog in the world and he never barks or anything."

This made me hesitate. I have been friends with many dogs in my life, but I never wished to invite them into my home. I don't even let anyone walk in shoes in my home, not to mention having a dog inside which understands nothing about cleanliness, as opposed to cats, the cleanest animals.

Still, I had to consent, since I liked Nadia and trusted she wouldn't do anything inconvenient if she stayed with me. It turned out that she was being extremely accurate – her dog was not only super cute, but actually the most well-behaved dog I've seen in my life. He never made a noise, and could have been mistaken for a cat. He was the same size as a cat, and slept as much. The dog was a crossbreed of Yorkshire Terrier and Chihuahua, with long fur and extremely long ears that pointed up. The only inaccurate thing was that she ended up staying for a month, rather than 4 days, but that was a good thing.

Meanwhile I developed a ritual of biking down to South Point every Sunday to have a lobster at Lobster Shack. Going all the way down to South Point, at the southernmost point of South Beach, was a bit far for weekdays, but great on a Sunday afternoon. I lived up north on 23rd street, which is almost on the border between South Beach and Mid-Beach. Whenever down south I would try to catch the sunset from South Point park. This was the best spot for it, since the entire beach side of South Beach faced east, away from the setting sun. On good days the whole sky lit up in bright yellow and orange at the horizon, some red merging with violet higher up in the sky, the water between here and the skyline of downtown Miami ablaze in orange and the palm trees silhouetted in black against all this color.

There was also one bar that had a sunset view – this was at the Mondrian hotel situated on the bayside. I talked with a bartender here, who was Cuban like the taxi driver I met when I first got to Miami, and who also talked about the importance of the freedom in Florida that allowed people to live. At this point, when I could see people laughing and talking as they sipped a caipirinha at the bar, watching the sun go down behind downtown across the bay, a DJ playing house music, I reflected on what's going on in New York and elsewhere.

Just as Switzerland was in the eye of the hurricane during WWII, an island of peace and stability largely unaffected by the destruction outside it, Florida was spared the anguish and devastation affecting Europe and the rest of America this winter.

Getting here was like *Escape from New York*, the dystopian 1981 film where Kurt Russell needs to escape from the post-apocalyptic city. Psychologically, the lockdowns in the winter were even worse than the ones last spring. New York was dark and frozen, with dusk at 4:00. Nobody talked to each other outside, imprisoned at home either in solitary confinement by themselves or with people they were tired of seeing all day in their small apartments. 52% of young people became fatter. 75% of college-age people developed depression, anxiety, or other problems. Even if braving the Arctic weather, there was nowhere to go outside. When you did see people outdoors, you didn't see their faces, just a hat pulled down to the eyes, and several layers of masks or scarves covering the rest of the face. (As if the fact that masks and cloths were useless for filtering microscopic viral particles could be solved merely by adding many layers of them!) In New York it was also a particularly snowy winter, with mountains of shoveled snow and ice on the sidewalks, an icy brew of slush and water at the end of each block.

The gloom of winter strikes one the most often not while sitting in the midst of it but during a sudden contrast, like for instance when enjoying Cartagena warmth for a few days and then suddenly returning to New York in January. Personally, I feel the realization the most in the beginning of May. In the first really warm days, when trees are beginning to turn green, at the same time as feeling optimism from the coming summer, at no other time do I come to a greater realization of how horrible winter truly is, since I see that enduring it for such an interminable, unending length of time, *one actually forgets* how good things could be! One forgets how it could actually be a pleasure to be outside, to go places, to walk aimlessly, to sit outdoors, to ride a bike – rather than it being an unpleasant chore, quickly scurrying from point A to B, tightening the feeble protections one has against the deathly wind. At the same time that one is happy in May for having reached the summer, there is a sadness that things have to be this way – that one needs to endure winter for so long that one actually forgets about the feeling of warmth.

This combination of elation tinged with bittersweet thoughts has often transfixed me as I stood outside, people obliviously passing on the sidewalk around me, in the glare of the sun on the first warm day of the year. Most people are not as sensitive to the oppression of the dismal days as I am. But they're also not as sensitive to the beauty of days like this in May. I wouldn't want to be like them.

It is hard to imagine, how much worse the corona restrictions, with all indoor restaurants and bars closed, made it for people remaining in New York in winter. It was completely different than the summer, when one could enjoy al fresco restaurants that set up tables over sidewalks and streets closed to traffic. But many people, probably a majority, supported the restrictions. I wrote to an acquaintance who lived in New York, telling her about

Miami. She wrote back, "But every single state is trending upward in cases now! We should all still be in Quarantine-Lite. Don't you think so?"

I replied that I didn't think so of course.

At the same time as sitting in their self-inflicted privations, the northern media lambasted the Floridians who were daring to live freely. For the rest of the country and the world, Florida appeared like a plague-stricken apocalypse. Alex, the motorcyclist who couldn't meet me in an indoor restaurant, was calling Floridians mentally deficient. He justified this ethnic slur by saying, "We've been making sacrifices and have made progress against the pandemic. But people in Miami and all over Florida are undoing all that effort! They're responsible for prolonging and exacerbating the pandemic!"

The Super Bowl, an annual championship of American football, was held in Tampa, Florida this winter. Looking up coverage of the event revealed the following headlines and commentary:

Vice magazine: "The real winner of the Super Bowl could be Covid-19."
Washington Post: "Hordes of football fans crammed into bars, clogged streets, and belted chants – many without masks, despite dire warnings from public health experts that the Super Bowl could become a superspreader event."
The Independent: "Wild, maskless Super Bowl celebrations in Covid variant hotspot spark superspreader fears."
Forbes: "Crowds of maskless Super Bowl fans seen partying in Tampa despite official warnings of superspreader events."

CNN: "CNN Reporter aghast at maskless, drunk Super Bowl crowds in Tampa: I ask the police, 'What are you doing about this?'"

These accusations, like every other that the media has made when they discovered that people don't want to obey their rules, are so full of spite they sound like a moralizing preacher trying to bootstamp his vision of austere Puritanism on a congregation that actually wants to live life and have fun. It is like Moses descending from the mountain and becoming enraged in finding that the Egyptian Hebrews are having a wild party rather than submissively waiting for the Commandments that he wants to impose on them.

Despite their dismal predictions, corona cases in Tampa declined after the Super Bowl.

* * *

There was one bizarre thing that irritated me in Miami: that restaurants would not write the real price of items on the menu, rather writing only 76.9% of each item's price, to which 30% was automatically added to get the final price.

When traveling in foreign countries one always needs to convert prices. One wouldn't pay a bill of 2 million dong or 209 dirhams or £37 without mentally converting it first to see what it is in dollars. In Miami, in one's own country, one needs to convert as well, from the restaurant currency to actual dollars. For instance, something that is written as '40' in the restaurant's currency units converts to $52. The mathematics of how a restaurant (or any other business) distributes its revenue to cover all of its fixed and variable costs – which portion goes to electricity, rent, sales taxes, property taxes, wages of the chef, wages of the waiters, and dividends to the owner – should not be an anxiety of the customer. Having a separate surcharge for sales taxes and 'service' (30%) is just as absurd and inconvenient as having surcharges for everything: electricity, insurance, and all the other costs. The 'service' portion does not even necessarily go directly to the waiters – everything first goes to the restaurant's revenue and is then distributed later.

Why stop at 30%? Why not have a 478% add-on? The $52 dish will be written as '9' on the menu. Then 478% will be added, itemized to describe where all that goes: towards electricity, the salary of the chef, garbage disposal fees, etc., adding up to a final price of $52. Regardless of what percentage addition is used, it wouldn't prevent someone from leaving an extra $5 or other tip to the waiter if they want.

Actually the best percentage would be something easy for the customer to calculate effortlessly. 900% would be ideal. Adding that would be the same as simply multiplying by 10. So '5.20' on the menu will convert to $52, which would be much more convenient to calculate than the arbitrary 30% addition.

Or, an even more simple way would be to write '52' on the menu.

In Switzerland it is like this, of course. It says 52 francs and you pay 52 francs, no more, no less. What could be simpler? Everyone is satisfied.

When I question waiters about the rationale for itemizing certain surcharges and not others they stare at me as if I am insane.

X
NADIA

X – Nadia

Nadia's stay at the other apartment came to an end and she relocated to mine, along with Chiara and the dog, Argo. The two demoiselles took over the large divan that was in a corner of the living room, under a painting by Signac – *The Port of Saint-Tropez*. It had two perpendicular sections, each of which was long enough for sleeping. They opened some of their suitcases near it, and for some reason the dog liked to sleep in the suitcases, burrowing under the clothes. At that time I was running low on supplies of food, that is to say, I had practically nothing, and Nadia said, "I'll get some tomorrow."

"We can get it delivered here," I told her. "Let's look online at what to get tomorrow." This happened to be a Friday evening, and I suggested to her to go to a club, called Do Not Sit on the Furniture, an obscure one on 16th street. We got drinks there and danced in the hot, crowded, and dark club which had illuminated décor hanging from the ceiling. The only "furniture" there was a chair, but it was hanging from the ceiling, thus not possible to sit on anyway. Although the place was small, it had among the best house music in South Beach. Today it sounded like something Monolink would play at Burning Man. With my hand on her bare waist I could not believe my good fortune at having met her and then all of a sudden living together. She was so charming that even a few minutes spent in her presence was something valuable to be savored, not to mention many days. "Did this really happen?" I wondered.

I drew my hand through her brown hair and lifted it, feeling the warm and moist back of her neck. I wished I could kiss her but didn't want to risk it. When the club closed at midnight we walked all the way home from there and I settled on the couch to watch a movie. The dog came and sat pressed against me. Nadia was preparing to go out again to some house party she knew about. She had an Hermès silk-twill scarf tied around her neck, which depicted a forest scene. It included, if one looked closely (which I did later on another day), tiny animals amidst the trees and meadows – stags, vixens, and peacocks. Just before leaving, she came over to give me a kiss on the lips goodbye. I said, "Wait," took her hand, and pulled her closer to kiss her more at length, then, smiling, she left.

This was surreal, like something in a dream that fills you with inordinate delight. The way that she kissed me when I pulled her back to me was entrancing. It was not, for instance, the way that I sometimes saw her kissing Chiara. Still, I wanted to refrain from flirting with her more, thinking it would be inappropriate since she's staying with me.

As a houseguest she was perfect – she cooked, almost always making something for lunch, cleaned, did laundry, bought some of the groceries and wine, paid for taxis, didn't interfere with my work, didn't make any disorder, and didn't wear shoes inside. Aside from all that, just to have her around, to see and talk with her, was a pleasure. She was beautiful and kind, and always in good spirits. (Chiara was gone many of the days and nights. She didn't take an active part but also didn't interfere in any way).

It was also good to be able to drink with someone, and Nadia liked wine even more than I did. I never have dinner without wine. Being from Geneva, it's unthinkable to me. From young people to great-grandparents, everyone ends the day with wine. It's something as natural and normal and necessary as eating. The only times when I didn't have a wine or a cocktail with dinner were when I was traveling in Iran or Saudia Arabia where it is prohibited. It was very good to meet a girl who didn't resist drinking like other girls. Chiara, for instance, practically didn't drink at all, and many others only consent to having some marginal amount. With some of them, it's as if they never want to relax and loosen up and have a *mania for sobriety*, maybe out of mistrust for their own actions in the event they get drunk. With Nadia this was never the case – she would usually be the one offering me wine and convincing me to drink more, and drinking with her was exciting.

All of a sudden there were scattered around my apartment combs and headbands, earrings, mascara, lipstick, feminine sunglasses, purses, wedges, mules, platform pumps, and tall soft boots. I liked having this cute stuff around. Nadia's most prized pair of shoes were black patent leather Louboutin Biancas, 140mm, although she rarely wore them because they were too high. She asked me to put them in a secure place to keep them safe. She was not tall – even when putting on the Bianca shoes she was a bit less than my height.

From her suitcase she took out a t-shirt that had a picture of Karl Lagerfeld and the cat Choupette, both wearing sunglasses, and was sad, reflecting, "What will we do without Karl?"

I agreed, "Yeah, he was the best. I have a book of his quotes. And another of his runway shows." I remember all the indelible Chanel fashion shows – one was in a French brasserie with the girls sitting down afterwards and waiters serving them – it was perfection; another was in an airport with a fictional Chanel Airlines.

She typically wore shorts and a polo shirt with snap buttons. The shorts were of the kind where you could see the pockets, being of shorter length than the pocket, and they looked good on her as she had long, thin, tanned legs. Encircling one of her thighs was a circlet of flowers tattoo, along with a revolver, looking as if it was inserted in the circlet like a holster.

Although I had stayed in hotels with girls, I had never actually lived with a girl before (not to mention two girls and a dog), and it was better than I imagined.

Chiara had the most beautiful, angelic long blonde hair. It acquired a new dimension of fascination when it was wet. Feeling the cool and heavy contact of this sodden, waterlogged, naiad gold just after she came out of the pool was like touching a rare and priceless material.

Seeing Sarita again was put on hold for an indefinite time since she had to go to Colombia to see a relative who had some health issue, and ended up staying there. If she was here it might have provided a dilemma since I knew her first, but in any case I liked Nadia a lot more.

Both Chiara and Nadia were unemployed due to the pandemic. Nadia was a bottle girl at nightclubs. This means those girls who take orders at nightclub tables and bring bottles of expensive champagne or other things and get a percentage of the sales. At a standard fashionable club in New York, Las Vegas, or Miami, the lowest cost of a bottle was around $700, and the prices went up from there. It is unclear why Americans considered this a good value. In the best clubs in Europe, a bottle would cost a fraction of this, and at the same time the nightlife is better than in America.

Nadia wasn't working yet because not enough of the big clubs had reopened. Chiara was, before the pandemic, in a small business office in New York that couldn't function with everyone remote and had to shut down. Both of them had only a small amount of liquid assets (which they lessened even further by speculating in risky investments like meme stocks and dogecoin). However, Nadia walked around with a Rolex Datejust with a pink dial and Chanel and Prada purses that were gifts some time ago from someone who must have been very wealthy.

I had a similar watch myself, but not pink. I took only one watch with me to Miami, on the basis of its endurance to water sports – for instance if I fell into the ocean at full speed off a jet ski or water ski.

I got Nadia and Chiara access cards, which were needed for all the doors, elevators, and the pool area at the hotel.

These were the times when Nadia was better, not drinking crazy amounts of alcohol, and waking up at normal hours. She reciprocated favors and didn't ask for anything. I could never have come to like her so much, nor could I have engendered any hopes for future prospects, if she had, for instance, various unreasonable demands, or if she was closer to the materialistic and opportunistic mindset one typically expects from beautiful girls working in nightlife.

For Chiara, in addition to the main problem of losing her job due to corona, everything else about corona restrictions annoyed her to the utmost degree, especially mask Nazis and travel bans. She didn't go to Saint-Tropez and Barcelona in the summer, and missed out on her annual trip to Mykonos, where she knew everyone and attended the most exclusive parties. She was constantly lamenting about overeating and gaining weight, even though from all the time that I observed, the slenderness of her waist didn't change by a millimeter. One could almost encircle it with one's hands.

I was glad that despite her chronic dissatisfaction, she could not find fault with my apartment here and was satisfied. Except for some minor things – like the level of service at the gym downstairs. When she complained about the gym lacking some particular equipment, Nadia and I exchanged a glance and both laughed at the same time, because we knew about this Chiara trait.

* * *

Nadia explained why she had so much tattoos all over her back – they were to cover numerous scars from a terrible injury in the wars. I thought Syria, but actually it was in Lebanon, where her family relocated because of jobs when she was 10.

"Lebanon, you know I'm sure, had civil war since the 70s," she said, while biting into a crescent of melon and hold a glass of wine with her other hand. "They say it ended in the 90s, but there was still something going on all the time. It was a shithole, but other than that it was a fun place to be. People partied, like nowhere else in the Middle East. The parties were insane. In 2005 Syria withdrew its army, right after that in 2006 Israel invaded; in 2008 Hezbollah took over West Beirut, where I was. I didn't pay attention to the politics. One day, I was walking on the street, minding my own business, then there was a flash and explosion and I fell to the ground. The next thing I knew I woke up in the hospital."

"In 2008?"

"Yes." She had ten surgeries over the course of a year, in her back, spine, and other areas. Alternating between being in the hospital and at home. She had lingering problems and fragility that make it unsafe to risk anything like skiing or horse riding. Also anxiety-related issues like post-traumatic stress disorder and panic disorder that made her start taking xanax. "Look at this," she pointed to a scar on her foot. "Just this required three surgeries – they had to put in a metal plate to hold the bones together, then they had to take it out later."

When she said things like that there was nothing I could have said to express sympathy. And she knew that, since she was talking about the very limits of endurable hardship. Surviving that was no less than a veritable miracle.

She continued, refilling our wine glasses as she spoke, "I couldn't go to school; couldn't apply to college. As soon as I got better my family moved back to Syria, thinking it would be better, but ironically, then the Syrian Civil War started, which is a whole other thing. Because of that though, they were able to get a refugee asylum in the US, and they were able to move to Houston. Houston, turned out to be, in many ways, worse than Damascus; that's another story. Anyway, one of the things I find ridiculous, is how panicked people are about corona, when such things as this happen."

How true, I thought. How perilous and unfair life is. That a 16 year old girl should endure something like that? Why does such a world even exist? Why would anyone think that the existence of such an evil world is a good thing? I admired her perseverance.

She said, taking a sip of wine, "The stupid masks and all these people yelling at you to wear a mask gives me anxiety."

"But you never wear a real one right?"

"No, I have a fake one that it's actually possible to breathe in, but it looks real."

I mentioned, "Lebanon just now implemented another lockdown."

"I know; I don't know what makes Lebanon extra stupid in this regard. Like, some countries are stupid, and some are just retarded. They're not letting people go outside at all. They're like imprisoned in their homes. And what is that going to do – seriously?"

She had a pleasant accent, reminiscent of that unusual accent children who grow up learning English in a non-English country have. It was neither here nor there – completely correct English but hard to attribute to a particular place. Her school was half in English, half Arabic.

"I was there in 2018," I said. "It was stable in those years. I rented a car and went to Balbec, in the northeast of the country, which was Hezbollah territory."

"Why? To see the Roman ruins?" she asked. She relocated to one of the bar stools between the living room and the open kitchen and crossed her legs.

"Yeah. I had read about it in the travels of Robert Byron and always wanted to see them. They were very interesting: huge ancient Roman temples in the desert. One of them is for the Roman god of wine. And no tourists – we had the whole site to ourselves. I went with a girl I met the night before at a party. It was interesting how it happened: as soon as I went out in Beirut, in Gemmayzeh, I met many people – everyone was friendly there – and they invited me to go with them to a club first, then someone's house after.

And I'm sure things like that happen with you all the time, but it hardly ever happens to me, only in unusual places like Beirut. It's hard for me to meet people...

"So I asked this girl if she wanted to drive to Balbec tomorrow and she said yes... On the way there were several military checkpoints, but they waved us through immediately when they saw us in a black Mercedes. We got to Balbec, looking for parking. It was just narrow, medieval streets with donkey carts, barely enough room for two cars to pass each other. I finally found a spot to leave the car; it happened to be next to a tank, with soldiers around it. We left the car, and saw something that looked like a rooftop café and wanted to see the views from there. Next thing I saw the soldiers from the tank coming into the building looking for us, asking where we were. They saw me and started shouting in Arabic. I had no idea what was going on. The girl translated for me – apparently they were trying to find me because I had left the motor running in the car!"

We had come to the end of the bottle of chianti we were pouring from and it was late so we didn't open another one.

Chiara came back home, saying, "Hey, I see you finished that bottle quickly," and sat on the divan composing messages on her phone. Nadia had some kind of electronic cigarette that was based on marijuana rather than tobacco. It's obscure how it worked, as it appeared to have a liquid inside. She inhaled from it and then, touching Chiara's chin so that she would turn her face towards her, exhaled the smoke into Chiara's mouth.

"How is it?" she asked.

"I like it. *Mi piače*." Chiara said.

Nadia seemed to like the sound of pronouncing that foreign word and repeated it. "*Mi piače*," while she came back to me and did the same thing, exhaling the smoke into my mouth, following up with a kiss.

"And when did you go to Syria?" she asked.

"It was a different trip. I took a taxi from Amman to Damascus, and then Damascus to Beirut."

"How did you get a visa?"

"It was hard. There are no consulates, as you know, or very few operating ones. I had to get a visa clearance directly from the Syrian Foreign Ministry, through an agent inside the country. Then I got the visa stamped at the border."

"Did they ask you, like, what the hell are you going to Syria for," she laughed.

"There were like 10 different checkpoints to go through. Besides me, the only other car I saw crossing the border was a UN diplomatic car. Yeah, the Jordanians questioned me – why would I be going to Syria? Where am I going after? But the Syrians didn't ask anything – none of them spoke English!"

"You don't have any Israeli stamps in your passport right?"

"No, I spent quite a lot of time in Jerusalem and Tel-Aviv but Israel doesn't stamp anymore. Any indication of having been in Israel though, would disqualify someone from entering Syria. So I made sure to remember not to wear my Israeli Defense Forces t-shirt on the day I crossed the border."

She laughed. "When was this that you went?"

"October 2019."

"Hmm. So about a year or two after the war ended? What was it like? Was the nightlife active again? Are there a lot of ruins in Damascus?"

"There were ruins all around it, in the suburbs – I was surprised actually; I didn't know the war reached that far south. Also, at the time Israel was occasionally bombing the Damascus suburbs because the Iranians and Hezbollah were assembling there."

"They were bombing Hezbollah? Good."

"The center of the city was totally fine though. A lot of amazing ancient buildings, like the Umayyad mosque, the Zaynab shrine, some Christian churches. Nightlife was small-scale, just one or two streets with bars, but pretty active on those streets. A lot of people drinking. They were very friendly – whenever I went to a bar, if I said I was from New York, everyone wanted to buy me a drink, ask me questions. The most dangerous thing in Syria for me was overdrinking from all the offers of drinks."

She laughed, "Yeah, that's Syria. We are hospitable to travelers and guests."

"And the girls were very beautiful."

"Yes, we are!" she nodded.

"There must have been few people traveling from New York there for many years. Americans are not allowed in the country – I used a Swiss passport of course. There were pictures of Bashar al-Assad everywhere. He's always in some nice-looking jacket. You get used to seeing him around everywhere. What do you think about Assad?"

"I can't answer this unless we have another drink," she said, pouring a small amount of jägermeister for each of us. "I hate Assad of course. I'm from Aleppo – the worst part of the war was there. He destroyed the city. Together with Putin and the Iranians. Aleppo used to be the biggest city in Syria; it's just as old as Damascus. Nothing is simple in Syria though – by now, most people I know, especially the Christians in Damascus, actually support Assad, because they know the worst thing in Syria is ISIS, you know, the psycho jihadists. He's against ISIS, so it's the lesser of two evils. Everything in Syria is bad; there is no good side."

She was right: talking about things like this demands having another drink. It is too heavy otherwise. Wine is the only way to alleviate the gravity of the things in life.

I asked, "Do you want to go back someday?"

"Yeah, definitely! We should do a road trip. Israel and Egypt too!"

XI
VITA NUOVA

XI – *Vita Nuova*

While I was drinking a cappuccino in the kitchen the next day, I saw Nadia come out of the washroom. She had been straightening her hair and spent a lot of time applying winged eyeliner and mascara. She looked angelic; I couldn't even say anything; I just stared at her entranced.

"What?" she inquired, but then smiled, knowing why I was looking.

On Sunday afternoons, the beach bar fired up a barbeque and I suggested to go there. There were rustic wooden tables in the sand under the shade of the trees. She wore black thigh-high suede boots and brought Argo. When we approached, it was already possible to smell the smoke from the grill, very beguiling when one is hungry. We got lamb chops, eating them off the bone.

I wondered – where was she going tonight for her to spend so much time with her makeup? Later on, I saw that she didn't go anywhere – she stayed with me at night, drinking wine and watching a movie. So unless it was the case that she had somewhere to go, and it was canceled at the last minute, then it turns out that she did all that hair and makeup just to spend a Sunday with me around the house, which is amazing.

We relocated to the barstools at the bar and had rosé and I left for a few minutes to the washroom. When I was returning, I could see her from a distance before I got there. Even in South Beach, and in the relatively refined standard of people at the 1 Hotel, she stood out among everyone. She seemed so beautiful, so captivating, so different from all the ordinary people around her, that it bewildered me as to why nobody was stupefied as I was by the cross of her tall boots as she perched on the chair, why everyone who was walking around did not stop in their tracks with the movements of her hand running through her hair, the way she adjusted her sunglasses atop her head, the spark of her eyeliner and blue eyes.

She asked me about work, "So what exactly do you do?"

"I'm in insurance. Did you see *Double Indemnity*?"

"No."

"It's a pretty good classic film noir from the 40s. Barbara Stanwyck is in it. So I do something like some of the insurance stuff they do in that movie. But much more sophisticated. We are doing political risk insurance, earthquake and tsunami insurance, piracy for container ships, re-insurance. It could be something very specific, like if you have a cobalt mining project in the Congo and you just want to insure against the risk of revolutions and insurrections, there's a policy for that."

"Sounds interesting!"

"No," I laughed, "it's horribly boring. I write reports about an assessment of the risk involved and whether we should underwrite a policy or not. Also I look at the bond portfolio. We collect a lot of cash for reserves against future claims and it has to be invested in bonds. So I kind of have to be a bond analyst as well."

"I'm a bond analyst too," she said matter-of-factly.

"You're a bond analyst?" I looked at her. "Where? When?"

She laughed, "James Bonds. I've seen every movie; I can tell you what countries he's visited, the cars, the Bond girls..."

"Oh haha. Who's your favorite Bond?"

"Sean Connery, for sure. Although George Lazenby is not bad."

"Yeah, Lazenby is alright. I'm well acquainted with him. Too well. When I was a student in Paris I was living for a year in a really bad apartment. I had no TV and almost no internet. I had internet from a USB stick which was limited to like 1GB a month. I only owned one DVD – it was the Lazenby Bond film. I watched that film over and over, a dozen times probably. There was nothing else I could watch!"

"We could have gone to see the new film, but it was postponed again!" She was referring to *No Time to Die*.

"Oh they postponed it again? Really?"

"Yeah, it's so stupid. Now it's supposed to be October of this year. It was originally April 2020. October would make it one and a half years it's delayed!"

"I wish they could just show it in Florida and let the rest of the world not see if they don't want."

"I know, right? There's no corona here. You can have 200 people in a club but you can't in a movie theatre?"

When the girls were gone during the day the dog kept me company, sleeping on a chair next to me while I worked on my computer on the balcony. I went to the pool to read and swim on every day with good weather – I had finished reading a collection of essays on Buddhism by Yoshida Kenkō and was now reading Gabriele D'Annunzio's *Il Piacere*, an 1889 novel about amorous affairs in the decadence of upper-class Rome.

I came back from the pool to the scent of apricots and strawberries in the apartment. In my absence, Nadia had come back and cut the apricots into halves and washed the strawberries into a bowl.

This was amazing. I'm astonishingly lazy; it does in fact astonish me how lazy I am – if I was alone it would be days before I would finally reach into the refrigerator and rinse and cut the apricots. To even imagine cooking something and then cleaning up after is something I view with real dread. In my New York apartment I don't even own a frying pan. But she did everything! (And this apartment was supplied with every conceivable kitchen utensil).

On another day when I went to the pool, Nadia came with me. I liked that she was not just looking at her phone, but reading a book, and commented to that effect, but she was vexed.

"Why does it surprise you?"

I had to explain that it's not about her, not that I think it's unlikely for her to do it, but that in general I'm always a bit surprised to see someone with a book. "Very few people read books. It's very rare to see someone holding an actual book. Look around now, how many do you see?"

In fact, at that moment there was not a single other person with a book at the pool. Books have become rarer on the subway as well, in the current century compared to the prior century. If I see someone reading literature on the subway I'm very impressed by this person.

* * *

In the warm violet velvet of the evening air, she brought me a glass of wine to the balcony. It was 5:00, so she knew I was finishing up the day's work. I still had some emails to compose; she stood behind me and playfully traced the nail of her finger along the back of my neck, my shoulders. The slightest physical touch from her, such as this, since it was not just a touch but a feeling of direct contact with her, sparked immeasurable felicity.

I finished the work and we drank wine while looking at the sea waves in the distance below us.

She asked me about my preferences regarding girls. I said, "I don't know. But I can tell you what I don't like – all American and Russian girls."

"Why?"

"The American ones – some are better like the ones who are in New York, but in general Americans are very insulated. They have no interest in the world outside the country; culture... I don't have even one friend who is an American. And they are intolerant to any differences in people. They dismiss anyone who is in any way different."

"To be honest you're an unusual person. But that's what I liked about you right away, I really felt you weren't like anyone else."

I laughed, "And that's why I liked you – you're not like them."

"But why Russians? They are the most attractive of all nationalities," she inquired, playing with the ends of her hair. The sky was changing color as the sun approached the horizon somewhere on the westward side of the building.

"That is true," I had to admit. "But in terms of personality they are the worst. Let me put it this way: every Russian girl is either a courtesan or a nun."

"Courtesan or nun?"

"Yes. There's very little in between. It's always either one or the other and both types are unattractive. Actually as different as these extremes are, they share the same point of view with regard to relationships. In Russia and in fact all the former Russian countries, Ukraine etc., they don't enjoy relationships *per se*. They only see it as something to tolerate."

"So are they lesbians?"

"Unfortunately, no," I laughed. "They seem to like girls even less often as guys."

I continued to go out for dinner by myself, and occasionally met various friends in the evening somewhere. Sometimes Nadia and Chiara both left in the evening and didn't return until after I went to sleep. I didn't inquire where they went.

Argo slept as much as a cat. He also liked to hibernate burrowing under blankets. One day I came back and didn't see him in any of the rooms. But then I saw an unruly pile of blankets in a corner of the divan, and I knew, "He must be under there." I checked, and turned out to be correct.

On many of the days, Nadia would do things on her laptop while I worked on mine. The most time-consuming thing she had to do was to complete ten 1 hour-long sessions with alcoholism groups that was ordered by a court due to her conviction for driving after drinking. (This is something that can happen to anyone. In many rural parts of the country, the police set up checkpoints and test everyone, catching many people even if they were driving normally). She did these sessions while drinking a coffee mug filled with wine, because they were so excruciating they could not be done sober.

We went to the rooftop bar at 1 Hotel, with her in white shorts and a cheerful little pink t-shirt with a silvery kitten on the chest. She always dressed modestly and simply and looked good.

Cocktails in Miami are expensive. But on this and some other occasions, she paid for my drinks. This made me love her more than I already did. When a girl offers to pay for things, it shows that she wants to be there. I was not concerned about small losses or savings of money. But the fact that she provides this evidence that she actually wants to be there – that is very attractive – it makes me more attracted to her. And the contrary is true – with someone who never contributes to anything, you can't know if they actually want to be there or not, and that is unattractive.

One day I was getting dressed to go out, to see a friend in South Point, and, as customary, I gave Nadia a quick kiss before leaving.

She said, "Kiss me for real; I'm not your cousin."

That was accurate, I thought. I picked her up and placed her on the edge of the kitchen countertop, kissing her for real.

It was truly a magnetic sensation of pleasure, one of those intense and profound sensations that one feels almost only at the beginning of a love affair.

When I came back home Nadia wasn't there. I went to sleep, and then later, in the middle of the night I woke up to hear her whispering to me, "My mouth is so numb with cocaine you might get high if you kiss me."

I kissed her as she got under the covers close to me but was confused, "What did you do – eat a lot of it?"

From this point on she deserted her section of the divan and only slept in my bed. She had a mild electronic weed cigarette and smoked it, which she did every day before sleeping. When going out she took combinations of whatever she came across: cocaine, ketamine, amphetamine, MDMA, GHB, DMT, mescaline, and some enigmatic drug she called 2C. (However, when I later discussed this topic with a friend in Medellin who was a pharmaceutical expert, he said that what is commonly marketed in Miami as 2C is not in fact the original designer drug, which is a psychedelic phenethylamine, but rather a cheap ersatz combination of MDMA, ketamine, and cocaine). Thankfully she didn't smoke cigarettes or opium, two of the most addictive things. In fact, all of these drugs were relatively benign in the way she was taking them and she wasn't doing anything really dangerous.

She also frequently took xanax, which is bad in combination with alcohol, and wine was something she was never a day without. Together, they make one lose memory of a whole range of things from the night before. People have discovered photos on their phone that they have no recollection of taking. Essentially, it's a sleepwalking state where one does things and forgets about it later. She legitimately needed some amount of xanax but not in combination with large amounts of wine.

The next day I was watching a movie and she sat next to me and seconds later passed out and her head fell on my shoulder. I turned to take a look at what is the matter with her and she slumped on my lap, completely unconscious.

She was easily able to get recreational drugs for free as a beautiful girl. But they are not actually so accessible for regular people. The US is one of the countries with a strong antidrug enforcement, unlike say, Portugal where Angolan dealers are visibly standing on every street corner in central Lisbon. During the day they are friendly: One asked me if I wanted a certain item and I replied in the negative. He then asked, "Well then tell me want you want. Anything you need." He started listing things he could get for me.

It turned out that I was indeed looking for something while I was taking a walk on the sunny May afternoon – I wanted a bottle of Portuguese wine and ginjinha to take home with me. I asked, "Actually yes, I do need something. Do you know where is the closest wine store?"

He knew, and walked with me for a block and around a corner, showing me how to get to the store.

At night, the Angolan dealers are less friendly – one was aggressively trying to get me to sample his product as I left a bar on my way to retire. I couldn't shake him; there was no verbal contention that was sufficient to convince him that a young man walking alone in Lisbon at the end of the night might perhaps not be interested in sampling his product and rather be intent on retiring.

The greater illegality and concealment of drugs in the US makes them more expensive – some of the rarer ones could sell for $50 or $100 for one pill or dose. And money alone is not enough to acquire them – one also needs the necessary connections among the underground world of thieves and hoodlums. If they don't know you they won't do business with you. Even to have someone vouch for you is often not enough.

*   *   *

Although Miami Beach was a good place, there was one other very notable location that was equally as free during this winter of lockdowns, or at least had become so in February: Tulum. A long time ago, I had already planned a half-week long trip to Tulum from Miami, taking advantage of my proximity in the Caribbean. So about a week after they moved in I had to leave them for a few days, although not doubting in the least that Nadia would maintain the apartment properly.

Tulum and Miami were free, but the rest of the world very far from it. In France people couldn't gather and couldn't travel more than 10 kilometers from their home. News came right at this time about how French police discovered and stopped an orgy in progress with 80 participants, charging them with violating the coronavirus curfew. Apparently there was also a lot of violation of "social distancing".

I hadn't been in Tulum in 18 years. The old Mayan ruins were exactly the same, and I encountered the same familiar iguanas amongst them as were there before. It was very sultry – even hotter than when I was exploring the old jungle ruins in Java or Cambodia. Besides this the rest of the town was not the same as it was in 2003. It had become an international nightlife destination. I met people from Barcelona, Geneva, Berlin, São Paulo, Mexico City, Los Angeles, and New York. Europeans and South Americans who could not come to Miami were coming here. A place called Gitano had the best nightlife scene out of all my days there. (There is also a Gitano in Miami in the Faena District).

On the plane I read Sidonie-Gabrielle Colette's *Claudine en ménage*, a 1902 novella about a Parisian wife having an amorous affair with a lady without knowing that this lady was actually her husband's mistress.

Coming back I got to test out my self-created corona credentials for entering the US. Everyone in Cancun airport checking-in to the flight was showing a negative PCR test as they were required to do. Then I approached and handed them instead a positive test! They were confused by this, as all these Kafkaesque rules were new and maybe I was the first person they were seeing bringing them a positive test instead of a negative. But it's much better, as the negative test is only good for 3 days whereas the positive test is good for 3 months! It had to be accompanied by a letter from a doctor saying that I recovered from corona, which I had, signed by myself with the name of a fictional doctor. I chose one with a long and unpronounceable Russian name, Dr. Ivan Petrovich Kotlyarevsky (same as the writer), which would give anyone second thoughts about calling anywhere and asking for this doctor. But nobody ever questioned the authenticity of these documents. The only thing they were concerned about was verifying that the dates are in the proper range and that my name matches my passport.

I would continue to use an updated positive test for 7 more times returning back to the US until the rule went away, saving myself much stress, hassle, and expense, as well as creating it for family and Nadia when they were traveling.

It was only after I started using this scheme that I discovered there was a notable historical precedent, for Sir Fitzroy Maclean, Bt, KT, CBE had used the exact same method while traveling in the Kingdom of Afghanistan in 1938. Maclean's travels to intriguing and potentially hostile places have always been an inspiration to me. While he was posted as a diplomat to the British Embassy in Moscow during Stalin, he evaded the NKVD's restriction on foreigners traveling to Central Asia and explored every city there. On one trip, ending up in Tajikistan, he decided it would be easier to cross into British India and fly back from there rather than make the return via the awful Soviet trains. But Afghanistan, at that time under the rule of Zahir Shah, was in the way. In Mazar-i-Sharif, he was informed that there was a cholera epidemic, and for that reason it was impossible for anyone to cross the mountain passes into Kabul. On the spot, he was able to create a medical certificate stating that he had already had cholera, and recovered! He also created this document for his driver, and they were able to get to Kabul and then Peshawar in India.

The major difference with the present day, though, is that cholera is actually a dangerous disease and not a cold. Also, unlike cholera, coronavirus is already in every country, except for some isolated islands, so what was the sense of all these unnecessary border restrictions? – which in some countries became so complex you needed to have the training of a lawyer to disentangle them.

When I got back to Miami from Mexico I called Nadia from the taxi. She missed me and came back home from an SLS pool party to meet me there.

In retrospect I don't know why I was so dim-witted that I didn't think to invite her to come with me. She did mention a while ago having someone's birthday soirée to go to the weekend I was away, and so I didn't consider asking her but I'm sure I could have convinced her to skip that insignificant thing in favor of going to Tulum.

She was still dressed in the swimsuit she wearing at SLS, looking stunningly beautiful. The light that flickered for a moment in her eyes made me inordinately happy. We took shots from the mezcal bottle I bought in the airport. I caught the infection of her desire and... it was incredible how suddenly things were happening, and yet, everything that happened over the past week had gradually and inevitably led to this moment – by this point it seemed so natural it was instinctive.

Prior to this nothing good had ever happened to me. That bears repeating. Nothing good had ever happened to me in life. I had been with beautiful girls before, but never one who I was in love with and who also liked me and who I thought I had a prospect with. That is an immense difference. She turned the balance over to the positive, making it such that for the first time, the positives in life outweighed the negatives and made life something other than just meaningless work for no reason. What else can be said? Up to now I had reluctantly endured the drudgery of life because I was told it needs to be endured and that someday something good might happen. Well, it had been a while and until now nothing truly significant had happened.

One day we were looking through some of the supplies that the apartment had in a closet – in addition to spare light bulbs and screwdrivers, she also found a headband with cat ears. Nadia laughed upon finding this and immediately put them on, and still had them on when we went out. We had dinner and a bottle of wine at an outdoor table at À La Folie, my favorite French bistro. Besides this, we also went for ceviche many times. Ceviche is one food Miami does better than New York, so I tried to get it often here.

Back in the kitchen later, I stroked and petted her hair.

"What are you, going to give saucer of milk next?" she inquired.

"What do you mean?"

"You seem to think I'm a sort of cat."

"Well..." I spread my hands in perplexity, looking at her, "Aren't you?"

"No."

"If not a cat, why do you have ears like a cat?" Did she forget she had the cat ears on?

"Oh, these are just decorative," she laughed, touching the cat ears, as if I didn't know.

This day her hair was straightened with an iron; other days it wasn't as straight and she put it into two cute braids.

Chiara came in, complaining about losing a lot of money in dogecoin and asking me what to do.

"I don't know. I only look at my portfolio once or twice a year, when I meet with my investments advisor at Citibank. Risky investments like dogecoins, yes they should be in everyone's portfolio, but a small percentage of your assets, like 2% or so."

"But this is the only way I can make money," Chiara said. "I have no income – so it's the only way I can possibly make anything."

"That is true, but you could also lose money."

"I know," she said, looking at her phone which showed the valuation decline.

Nadia exclaimed, "Argo, don't touch my purse, it's Chanel." The dog was curiously examining the purse she left on the divan when coming in.

We ate some madeleines and financiers (another cake similar to a madeleine but a different shape). Nadia tended not to use any American slang, which was good. I didn't even understand some of the Brooklyn slang my friends in New York such as Georges insisted on using, despite the fact that none of them were actual native Americans. She also never happened to pronounce a single vulgar thing. She was entirely *comme il faut* and was indistinguishable from anyone coming from a patrician background, even though her background was quite turbulent.

We went down to the lobby bar to meet some acquaintances of Chiara who were visiting the island. Nadia put on a jacket on top of her dress. Chiara admired her – "You're really beautiful in that dress," she said.

"Thanks," said Nadia, "I like your skirt," touching it. And they interlocked the fingers of their hands as they were walking out the door. Nadia looked back, saying, "Come Argo!" The dog lifted his ears, and happy to go with us, ran ahead of us into the hallway, tail wagging. Miami is very open about bringing dogs everywhere.

Downstairs, as always, it was the fact of having Nadia that made anything about the gathering pleasant. Without her, there would be nothing interesting – just another conversation with various people. With her, everything was different; she made everything better just with her presence. Everyone who came into contact with her aura felt uplifted. Her existence makes the world a better place.

When we went back upstairs in the elevator, she put Argo on her shoulder like a parrot, and he stayed there until we were back in the apartment. She then poured the dog off onto the divan by inclining her shoulder.

I always wanted to rent a motorboat in Miami, but it turned out to be more difficult than I thought. Although I had a Florida boating license, even with the license, any boat above a certain size could only be rented with a driver, which wasn't fun. I wanted to drive the boat myself and go with Nadia wherever we wanted. Even with the smaller boats, not every owner was willing to rent to individuals. I found one fast boat that was possible to rent and we took it for a day from the marina on Virginia Key.

They explained the main difficulty to be mindful of: the water in Biscayne Bay was very shallow – so shallow even a small boat could get stuck in it. There was a map of the deep channels, and it was essential to consult the map and stay only within those areas. The water within a few dozen meters of the land was deep enough. Also, there were various confusing buoys of different colors that needed to be passed either on the right or the left (I didn't catch that part, when was it right and when left?), speed limits, bridge passages, and sea police. All these restrictions were worrying, but Nadia brought a flask of Colombian rum on board and everything was fine.

We first found the Miami River, a narrow waterway lined with skyscrapers on each side, and went into it as far as Kiki's. There were several yachts there of such an abnormal size that it wasn't clear how they could possibly turn around in the river.

Stopping the boat off the coast of Brickell Key, I took photos of Nadia, who took off her shorts and was just in a swimsuit. As she continuing adopting various poses on the edge of the boat for photos, it was so beautifully bewildering I felt I was no longer in reality.

I let her drive through some narrow bridge passings, where we had to wait for traffic of other boats to pass, then past Joia Beach Club to Star Island. Testing the boat's maximum speed, we went north through the Bay and then down through the narrow channel that goes to Mid-Beach. We drank the rest of the rum here (mostly her) and went back to Virginia Key, where, conveniently, there was a good restaurant near the marina, Rusty Pelican.

* * *

It wasn't possible to extend the apartment any further than beginning of March – another tenant was already scheduled after I left. So that was it – she went to Fort Lauderdale to the house of a girl she knew, since she wanted to stay in the Miami area to look for nightclub jobs.

Chiara stayed another week in Miami with someone then returned to New York.

It was a sad parting for me, since I didn't know what would happen. There was a hope of a continuation and she was saying she will come to New York in a month. But sadly, she committed to nothing specific, and was so vague regarding the future that I unfortunately felt there was not that much chance. I imagined that it would be hard to retain the attention of such a beautiful girl, who knows so many people, especially while living in far-apart cities. But I didn't want to discuss any of this with her and risk parting on a bad note; so we had a fond farewell and separated.

XII
NEW YORK

XII – New York

When I got back to the city in March 2021, after being gone for more than 3 months, the people there, sullen and downcast, looked as if they had survived an apocalypse. The city seemed destroyed. Why? It's the same exact virus in Miami and New York. I had almost forgotten that corona was still a thing. It wasn't an issue or a concern in Miami. Why such a difference here?

March is a month that is deceptive in its climate. The greater amount of sunlight and higher temperatures make one think that the winter is nearly over, but this is not the case. Throughout the entire month, a vile wind picks up, a wind so cold it destroys all expectations of an end to the winter. For Ernest Hemingway, March was the saddest month, because at this point you've had so much of winter you can't stand it anymore, you can't endure any more of it, and it looks like it might be actually ending, but it is not.

> You expected to be sad in the fall; part of you died each year when the leaves fell from the trees. But you knew there would always be the spring. Yet when the cold rains kept on and killed the spring, it was as though a young person had died for no reason.

Returning to New York, the shivering cold was only exceeded by the coldness and hostility of the population.

Once again I was the only person on the subway without a mask – nobody else besides me. This was rarely commented on but one time an angry woman confronted me about it, on one of my first days back. I shrugged, saying, "I'm from Miami."

She replied, "Well, this isn't Miami. It's New York."

"Oh. So what's different here?"

Even on the street people wore masks – the most frightful were the ones with a cap lowered to the eyes, or the ones with sunglasses and a mask. You couldn't see any part of their face at all, and they looked non-human. At night on East 8th street, young people going out were all muzzled. Some people were sitting at the same table, outdoors, and still kept their mask on. Some decided that wearing one mask was not enough – they would wear two or three on top of each other. When you saw a person with just one regular mask, you didn't know if they are doing it voluntarily or are being forced. But when you saw someone wearing two or three, you knew you were seeing a true religious believer of the faith.

Indoor restaurants were recently reopened again, but with capacity limits, mask requirements when leaving the table, and no ability to order a drink without also ordering food.

This effectively meant there were no real bars or nightlife. Some bars disagreed with the absurdity and sold very small things, like an olive for 50¢, that qualified as the "food". But other bars were religious about the regulations and said you need to order something substantial, zealous about the new mandates. "We're in a pandemic!"

What a stark contrast to Mynt, Treehouse, Mila, and other places. I was unprepared for this level of absurdity after being in Miami all winter, where people chose not to be in a pandemic.

There was a take-out place in the East Village where I tried to get a drink and have it while sitting at one of their outdoor tables. They informed me I must order a minimum amount of food as well, otherwise it was impossible. I wasn't hungry, but I was fine with ordering some small snack. I started looking at their options to determine what I could get that wouldn't be too big. But they started yelling at me for daring to order without having a mask on, even though they were behind a large barrier of plexiglass. Like the Soup Nazi from *Seinfeld* ("No soup for you!") they were refusing to sell anything to me because I violated their protocol. And, what infuriated them further was that rather than leaving immediately I was trying to engage in a discussion to understand and question their dogma. But their beliefs weren't supposed to be questioned – they were astonished I didn't know that, the same way a store in Kabul during Taliban rule would be shocked at a woman coming to them without a veil, or a "white" store in Alabama during segregation would refuse to serve a black person.

Some people, later on, were keen to remind me that they stayed in New York the whole time and were never lacking in social events, consistently going to parties even during the worst shutdown times.

But their experience is not exactly relevant. The people who say this are from the social elites. They have always had interesting and alluring parties to go to, both before the pandemic and during it. Nothing has changed for them since they have their own exclusive circles. Not having this, I rely on ordinary nightlife. The accomplishment that I achieved, was that I am not from this elite, but still managed to party. This was by having the resourcefulness of knowing where to go, having two good passports, and knowing not to have an irrational fear of corona. I knew to be in Krakow, Bodrum, Tulum, and South Beach.

During these two years 2020 and 2021 I got sick occasionally, about the same number of times as was normal in the past, and never severely. The thought never occurred to me to go wait in line at a clinic, potentially exposing other people to whatever I have, in order to take a corona test, because what would I do with that information by the time I got it? If I felt sick I wouldn't feel like going out and seeing people anyway, regardless of the type of illness it was. I'm not like one of the those people who we've all seen, who shows up to gatherings declaring how sick they are and then proceeds to socialize among everyone, sharing food, kissing on the cheek, oblivious of the chance of infecting others.

With regard to corona, it turned out that between 90% and 95% (depending on the study) of people who tested positive for it, were actually not contagious at that point. So if they used that testing information to isolate themselves, even while asymptomatic and feeling fine, 90-95% of them were doing it for nothing.

I did a standard check-up in the spring, and thankfully the doctor was a rational person and didn't require me to wear a mask (which doctors have never required patients to do for all the years before, even when patients came to them sick with flu). She also didn't wear one. If either of us had masks blocking our mouths, I don't see how we could have been able to carry on a normal articulate conversation. The check-up results showed no diseases, and showed that I have immunity to hepatitis A, hepatitis B, and other things (from prior vaccinations). It also, unexpectedly, showed I have immunity to SARS CoV-2. Knowing this, I thought, why would I go and get a vaccine against it?

Instead I simply printed a blank vaccine card on paper of the same thickness and wrote the necessary vaccine information myself. This became obligatory later in 2021 for many border crossings as well as for living in New York. Restaurants and bars were not allowed to let people in without seeing this, and companies could not employ anyone without it. Without a vaccine card, one couldn't eat or work in New York. Thankfully, unlike Europe, the US made both tests and vaccines very easy to fabricate.

A perplexing thing about the contagion of corona belief was that I always believed Americans to be extremely hardy and impervious to the elements. I envied their hardiness, being much less capable of tolerating weather extremes than they are.

New York is known for exceptionally brutal winters. The weather would fluctuate, but typically each winter would see at least a few days of a -20°C or lower wind chill. For instance, on one day in 2018, when I was going to work in the morning, the wind chill was -26°. Knowing this, I made the necessary preparations – I gathered the multitude of specialized gear necessary to weather such extreme conditions. I put on a waistcoat, jacket, a knee-length leather coat lined with fur on the inside, shearling gloves, tall boots, one standard scarf, a second closed-end scarf typically used for skiing, and an extra-thick Siberian fur hat. Everything was covered except my eyes, in a narrow opening between the second scarf and the hat.

Finally, after the lengthy process of dressing, I ventured out, with this gear certain I would survive the journey if I did it fast and did not linger anywhere. On 57th street, crossing my path in the opposite direction was a man in a light jacket, the kind you might wear in the summer. He had no scarf. In fact I could visibly see the exposed skin of his neck and throat; I could actually see it! Many Americans apparently do not own a scarf. What would likely be a fatal exposure to a deathly acid wind for a Frenchman or a Turk was only causing him a mild discomfiture at most. He did not even bother to zip his jacket up. He was not even quickening his step but walking at a leisurely pace. Many such examples are seen every day in New York.

Although it perplexes me, I don't oppose his freedom to wear whatever he wants. The irritating thing is rather that such a hardy race as this, parading around their invulnerability to illness and cold, were at the same time spearheading an effort to make everyone wear masks and submit to travel restrictions on account of a mild cold circulating around.

During the pandemic I've seen, at 5°, people wearing shorts and a T-shirt, together with a facemask. Obviously not concerned in the slightest about damaging their health through exposure to cold, but very afraid about the nonexistent chance of catching a molecule of corona outdoors.

The other irritating thing is that waiters assume I am also a member of this hardy race of frontiersmen and attempt to murder me by giving me a glass of cold water filled to the top with *ice* when I had just come in from a -10° Arctic deathzone outside.

When I ask Americans why they like the winter, they say, "I like the changing of the seasons."

"So you like the fact that six months, half the year from November to April, is bad weather?"

Personally I would rather have good weather all year than to have seasons change.

Another consequence of Americans' light dressing and acceptance of discomfort is that there is nowhere to put all one's clothes, hats and scarves in many restaurants and bars. Sometimes I came to a restaurant and could not locate a closet or even a simple hook on the wall where I could hang my long knee-length coat. I ask the waiters, "Where can I put all this?" needing to start explaining that it is winter and hence because of the season I am wearing many things.

They would inevitably be speechless, as if we are in the tropical heat of Miami and I was the first person they ever met asking this question. But we're not in Miami – it is a -10° wind chill outside. Looking around, I could see some people sitting on stools, with their coats crumbled underneath them, parts of the coat touching the floor. Many times I just had to leave the restaurant and find another one with a closet or a proper hook. Meanwhile, finding a place to leave my coat has never been a problem when I was in Geneva, Moscow, or Tokyo in the winter, but in New York they like to pretend that winter doesn't exist and are surprised when someone tries to bring a long coat to a bar.

* * *

Of course I wanted to marry Nadia, but suspected that it was impossible. It was very likely that, regardless of dalliances, she probably wouldn't want to make a permanent commitment to someone. Many hints she gave led me to believe that to have her attention for a little bit was possible, but such a beauty could not be expected to settle permanently when she was bombarded with a never-ending choice of wealthy prospects.

When she was working in nightclubs before, she regularly made the acquaintance of rich and glamorous people, for instance Antoine Arnault and Calvin Harris. She talked about being taken on first class flights to Dubai and London, about parties on enormous yachts, and $50,000 Nebuchadnezzar bottles.

Up to now, during all our acquaintance she had always been in proximity – I saw her every day. When she was, for the first time, at a distance from me, was the moment I had the revelation that Nadia at a distance is a completely different person than Nadia in proximity. I found out that her communication was in fact one of the worst of anyone I've ever known. It was as if her charm could only be contained in one place in her personality, namely the brightness and joy that she emanated to her surroundings wherever she went, and so much charm went there that there was none left over for her to have any when communicating long-distance.

Until I came to understand that this was a standard trait of her's, – until I became, if not accustomed to it (no amount of time could make me accustomed to it) but at least knowing to expect it – it made me unhinged. We were in the middle of discussing her plans to come to New York (over text messages since she rarely spoke on the phone) and she didn't reply for 2 days. By the end of the day she still hadn't responded, and I thought that's fine, it can wait till tomorrow. First thing when I woke up in the morning I checked my phone, because maybe she replied late at night: There was nothing from her.

Slowly and gradually during the day my mind's volume was having all its hope draining out and instead increasingly being filled with heavy despair which was sinking me. Whatever I was doing, at work, or when meeting someone, the bewildering question of why she isn't replying was always in my thoughts, like a leaden spectre, driving away all thoughts of distraction, preventing me from focusing on anything. Hardly anything happened in the day without reminding me of this uncertainty. My thoughts veered violently between poles of optimism and pessimism. After a night of terrible sleep, I again looked at my phone in the morning, and again nothing from her!

At this point, naturally I thought that either she died or was lost forever. I was devastated. Why did I suddenly lose her without a word?, I thought. What happened to her?

Then after 48 hours she finally replied. Bizarrely, she acted as if nothing was the matter. She was cheerfully confirming plans and even chatting a bit.

When she finally came to New York and stayed with me, I was thrilled to see her again, but had to quickly adjust my expectations. She spent almost all of her time away. She had even more acquaintances in New York than in Miami, and spent every day and night traversing the city and drinking and doing drugs with them all. One day she had a "thing" happening in New Jersey. I couldn't gain an understanding of what these things were. House parties where people do large amounts of weird drugs all day? Another time she needed to retrieve a box of her possessions from a storage unit and mail it to herself in Fort Lauderdale. But actually, she met up with some people in a bar before this and ended up drinking so much she couldn't go and do the task, requiring me to later do it for her after she left.

With her need to see everyone she knew and a limited number of days, she was only able to have dinner with me once, on the last day. We went to Le Baratin, a crowded French bistro in the West Village that, unlike most other places, didn't follow rules on capacity restrictions and did not care if people wore masks when they were standing.

As always when spending time tête-à-tête with her I forgot everything except how much I adored her. And, I didn't know this yet, but after this downturn the sweetest and best part of our relationship would come later, in June.

Later on she would tell me she misses me, would insist I visit her in Miami. The kind words with which she would express her desire to spend time with me, in contrast to the lack of attention in her New York visit, I had at that future moment sought to attribute to a genuine change of heart. In fact they were simply the reflection of one of those changes in a situation of which we do not know, and which are the whole secret of the variations in the conduct of women who do not love us. The simple truth was that she had a greater preference for others (she even traveled to San Francisco to meet with one of them) and for whatever reason, by the time it was May, things had not worked out with any of them.

Dissimulation is a recurring theme in *À la recherche du temps perdu*, and the world of Proust is a world where nobody can be trusted and everyone lives in deceit. Odette de Crécy and Albertine are experts in deception. Nadia, however, didn't need to deceive; all she had to do was omit. Since we were far apart, and communication was so sparse, merely by omission she could have me know about her life only what she wanted me to know, and nothing she didn't want.

Charles Swann's suspicions with regard to Odette were incorrect – the men she was seeing were entirely different than the ones he suspected, and a far greater number than he supposed. She would, in fact, have orgies with 5 or 6 at the same time, organized by the Baron de Charlus, a friend of Swann's. Nadia, at least, was not a nymphomaniac and did not do that.

XIII
TIME DOES NOT EXIST

XIII – Time Does not Exist

I happened to meet a close friend, visiting from out of town, who I had not seen or talked to for 7 years. What struck me was that he saw me as the way I was 7 years ago. Given a certain situation, he was assuming how I would react, but it was not "me" he was thinking of, but me from 7 years ago. I wanted to say, "That's not me; I'm a different person than I was before."

And in fact it would be odd if we did not change our opinions, preferences, or tastes throughout our lives. If we continually learn, travel, and experience new things, we have to incvitably evolve our thoughts and even preferences, since it is impossible to come into the world already knowing everything. Even within the timeframe of this book, which is approximately two years, the person I was at the beginning is not the one I am at the end. Oftentimes one's opinions and sometimes even one's knowledge is merely a result of a perception of knowing, while the truth can elude one for decades until it is finally grasped. Actually I feel like the more time that passes, the less and less I know, because the more I end up knowing, the more I realize I don't know.

Reflecting on the observations of my friend, I realized that personality is not something that exists in our minds, but rather is created by the thoughts of others, on the basis of our communication with them. Thus, our personality exists in the perception of others, and it is not one tangible unitary thing, since as many people as exist with whom we have interacted, as many different versions of our personality exist in all of their perceptions. We have some control over it, but ultimately, it exists in other people, not in us.

Going further along this line of thought, we can see that all these people who collectively hold our existence in their minds, will soon be dead. So, in the long-run, we do not exist. I was talking about this with Nadia in the 1 Hotel beach bar. I said, "Only in literature can someone live forever, because an author creates his own world and the full image of a character. Emma Bovary, for instance, or Anna Karenina, is more real than you or I. Anna was created in 1875 and is just as unchanged now as all the years since then. Once we're gone, and everyone who knows us is gone, she will still exist."

"How can you say," she asked, "that a fictional character that isn't real, is more real than real people?"

"It's precisely because the character is fictional, that she does not have a lifespan – she can be eternal – while for us, reality is defined only as this tiny moment right now."

"So what do we do in this moment?" she smiled seductively.

"Well, to start with, we should drink," and we clinked our glasses of wine to that.

But the wine made me reflect more. I recalled Proust, specifically the climax of his 3500 page novel, where he has a déjà-vu related to the feeling he has when stepping on an oddly-shaped paving stone outside a building and then spends 80 pages deliberating on perception and time, and on reconnecting with the perceptions of former time in the mind.

He wrote about how it is only through art and literature that we can approach a knowledge of how another person sees the world. That art is a means of both rediscovering and translating perception, not just of things, but of subjective, conscious experience. Without art, there would be no way to know how anyone else perceives the world, since our perception of everything in it and in life differs from that of everyone else.

Taking a look at practical work such as farming and industry, can we say it is truly productive? Not in the long run – it is just another part of *samsāra,* the wheel, the cycle of death and rebirth. Art, however, exists beyond the temporal, surpassing time.

Its value lies precisely in the fact that it has no practical value. It brings reality to the world, a world which otherwise doesn't truly exist, since its most important element, the subjective perception of life that we individually experience, is located only in our temporary thoughts, strictly bound by time. Outside of our minds, art is the only other place where the world exists.

Swiss people in particular are very keen on capturing time, with our centuries of horological clockmaking, structuring life by the movement of the cogs and tourbillons. A train will apologize if it is half a minute late.

We cling to time, as if even an infinite amount of time would help. Would more time help? It would not. Since what can really be achieved in this illusory life? – Life would remain as always divided between the struggle against hierarchy and the struggle against boredom. Zero time is rather what is needed.

Since the world doesn't matter and doesn't exist, time doesn't exist either. An unlimited amount would achieve the same effect as zero. Proust, Nabokov, Bergson, Hesse, and Borges have written a lot about time, but none of them have come to the conclusion that time doesn't exist because it doesn't matter.

More can be written about that, but no, let's not lengthen the chapter.

XIV
ZERMATT

XIV – Zermatt

It was a good time to go skiing – the slopes in Switzerland were nearly empty, and I could blaze for miles through the untouched corduroy, gaping at the sublimity of the Matterhorn and hardly seeing any people.

There were again the empty international terminals and empty planes. I had the feeling of being an actual real traveler – "bound for mysterious lands and distant climes," as Mark Twain put it – not being funneled with a crowd heading the same direction but doing something unique that nobody else was doing, on a special undertaking. The mission was to ski.

Switzerland was the only place in Europe it was possible to ski this winter. France and Italy shut everything down. In France at this time there was a 19:00 curfew and people weren't allowed to travel more than 10 kilometers from their homes, worse restrictions than during the Nazi occupation in WWII. Austria permitted skiing but only for local residents, no travelers, and with a heap of various restrictions. (Some Bavarians, however, were able to portray themselves as Austrians, knowing the language, and to ski in Kitzbühel, according to an acquaintance in Munich).

Although Switzerland welcomed any Europeans from anywhere, in all my time there, I didn't meet one person who had come to ski from another country. The only ones were from inside Switzerland, like Geneva and Zürich. I asked my friend from just across the border in Stuttgart to join me; he refused. He is Mexican and said he was afraid of problems entering back into Germany if he left. I asked, "How would they know that you left the country?" As far as I knew there were no German border guards patrolling the

Swiss border. France, on the other hand, actually had police on the border, and asking anyone to come from Paris was out of the question. Meanwhile I came all the way across the ocean from New York without any inconveniences at all. By now most countries worldwide, if they were open for travel at all, were requiring at least a negative corona test to cross borders. But both Switzerland and the US accepted the positive test as an alternative, and I used it (a fake one) for both.

Since it was mid-April, I decided to go to Zermatt, the highest elevation ski area in Europe, some parts of it so high you can ski in the summer. I landed in Zürich, with my skis and gear, and within a few hours train ride was in Zermatt, greeted by the angular eminence of the Matterhorn, the giant tooth of ice and rock. The town at the foot of this towering pyramid consists of old chalets and winding alleys, and has the charm of having no cars permitted. Everyone gets in by train.

I picked up a copy of the trail map and stared at it over dinner, salivating at the prospects. The map of the ski area was so big it stretched into another country, Italy. (Normally, it would have been possible to ski into Italy, have lunch there, and come back. But now, everything in Italy was closed). The map's rich variety of conveyances for getting up the mountain – aerial tramways, funiculars, télécabines, and a cog railway – revealed Swiss ingenuity, unlike say in the Andes in Argentina, where there are beautiful mountains but the infrastructure is lacking, leading to just a few chairlifts and long queues for each one. Here in Zermatt you would find the world's highest tricable lift, heading up to the Klein glaciers at 3820 meters.

The pandemic changed the way I perceived certain states. At one extreme, Australia I would mistrust forever; just the example of their mistreatment of Novak Djokovic is enough cause. In Switzerland, I had always felt at home, of course, and now additionally felt this way in Florida and Türkiye. But no longer as much in Bavaria and Austria, which formerly I loved more than anywhere else in Europe and admired even more than Switzerland. I always felt that Switzerland was a little lacking in hospitality compared to Austro-Bavaria, the land of *Gemütlichkeit*, dirndls, and Oktoberfest. Not anymore. The way I was welcomed in Switzerland in April 2021 – at the hotel, at restaurants, everywhere else – changed that. And it wouldn't have mattered if I was a citizen of Geneva or any other state in Europe, since I said I was coming from New York and nobody knew who I was. There were still lingering restrictions in Switzerland that only allowed restaurants to be open outdoors. But, for the benefit of travelers, hotels were an exception to the rule, so indoor restaurants and bars were open there. Also, hotels made reciprocal arrangements with other hotels, to enable someone to go to a restaurant in one where they're not staying. Not the ideal situation, but still leagues ahead of the situation across the border in France with curfews and shutdowns.

As I looked out my window the next day I was disappointed to see gray clouds, the cog train struggling through the fog. I gathered the ton of ski gear necessary: Authier coat, gloves, mirrored ski goggles, etc., went to the hotel's ski room where I put on boots and took my skis and sticks, then walked to the underground funicular station nearby. There were almost no people on any lift, since there was no one in town from the rest of Europe outside

Switzerland. When I got to the top – brilliant sunshine. Visibility for miles, a bright blue sky, and, to add brightness to the day, at this moment I happened to get a nice note from Nadia on my phone, ending with the kissing cat face icon.

At the tops of the mountains, in the wide pistes above the tree-line, I could race for hours, inclining the knife-sharp edges of my skis into the freshly-groomed snow to make precision arcs, all the time bewildered, actually stunned to disbelief by the beauty of the high Alps all around. Many times I felt that I was committing a transgression by not taking a picture or a video of what I was seeing, that this cannot be left to just memory alone, but I did not have time to stop; I was enjoying it too much, so I had to hope that memory will be enough.

Lower down, amidst the pines, I would find some fresh virgin powder, the most coveted of snow to ride in, untouched, deep soft powder. This was a dream of swaying in between trees through sugar, occasionally finding a jumping off point from a boulder, and landing up to the waist in soft snow, only to continue down the slope due to inertia.

I came back up the mountain to search for a steep off-piste and I finally found one off the Stockhorn. I looked down – a kilometer of uninterrupted virgin powder heading straight to the bottom. Some other skiers on the piste stopped, watching me as I prepared myself to make the descent. I jumped off the piste and into the vertical sea of snow – it is like falling in slow-motion through velvet, half submerged. Each turn must be made accurately to remain in control of the speed, but to think about what one is doing would be fatal to stability; every motion must come naturally and thoughtlessly.

After this descent I went to have lunch at a restaurant in Riffelberg in the middle of the mountain. But the effect of all this on my senses remained. I felt a heightened sense of perception of everything around me. Colors seemed more vivid; outlines seemed sharper. I was riveted by a skier's bright red coat against the whiteness of the snow. As I sat under the bright Alpine sun, eating a schnitzel and drinking a beer, observing the world, I felt as though a layer of dust had been removed from my senses and everything was clearer. I noticed details I hadn't noticed before, like the perfect way a cable car climbed up the mountain in the distance, the towers perched precariously on a cliff face. An Alsatian hound walked by, a child riding it. For a brief moment everything seemed perfectly constructed in the world around. Only briefly; the luminous state faded eventually because I realized the pain of being alone.

In late afternoon, having squeezed every descent possible out of the day, it was time for après-ski at one of the outdoor bars on the slopes just before one descends into the town. There were a lot of young people drinking here and I met a blonde Luxembourgish girl living in Zermatt and a Swiss-French lad from Montreux, the same town where V.V. Nabokov lived when he wrote *Ada*. My cousin from Geneva came, with his wife, and I had dinner with them in town. The next day I skied with the fellow from Montreux, but it did not alleviate my loneliness. I missed Nadia.

On the trains I was reading *Mémoires d'Outre-Tombe*, the memoirs of François-René de Chateaubriand. He mentioned witnessing a cholera epidemic in Paris in 1832. What is interesting is that despite the extreme and lethal danger of this epidemic, Parisians were unconcerned. "Everyone continued to attend to his business, and the theatres were full." Meanwhile, in the current day, during a severe cold going around, Paris has resorted to a 19:00 curfew and total restrictions on traveling a short distance from your home.

When I got back to JFK airport in New York the passport control officer asked me what was the purpose of my travel. I replied, "Skiing." He was fine with that response and did not react. I have the right to go skiing, after all, pandemic or not.

As soon as I got back I had another trip to CDMX – Mexico City – staying at the new Sofitel in Reforma. I had not been in a city outside Europe/America since Istanbul in September 2020, and I realized how long it's been. The smell of the car exhaust in the street was different than that of anywhere I've been for a long time, and I enjoyed this smell because of its uniqueness – just for the reason that it felt good to be in a place that was different.

I visited the Palacio de Quetzalpapálotl and the pyramids of Teotihuacán, noting the Patio of the Jaguars – red tinted frescos depicting jaguars with conch shells in their mouths.

In terms of corona restrictions it was almost normal, apart from the bigger dance clubs being not open yet, and the occasional mask request (*"mascarilla"* here). Casa Franca, my favorite jazz club in the world, was open. For parties I was relying on my friends there to direct me to semi-secret places not on the map that were operating normally. Mexico is a place where there may or may not be rules, but they don't apply to everyone, and it's always possible to get around them. I was lucky that one of my friends, Catuxa, was a Mexican model. She introduced me to her friends and each of them was also a model, all from different countries: Montréal, Minsk, and Montevideo. Normally, they would be working in various parts of Latin America. CDMX was the center of the Latin American film industry but there were also many film and modeling jobs in Brazil and Argentina. Now, they explained, everyone was centered only in CDMX as other places were shut down and it had the most freedom. Not one of these girls was single though.

I talked with Alizée, the girl from Montréal, and she told me fascinating things about what is going on there right now. Prior to the corona pandemic, I assumed Canada was so similar to the US that it was essentially like another state, the 51st state. Actually this was not the case – Canada was extremely different. It was far worse.

Alizée said that she just now escaped from Montréal to Mexico. Her usage of the exact word "escaped" indicated how bad it was there. The government of Quebec had identified that another coronavirus wave was happening and severe measures were reintroduced in April 2021. The border between Ontario and Quebec was closed. Canadians could leave the country but if they did they could not come back. In Montréal everything was shut down again: schools, businesses, restaurants. And there was an 8:00 PM curfew.

Alizée described a recent incident, "I was at a house party at someone's apartment and there was a hot tub on the balcony. I was in a swimsuit, in the hot tub, and people suddenly started saying the cops are here. Someone informed on us that we were having a party. You aren't allowed to have more than a certain number of people in your house or you will get fined. We actually climbed over the railing of the balcony to the neighbor's apartment, and were knocking on the door there so he could let us in. Still in a swimsuit, and it's April, so it's freezing cold in Montréal..."

I asked, "Who would get fined – everyone, or just the person who lives there?"

"Just the owner of the apartment would get fined, but we didn't want that to happen, so as many people as could climbed over to the neighbor's balcony!"

This was the kind of crazy police-state fascism that was happening just across the border in Canada. Like in some European countries, people weren't even allowed to do what they wanted to do in their own homes. Neighbors would rat you out to the police. Who could imagine that in the 21st century things like this would happen in Western countries that we imagined had some semblance of human rights?

I already knew it was true that Canadians couldn't travel. I have a friend in Toronto, so close to New York, but as much as she wanted to leave to enjoy Miami or Tulum in the winter, she couldn't because there would be restrictions going back, assuming it was even possible. It was the same when I invited friends from London to join me in Europe or Türkiye. They were governed by a color-coded map of constantly shifting colors that allowed certain trips and disallowed others.

* * *

On the way back to New York from Mexico, I ran into particularly zealous mask Nazis on American Airlines. This was despite the fact that everyone on the plane, in order to enter the US, had to present a negative corona test within the last 3 days (except for me, but that's besides the point since they didn't know my documents were falsified).

What was the reason to be so stringent in enforcing these masks when everyone on the plane had a negative test? I know the obvious answer that is given to this question: "Because it's a rule." Does every nonsensical rule need to be blindly enforced?

As soon as I entered they observed that my flimsy, home-made mask that was completely open at the bottom was unacceptable for their standards. I switched to another one I had, a lightweight black cloth one. But obviously I could not sit completely covered with a hot muzzle for hours. The flight attendant, like a drill sergeant ever vigilant in catching misbehaving delinquents, criticized me for not covering my nose. I complied with his orders and lifted it; he said it's not high enough (!), he could still see a part of my nose. I lifted it even higher, right up to my eyes. Later in the flight, I was watching a James Bond movie while drinking a Ginger Ale. I don't like to drink carbonated drinks very fast; I was taking my time, taking sips from the cup as needed while holding it in my hand. I was sitting in the very last row, my entire row was empty, and nobody was complaining about my lack of mask. The flight attendant approached again, saying, "You're drinking too slowly. Everyone else has already finished."

"This is how I drink though." I was shocked he was actually blaming me for drinking too slowly.

"So then you need to put your mask back on, and only lower it in between sips."

I could not understand this level of absurdity. I asked, "Why is it so important to you, personally, that I do this? Nobody else is around. Why do you feel the need to enforce this at this moment? You can't make a reasonable exception?"

He did not respond but left and several minutes later brought me a piece of paper and told me to read it. The paper, on some government letterhead, said, in summary, "This notice serves as a warning that you may be in violation of federal law. Persisting with your actions could lead to fines and/or arrest." I read the paper and had to comply with the mask Nazis. What else could I do?

Upon taking the first step off the plane, I tore off the mask, in great relief, because now I could actually breathe again! While walking through the sleeve connecting the plane to the terminal, I noticed that the people walking beside me were still wearing a mask. I told one of them, "There's no need to wear this anymore – we're off the plane!"

He mumbled something I couldn't understand, since a mask was blocking his mouth. I told the old woman next to him, "This airline was the worst of all I've taken regarding masks. And before this flight everyone had to take a PCR test as well, so why all this?"

The irony that I, the only person on the flight complaining, was also the one person who had not taken a negative test did not bother me. These rules were all absurd and the fact that I cleverly exploited a loophole did not change the absurdity I was trying to defy. I aspired to Oscar Wilde's admission, "I am one of those who are made for exceptions, not for laws."

The old woman asked, "So what was the best airline regarding masks?"

"Swiss Air to Zürich."

The man I had talked to first angrily said to me, "I hope you get fined in the airport."

* * *

Back in New York, vaccines had already been distributed to practically everyone. I happened to be in a hotel lobby and a television was on showing the news. I never watch the American news, but this time I stopped to look and I caught an interesting tidbit about how the corona believers think. A woman was being interviewed outdoors in a park about why she is still wearing a mask everywhere she goes. What she said was so astounding the exact words have been fixed in my memory verbatim ever since. She said, "I've been fully vaccinated, and I know that I don't need a mask now, especially outdoors. But it's important to maintain the *culture of mask wearing* until everyone is vaccinated, including all children."

The culture of mask wearing. This was just a chance observation of one time glimpsing what the media is showing people in America. They may have been saying even crazier things than this – I don't know.

By the middle of May, the various rules in New York about capacity limits and food went away and bars and clubs were fully normal for Summer 2021. Government rules requiring restaurants to enforce mask wearing when a person walks the 10 meters from the door to the table went away, and immediately most restaurants stopped saying anything about masks. But a few stubbornly continued the same way as before, so now it was plainly visible which staff had been just reluctantly complying with government orders and which were actual zealots who were humiliating us just because they wanted to, either from sadism or stupidity. These places continuing to enforce masks even after the government didn't care, earned a permanent boycott from me. Meanwhile, the places which I remembered refused to enforce rules earlier when the rules were in effect, earned my permanent respect.

I went to Los Angeles for a weekend and then San Francisco for a week, working out of my company's office in downtown. Everything was relatively normal in California (although at other times, I heard the restrictions were even worse than in New York).

It perplexed me why mask usage on the subway in New York persisted for so long, even after people stopped wearing masks anywhere else in the city. They would exit a super-crowded, unventilated bar, like Red Lion on Bleecker street, where nobody had a mask, then go in to the subway, which was much less crowded and put one on. What was the logic behind that?

A disturbing incident occurred around this time that made me reflect on the culture of Nazism. I was entering the Morgan Library museum on 37th and Madison, and there was two different sets of doors, on the left and on the right. After the doors was a vestibule, then another set of doors. The ones on the left were wide open, so I went in through there, not wanting to touch the unclean door handles of the doors on the right that were closed.

A guard stopped me, pointing to the floor. There were arrows painted on the floor indicating that the way I had entered was actually supposed to be the way out. Apparently entry was forbidden in this direction.

What followed was pure Kafka. Kafka himself couldn't have come up this level of absurdity. I said, "Okay, I see, but I have already entered by mistake through these doors."

"No, you have to go back out and re-enter through those," he said.

I looked around. There were no people around us. If I just stepped two meters to the right, I would be in the same location that exiting and re-entering through the right-side doors would lead me to. I said, trying to move towards that part of the floor, "But I've already made the mistake and entered. It's too late to undo that. If I just move a bit in this direction, I'll be in the place you want."

"No!", he was becoming aggressive. "You must exit right now! You cannot enter the building if you came through these doors."

"Why?"

Same answer.

"Can I go through here, and then enter through those doors there?" I asked, pointing at the vestibule.

"No, you must go back all the way outside."

I really wanted to see something in this museum, an original Gutenberg Bible, so I gave up and went through the pointless ritual. I exited from the left-side doors, went through the vestibule, went outside, then demonstratively walked over to the right-side doors, went through them, then the same vestibule I was just in, then the second set of right-side doors. I was now in the building again, just two meters to the right of where I was before.

"There, I did it. Everything is different now?"

A woman who apparently worked in the museum had been observing the confrontation. Once I was in I asked her if this harassment was right. She said, "You should have just done what you were told to do."

That was amusing. Why would I do something that I know is completely nonsensical just because someone tells me to do it? What was bothering me the most was not the effort to walk a few extra meters and get my hands dirty pulling the door handles, but the farcically Kafkaesque nature of the task they were demanding of me.

It was a similar nonsensical injustice that led to the founding of the Swiss Confederation 700 years ago. According to legend, the mountaineer William Tell was visiting the town of Altdorf and was told that he needs to bow before the hat of the Austrian overlord, which was placed on a stick in the center of town. He asked, "What if I refuse to bow before this hat?"

"You will be arrested."

His refusal sparked a rebellion and the formation of Switzerland. This was so long ago it was even before the time of Dante, Petrarch, and Boccaccio. The Renaissance was just beginning in northern Italy; the rest of Europe was in the Dark Ages and the Byzantine Empire still existed in the east. Since then Switzerland has stuck to personal freedom and armed isolationism, with its population armed with guns, its mountains fortified, its roads and bridges lined with camouflaged tank traps. As a result it was the most peaceful nation in Europe these seven centuries.

The encounter with the guard made me recall Dostoyevsky's *Memoirs from the House of the Dead*, his powerful work reflecting on his years of imprisonment in Siberia. He writes,

> These advocates of the application of the law definitely, do not understand, and are incapable of understanding, that the mere literal fulfillment of the law, without reason or comprehension of its spirit, leads straight to disorder and has never led to anything else. 'The law says so; what more do you want?' they say, and are sincerely astonished that anybody should demand of them, in addition to the letter of the law, sound judgment and sober minds. These last in particular seem to many of them a superfluous and shocking luxury, and an intolerable restraint.

So many times during the course of the pandemic, when I inquired about the rationale behind various peoples' demands that I do one thing or not do another, I would get the same unthinking response, repeated over and over, "But it's the law!" And they would stare at me as if I was mad, as if I had been questioning an axiom of mathematics, as if they had never even heard of such a thing being possible as a bad, unfair, or cruel law, as if slavery and alcohol prohibition were not once laws even here in America.

Then I thought about another thing related to this: where did all these goons and mask Nazis come from – all the ones that have suddenly materialized to enforce nonsense like arrows painted on floors, and masks at the entrance to groceries? The answer is that they were always here – we didn't know because nobody before this had given them any power, to harass people who are just minding their own business trying to go about their lives.

When I was in Siem Reap I questioned an elderly local about Pol Pot. The communist regime in Cambodia had murdered at least 1.5 million people, nearly a quarter of the country's population, many of whom were beaten to death with clubs, hoes, and pickaxes. He disagreed with my assumption; he said no, it can't be blamed solely on foreign communist influence – everything that happened in Cambodia was done by the Cambodian people.

But how? The Cambodians are a gracious, Buddhist people, similar to the people of Thailand. I realized that every society, no matter its culture, already has within it enough people to be able to find and recruit any number of goons, as well as enough people who will submit to any rules without saying anything.

*   *   *

Meanwhile, things had improved for Nadia. She got a new job in a nightclub in Miami and started working again in the beginning of May for the first time in more than a year. We had been corresponding more and more and she had seen pictures from all my travels. (Travel, in addition to bringing us closer to people who we visit while traveling, also brings us closer to everyone else that we know, as it give us something meaningful to share with them, other than the humdrum and largely repetitive events of daily life in the cities where we live, which, although they might be interesting if the city is an exceptional one like New York, have nowhere near the colorful appeal of distant lands).

My friend Georges was going ahead with his wedding plans in Saint-Tropez, and I invited Nadia to come with me. Meanwhile she was inviting me to visit her in Miami.

She needed an apartment in downtown Miami close to where she worked. I was considering buying an apartment there and renting it to her. I would have to sell half of my investments to do so, but having real estate in Miami would be an even better investment in the long-term. However, this would not work due to the many months required for a transaction to close. She needed an apartment as soon as possible, so she looked for one to lease, and eventually found one. I helped her very substantially in many of the costs associated with this (for instance, she had no furniture), and my rationale was that in addition to helping her, I was also making it possible for myself to have a place to stay in Miami next winter. (I was assuming my company would return to the office well before the winter, but even in that case I was sure that there would be flexibility to work remotely for at least a month. What actually happened was some new variants of corona emerged and the office return didn't occur until the following spring, a year from now). She involved me so much in the search, selection, and upfront costs, I almost thought of it as *our* apartment.

A problem was that all this time since February when we lived together in South Beach, she continued to have the same kind of erratic and unreliable communication. It was stunning how poor her communication was. I already accepted that she doesn't prefer or have time to actually chat about things, like most people normally do. So although she was one of the closest people to me in the world, she was ironically the one I had the least ability to regularly communicate with, rarely able to know what is happening in her life or to be able to share what's going on in mine.

That was unfortunate, but it was fine, as long as I could count on her being there when it was really needed. But I could not – it was always unknown, when I sent her a message, whether it would be read at all, and whether a reply would come soon, or in two days time, or never.

Communication is important because without communication there is nothing. Nothing connects two people without it. You do not know anything, there is no present, no future, the person might as well not exist if you do not trust that they will reply; their existence is equivalently as real to us as the existence of a citadel of unicorns and hippogriffs on the far side of the moon that we cannot see because it is hidden from any method of communication.

Maybe because of the trauma of having so many people in my life vanish suddenly, I was like a dog, who, when its owner leaves on a journey, doesn't know where they are and whether they will ever come back.

Of all the things about Nadia that were unusual, the one and only thing that I absolutely could not find a way to understand, far most inexplicable to me than her drug use or anything else, was her inability to reply to messages on a phone. It was some kind of pathological incapacity that had no cause, motivation, or catalyst. It happened not just with me (Chiara tried to mail her flowers for her birthday, but couldn't get a response from her asking about her address so had to ask me for it) and also led to problems for herself as well. (In her new apartment, she suddenly remembered that she still didn't get a coffee table that I promised her. I said, "I tried to get one for you, I sent you a few options, several times, you never responded.")

Some might argue, "She's very beautiful, so she doesn't have time to respond to people." There is certainly a lot of strong logic in that statement, (I'm not being sarcastic – there is actually some logic in that) but on the other hand, we all know other girls who are beautiful and privileged and still manage to respond to us efficiently.

It can also be said that knowing that she has this trait, I should have lessened my expectations and stopped getting upset. But I could not, since she would sometimes choose the most uncomfortable moments in which to not reply for two or more days. For instance, sometimes I found out from her that she was experiencing a certain problem, like she was ill or was stranded in some airport because she missed a connecting flight. And then I would be unable to get an answer for days about whether she was okay, leading to unnecessary worry, something she could have so easily prevented me.

I was making plans to visit her in mid-June, everything was set, and there was one last step remaining, to confirm dates with her before buying flights. We had been corresponding quite a bit and I sent her a question in the middle of a certain day.

And it was at that moment she had to disappear. It took her two days to reply, even with a reminder I sent her after one day. Then at some unexpected moment, she finally responded, confirming dates, eager to see me soon, and I was so relieved I forgave her for everything.

Was it rational to have this much uncertainty every time she did not respond for a long time? I don't know. Unfortunately, what she was doing was indistinguishable from the actions of someone who doesn't care at all. Each time, it required a great deal of self-convincing to reject that explanation, which is the simplest one, and to imagine that there are some more complex explanations preventing her from acting normally. In the absence of communication, there was simply no way to tell which is was. In the painful intervals, in the numerous days I spent waiting for a response, I had no idea what is going on with her and what is happening between us. I supposed that if she didn't care about responding, then she's capable of anything, even suddenly deciding she wants to become affianced with someone and deciding to no longer see me again and to stop responding forever and let me figure it out. The effect of this was that I gradually started to avoid writing her unless it was very important.

XV
∆

XV - Δ

Nadia had an apartment not far from the center of Brickell, where it was possible to get around by monorail and taxi without needing a car, in a brand new high-rise with pools and other amenities. It was possible to get good value in downtown Miami, unlike New York, because it was still a relatively new and developing city. In Manhattan, not only were rents about 1.5x higher, but one also got very poor quality, in decades-old buildings, for the higher price.

I visited her in June right after she moved in. She was working on weekend nights, which was contrary to my work schedule, but she took Saturday off.

The disbelief of finding another moment of enchantment in this world, indulging with her in the pleasure of passionate desire, or even just being in the same room with her and talking about plans of where will we go out that evening, was something so contrary to the normal course of ordinary life, that the mind doesn't register it; one drifts incredulously through an alternate reality, since her gestures, her expressions, the intimacy of being a couple when we went out and came back home, the electric warmth of her body as it touched mine, were all things belonging more to the daydreams of decades than to what I perceived to be life. She was a flaming light in a vast tract of time unlit, unlived. How well her presence gave expression to the promise of happiness. One night she wore a short little black crêpe de chine dress with a strap asymmetrically over just one shoulder, with violet platform heels. For the first time in months I could savor her presence for an extended period of time – a stiletto heel hanging off her foot as she sat with crossed legs, the texture of her dark brown hair when I touched it, the scent of perfume on her neck, the adrenaline of downing a big shot of tequila with her to start the night, carefree laughter about things we both found amusing. The curve of her lips was perfection, enticing me to want to taste her mouth. We would talk for hours at night, about what I don't remember, sitting on her bed refilling our wine glasses with red wine. She tied her hair up so that I could massage her neck and shoulders.

With her, it was as if all my feelings and desires melted and dissolved together in a single river of sensation. Reality felt altered because reality was in her – she was the one who gave reality meaning.

I thought of a certain passage of Baudelaire:

> La mousseline pleut abondamment devant les fenêtres et devant le lit; elle s'épanche en cascades neigeuses. Sur ce lit est couchée l'Idole, la souveraine des rêves. Mais comment est-elle ici? Qui l'a amenée? quel pouvoir magique l'a installée sur ce trône de rêverie et de volupté? Qu'importe? la voilà! je la reconnais.
>
> À quel démon bienveillant dois-je d'être ainsi entouré de mystère, de silence, de paix et de parfums? Ô béatitude! ce que nous nommons généralement la vie, même dans son expansion la plus heureuse, n'a rien de commun avec cette vie suprême dont j'ai maintenant connaissance et que je savoure minute par minute, seconde par seconde!
>
> Non! il n'est plus de minutes, il n'est plus de secondes! Le temps a disparu; c'est l'Éternité qui règne.

We fell asleep, and Nadia nestled up to me, pulling me against her with all her might, as if the closer the embrace the more it could remedy the long period of time when we were apart.

Later at night, she woke up, searching for her electronic weed stick, which she found under a pillow. She lay with her head on my chest, watching the artery of cars on I-95 through the window high above, occasionally inhaling smoke and turning to blow it into my mouth.

We went to the rooftop bar at the nearby East hotel every night, at the time the best bar on the mainland in Miami, not counting the island of Miami Beach. I got flights to visit her again in July and we also planned to go to Rome and Saint-Tropez in September. Saint-Tropez would have also been accessible from a stopover in Paris or Barcelona, but she had already been to both, so we decided on Rome, which had a direct flight from Miami as well as flights to Nice.

Leaving Miami in June it was impossible to think on this whole situation without incredulous delirium. I've never had such intimacy and long-term prospects with a girl. I tried to remain composed, because there were many uncertainties, especially with her being all the way south in Miami. To confirm, I asked if she wouldn't date anyone else and she said no, which was a relief.

She posted videos on instagram, which could be a bittersweet thing to see, since it meant seeing her without communicating with her – it's beautiful but it made me miss her more. Is some she looked exquisite, in some, unbearably cute.

In one videoclip she took while laying by the side of her pool, she looked exasperatingly beautiful. After some time passed without her it became genuinely surreal that this gorgeous girl is out there in Miami and I have her.

From the moment of waking until the end of the day, it was invariably to some thought concerning Nadia that I related every sensation. If I was reading a travel magazine about a hiking trail in Rio de Janeiro I would think whether she would like it; if I was listening to music I wondered what she would think about it. It didn't matter that she didn't even like hiking at all and didn't like that kind of music – everything was still associated with her because she was the first thought through which every other thought went, carrying her with it.

One reason our opinions aligned with regard to corona was that Nadia was capable of perspective. She was a casualty of a Hezbollah attack, had been ill from bad combinations of drugs, and had seen friends die from overdoses. To overreact to a cold going around would be out of perspective for her. Also she had an instinctive disregard for authority, rules, and conformity. With some people, this could simply come from nihilism (making vice an ideal), but with her I knew it did not, since she also had integrity. Rather, her defiance of society came from authentic individuality, in the sense of what Nietzsche described when he wrote about authenticity and value-driven ethics in the 1880s. Once her family tried to make her wear a hijab for an important religious occasion and she refused, out of principle, and remained the only one without covering her hair. When she told me this it reminded me of Mary Shelley's very progressive Safie character, a girl who escaped 1816 Constantinople, the capital of the Islamic world, to have a better non-religious life in Germany.

140 years have not made Nietzsche's ideas understood by the majority of the world's people. While Christian religious dogma has faded, most of mankind still regards

values as something imposed and external rather than coming from within. Herd mentality persists.

I actually made the suggestion to her, that she get a coronavirus vaccine for real rather than having a fake paper, since she spent so much time working in a packed club, interacting with people traveling from all over, sharing drinks. But she refused, just because she wanted to do the opposite of the mainstream.

Predictably, Nadia didn't subscribe to any political party dogmas and took an independent view on everything. Her opinions on most issues turned out to be more or less libertarian. She disliked BLM because the movement is "racist and anarchist." She liked Trump's political outsider status and the fact that he was a businessman. Of course, she also liked the fact that he was against excessive corona restrictions.

*   *   *

I had dinner with Georges at *Evelina*, a restaurant in Brooklyn, and we discussed plans for his wedding in Saint-Tropez, while eating octopus and lamb chops. I was seeing him for the first time since meeting Nadia and wanted to tell him about her. Not being able to have a consistent communication with her, the next best thing was to talk about her with someone else.

First I was showing him Lucrezia's instagram page because both of them worked in a similar field and he wanted me to introduce him for business. He focused on one of her pictures from Miami which contained her and a few other girls and said, "Wow, who's that girl there? Do you know?" Apparently one of the girls in the photo was stunning enough to stop what he was doing and inquire about.

I looked at the picture, and saw that by chance Nadia was in it. "This is Nadia, actually."

"That's Nadia?" he asked, zooming in to it, "Wow."

Lucrezia was generally considered pretty, up until she was placed next to, and compared with Nadia.

While we talked I explained more about her, "It is in fact completely surreal to me, this whole thing. It's like too good to be true, that why I don't even believe it at times, that she is actually there, and that we have something..."

"That's good – that's how it should be. I'm happy for you."

"But I'm almost sure that getting married isn't possible."

"Do you want to get married?"

"Yes, but I think there's no way she would want to. She knows she can do better."

"You've gotten this far though. You think too little of yourself."

"I don't know. She has so many acquaintances. And she's constantly meeting more. She works in a club."

"See how it goes. If not, maybe you'll get someone better, someone who doesn't work in clubs and do drugs all the time."

"No, that's where you're wrong. Sometimes I catch myself thinking it would be great if she was a normal girl. But that's not correct, to think like that. Picture this – if she was completely normal, if she wasn't so messed up, then she wouldn't have liked a messed up degenerate like me in the first place."

Another time I met Lucrezia at Decibel, a cozy dimly-lit Japanese bar in the East Village reminiscent of the Golden Gai bars in the back alleys of Shinjuku. She had a good grasp of reality and how things work. She had only met Nadia a few times at Miami parties but admired and envied her. She was actually shocked that Nadia had agreed to go with me all the way to Europe. Her surprise was natural since she herself would never deign to consider dating me, and yet Nadia was a girl she looked up to and sought to emulate.

"Wow – a girl like her doesn't go to Europe with just anyone. Do you know how many offers she gets, and much better and more glamorous offers. You're not even taking her first class right?"

"No."

She re-crossed her legs while sitting on the bar stool. She was wearing Dior stretch-vinyl boots with stilettos – they were as tight as a stocking. "You are lucky – I don't know how you did it. But savor it while you can my friend – such a thing might happen once in a lifetime."

"But those guys who are so wealthy they can take her on first class flights and stuff like that, their interest in her is likely to be only temporary. Guys like that wouldn't be with one girl permanently."

"Yes, but does she care?"

As much as she tried to downplay my chances, I was pleased about being able to surprise Lucrezia's expectations of me. She was certainly right about how lucky I was to have Nadia agree to long-term plans, which indicated her affinity towards me. Consider how indecisive most girls are, including ones far less glamorous than her. If you offer something too early, a trip or a restaurant reservation – "I can't plan that far ahead." If you wait until later – "Already have plans". The reason that these girls are unwilling to commit to anything is not that they can't plan that far ahead; it's because they do not like us that much and they don't want to miss out on something better.

* * *

Around this time word spread of a new and very dangerous corona variant circulating around: *the Indian variant*. First let me back up and recount the events in India leading up to this.

In late March 2020 India decided that the entire country – a population larger than that of North and South America combined – would be under lockdown for 3 weeks. Unlike Americans and Europeans who could afford this luxury of not going to work, many Indians literally faced starvation if they could not earn wages for 3 weeks. The biggest exodus since the Pakistan Partition of 1946 began as millions of workers in the cities tried to get to their home villages hundreds of miles away. While there were still some trains and buses available, crowds swarmed to fight for the last seats. Police beat the crowds with sticks because they were violating social distancing. Without any more transportation available, people walked for days, many dying of hunger or exhaustion along the way. (At least they didn't catch corona – that's the most important thing).

In some of the places they arrived, the villages turned them away, reminiscent of medieval villages in 14th century Germany – such as those described by Hermann Hesse in *Narziß und Goldmund* – that built barricades against travelers from fear of the Black Death. Sometimes, when they were crossing the border between two Indian states, they were hosed down by trucks with a chemical antiseptic solution, as if they were radioactive.

Prime Minister Modi promised a lockdown for only 3 weeks, saying that unless this is done India won't recover for 20 years. At the time, I was doubting that this would have any effect and expecting them to prolong it. Predictably, after the 3 weeks were over they saw it wasn't enough and extended the lockdown. Then again and again. It ended up turning into 9 dreadful weeks.

In the winter of 2020-21 India opened up completely and Delhi and Bombay were one of the few places in the world besides Miami were clubs were open. However, the 9 weeks of lockdown apparently failed to stop the proliferation of the virus and its new variant, which came to be known as Delta. By March 2021 India had an even bigger wave than the previous year. Was the lockdown worth it?

The variant spread worldwide, causing setbacks to Europe's reopening in the summer and making vaccinated people in New York decide to put on masks again out of fear. Some stores, like Zara, re-introduced a masking requirement, which of course made me boycott those stores and only go to the ones without this.

Around this time I was looking at an apartment for sale in New York. I made an appointment with the real estate agent and met her at the location. When she saw me walking around, examining the apartment without wearing a mask she jumped back, retreating into a corner from fear and keeping as much distance as possible between us. "Do you have a mask?" she shrieked.

"No, of course not. Why would I?" I was unaccustomed to these kind of demands.

She said, "In case you don't know, 200,000 people died in this pandemic."

"What does that have to do with masks? What does the mask do?" She was already yelling at me to leave.

For Europe, this third wave caused by Delta was a lot smaller than the severe and lengthy wave over the previous winter. In Miami it was the reverse – the wave in Summer 2021 was bigger than in the winter. But being big doesn't mean that it put a strain on the hospital capacity or changed anything. In fact, any remaining corona restrictions had ceased entirely by this point. Reasoning correctly, Florida ignored this wave and this variant, and it passed unnoticed.

The good thing about Delta was that it caused my company's office return, which was planned for August/September, to be postponed indefinitely. I was happy about this. I could still go to the office whenever I wanted, but no mandatory return meant I had more flexibility to travel. On my desk in the office overlooking Bryant Park, I added a small desk flag of Florida, having affinity for the state now, next to my flag of Switzerland.

My "commute", a mile-long walk, took me past some of the most beautiful places in the world, past world-renowned, iconic buildings. I tried not to lose appreciation for this benefit, like many of the people scurrying about on the same street without looking up, their eyes on the pavement. Otherwise I would be little different than the people commuting on an unsightly traffic-clogged highway in central New Jersey, along swampy petrochemical plants, or waiting for a bus alongside unsavory people in a slum part of East Brooklyn.

*   *   *

I visited Nadia for a week in July. Every red light the taxi stopped at on the way from the airport seemed to last an age. Every minute of delay irritated me. The driver, an old Spanish man, was moving like a sloth. When the car was finally making its last drowsy turns towards the block where she lived I could audibly hear the adrenaline pounding in my heart.

She met me in the lobby and we kissed; I could barely articulate any words.

By now she had been working for two months, and I suspected that the work was a strain on her. Each one of the three times per week she was working was an entire night of free drinks and mandatory drinking, sometimes ending in more drinking after the club closed. It was also preceded by drinking in the several hours as she's getting dressed and preparing to go. Getting used to this, on the days when she wasn't working she would also drink more than she did in the past. When I got there the entire cabinet under the sink was full of empty wine bottles she hadn't had time to dispose of yet.

I brought her a 225g tin of black caviar from a Russian store in Brooklyn, as well as a tray of uni from a Japanese store. She also had some salmon sashimi, so we enjoyed the delicious luxury of sashimi and sea urchin topped with caviar.

This day happened to be the final game of the Eurocup: England vs Italy. It was the 2020 Eurocup postponed to 2021 due to the pandemic. We watched the game in a nearby bar, Italy winning on penalties, the crowd in the bar mostly Italians and riotously cheering every favorable shot or making anguished gestures of despair at every missed one. After that Nadia was getting ready for work, trying on various outfits, doing her hair and makeup, while I drank more wine with her.

"Give me my shoes over there... Not those, the ones with the high heels... Thanks. See ya."

I went to Casablanca, a seafood restaurant on the edge of the Miami River and then a bar downtown, and went to sleep. Around dawn she returned, very loud and even confrontational, and promptly passed out.

One source of potential incompatibility between us was the immense divergence of experience. She was 5 years younger than me, but despite that had 10 years more experience. She started with relationships at a very young age, as soon as she was capable. In the 15 years of experience that she had, she was already accustomed to a constant succession of relationships. Whereas I only started seeing a bit of life when I was at the age that she was now!

And even then, I have only made good connections in foreign lands, where I was only a brief time, never in the place where I lived. In the city I was living it has always eluded me – until January 2021, the peak of the corona pandemic, with Nadia in Miami.

During the weekdays it was very difficult to wake up at 8:30 and drag myself to the business center downstairs in her building, where I would have espresso and try to get through a day of work. I came back upstairs around 12:00, hoping to have lunch with her, but she was still sleeping it off, although she had relocated to the couch. I came back after 3:00 and she was finally up, but very hung over. She couldn't speak, couldn't be touched, and was barely able to do anything. But she managed to make some food. Unfortunately, she was unable to ever drink coffee because she said it added to her anxiety. It's too bad because coffee would have benefited her each morning. Without the use of coffee, and rarely having any cocaine, she had to resort to the next best thing for energy: shots of tequila. After this she felt a little better. She made an elixir of tequila mixed with limes and tea, which we took with us when we went to the pool.

It was amazing how tanned and beautiful she was. She had her hair in two cute braids. Her blue eyes were even more striking in the unusual combination with her tan and brown hair.

We did not drink much that night, but the next day she was even worse. Although we went to sleep at the same time, she could not be woken up, even when I came back upstairs at 12:00. She said she was feeling awful and needed xanax, which she had completely run out of. For obscure reasons, she didn't have a prescription and was always getting the pills on the black market. After some more time, she found the energy to call a dealer who said he could give her some. I offered to get a taxi and take her there, but it was still another hour before she could get out of bed in order to go. She said the air was making her suffocate and she couldn't breathe. The dealer was in South Beach. I accompanied her as she went, in an edgy and dismal mood, and made the transaction. We had a rum and coca-cola at the rooftop of the Palace gay bar on Ocean Drive. Overlooking the sea and palm trees, I remained silent for a while. At length I asked, "Are you okay?"

"Yeah, I'm fine now."

She was herself again and we went for a walk down Ocean Drive until reaching Intimo, the Peruvian restaurant in Sofi. Although it was the wet season, it did not rain as much as I thought it would – not as wet as the monsoon in South Asia for instance.

Back at her house, we intended to change clothes and then meet my Chilean friend Carlos who was visiting town.

But she passed out on the bed and I couldn't rouse her. She told me to go by myself.

Xanax is a benzodiazepine and alleviates physical symptoms of irrational acute anxiety and panic disorder. But the downside is its incompatibility with alcohol as well as eventual dependency that leads to withdrawal problems. For instance, one new source of anxiety that arises is the worry about running out of xanax when one needs it.

I was wondering how, with this extra difficulty that most people do not have, she could possibly cope with various things that normally give everyone stress: jobs, airports, the myriad of confrontations that arise in all aspects of life?

The day after that she was better and we went on a double date with another couple to Hutong, a Szechuan restaurant. The girl was one of her best friends and the night turned into a lot of drinking. It seemed that she was almost always hung over, and would never feel alright and be in a decent mood in the morning until she started drinking again. I tried to convince her to change something but she said there was nothing she could do. Because of anxiety disorders, she had to either take xanax or drink alcohol. The xanax she could reduce at times, or not take at all, but not having enough alcohol would cause immediate withdrawal symptoms.

If someone has an alcohol dependence syndrome, withdrawal from it can be so bad it can potentially be fatal. I could drink every day for months, then go to Saudi Arabia, not seeing any wine for a week and be totally fine. But Nadia would have significant physical withdrawal symptoms if she was two days or so without alcohol.

That said, even if she did not have a physical dependence on it, that would not have changed the end result, since she enjoyed drinking and would do it anyway. And she frequently overdid it, since it is hard to know when it has become enough for the night.

When I saw her after a bad night, still passed out in the unwelcome glare of the morning sun, her hair disheveled, I still thought that she looked perfect – for the reason that regardless of what state she was in she still looked like herself, like Nadia. In fact, whenever someone presented me with what they thought was a drawback or fault of Nadia, I brushed it aside with the circular logic that it's not relevant, simply because Nadia is Nadia.

Her health was undamaged from all this. She was not nearly as bad as, for instance, F. Scott Fitzgerald and his wife Zelda. Fitzgerald (the author of *Gatsby*) completely destroyed his health from overdrinking throughout his 30s, was hospitalized several times, and then died of it.
Still, the direction she was going was detrimental and unsustainable. I wanted to help her, but it wasn't possible. She resisted even the mention of any change when we spoke about it. Also, I wished that she could find a more stable job but we couldn't come up with anything else that she could do. Even if, after acquiring some training or credentials she could somehow obtain an office job, she said that she would be too bored to be able to do it. The advantage of being a bottle girl in a nightclub was that she enjoyed the environment, she could drink, and it didn't feel like real work.

When I was flying back, she gave me a xanax to take for the flight. Since I knew that alcohol magnified whatever effects the pill would have, I made sure to drink an ample amount of wine to test it. However, I felt nothing at all beneficial from it. The flight went normally. I tried to sleep but I couldn't – instead I watched movies. Getting from the airport to my house was a bit more blurry, and then I prepared some food, sat down on my couch to eat it at the coffee table while watching TV, and passed out before I could start. I woke up an hour or two later with the food cold.

The next day, I was asking my building's doorman if a package that I had been anticipating had come yet. He insisted there was nothing for me, and yet I had an email saying a delivery had already been made. This confused me until the following day, when I discovered the missing item in one of my closets. Now, I was finally able to piece together the events. Apparently, I collected the package the night I arrived from the airport, unpacked it, discarded the packaging, and put it in a closet, then completely forgot about all that. Such a lapse of memory had never happened to me before.

Experiencing this, it started to become somewhat less surprising how erratic Nadia is. And yet in her day-to-day life she seemed normal and almost fine. I felt if she just moderated a little bit more, she might be completely fine.

XVI
SEVEN SEAS

XVI – Seven Seas

Writing and travel are both explorations of life, but in opposite directions – one is towards the external world, the other towards the internal world. In both travel and in writing one seeks to reach something, a new perspective or point of view; to discover certain truths.

Travel is a movement through space but could also be a movement through time or a movement through class. Given that our identity exists in the perceptions of other people, by traveling to a place that is very different, one is changed into someone entirely different.

I met a beautiful Japanese lady in Saigon, Misako. She asked if I had ever seen the series *Gossip Girl*, which is set in New York. Of course I had.

"You remind me of one of the characters in this film," she said.

I was ready for this. People had sometimes compared me to Dan Humphrey in the past, the poor and socially clumsy writer from Brooklyn. But she said something completely different and unexpected: She said I reminded her of Chuck Bass, the suave, always well-dressed Manhattan *bon vivant*. This was astonishing – I never thought I could possibly be compared to him. Indeed, I thought, it is not by staying at home and being the same self that we encounter our best selves. The habituations and the furniture of daily life at home does not change for years and keeps us tethered to who we are there, which might not be who we are somewhere else, in different environments. How can one change from Dan Humphrey to Chuck Bass merely by crossing the Pacific Ocean?

It was my first time in the Far Orient, in 2016 – on my very first day in Saigon I met Misako at a rooftop bar. I saw her in the midst of a group of people, cute flared skirt in a triangle from her very narrow waist, stilettos and tiered chandelier earrings, and used the most simple and classic, but effective stratagem to talk to her – I asked if she could take my picture with the view on the edge of the rooftop, and after she did, we continued talking and got drinks together. A closer look disclosed her skirt to be part of a pink and white Fausto Puglisi dress, with a black cinched waist belt. This is an obscure Sicilian designer who was made famous when Zendaya wore a dress by him for her first Met Gala.

We ended up spending the whole weekend together, exploring the coiled incense-filled Buddhist temples and pagodas in the western part of town, eating pho and bún cha in sidewalk eateries. She wore another pink skirt and opaque black stockings – tight against the contours of her slender legs. She was in Vietnam on business, being the owner of a Tokyo import/export company with several dozen employees. She was staying in the best suite at the top floor of the best hotel in town, Reverie. My hotel was not as good; I stayed with her.

She once said to me, "I didn't know it was possible that someone so good-looking could also be so intelligent at the same time." I tried not to appear surprised, but secretly I was dumbfounded – it was the most astonishing thing I ever heard anyone say to me, since back in New York few people would be kind enough to categorize me as particularly intelligent, but even if some would, even fewer would ever describe me as good-looking.

We got along perfectly – besides Nadia I don't think there ever was anyone I got along with so well. There one problem though, a major one: she was already married. We only met one more time after this – the following year I was in Hong Kong and she happened to be there at the same time.

She was too busy to plan anything with; I didn't even know she was in Hong Kong until I got there. I was staying at the Ritz-Carlton, the highest elevation hotel in the world. Looking out towards the island from my room on the 115th floor was like being in an airplane. She was at the Landmark Mandarin Oriental so I descended down to Earth, then took the train to the island to meet her there. I saw her in the hotel as she was finishing up a business meeting – she was dressed in a Chanel tweed pencil skirt and jacket, with stockings and Manolo stiletto heels, her look consistent with her position of authority in her company. I gasped inwardly in new rapture.

She told me to be discreet and careful not to give anything away, as there were many people who knew her at the hotel. We went to the Sevva rooftop nearby, watching below us the romantic double-decker trams making arcs around the glass Bank of China tower, then snuck back into her hotel late at night undetected. I was in Tokyo twice after this but she traveled on business so often that both of those times she was out of town when I was there.

Even the well-traveled Paul Theroux, whose career consists of traveling and who has been in the most obscure and remote places, wrote that he felt disoriented, backward, and foreign in Japan. That is odd, since I, on the contrary, felt nowhere more at home and comfortable than in Tokyo. I typically get bored quickly anywhere except in a really big cosmopolitan city, and Tokyo is the biggest of all. Each one of its distinct neighborhoods is like the size of a city by itself.

But more importantly, I somehow felt in tune with Japanese culture. I liked the sensitivity towards æsthetics, evident in things like appreciation of the *kawaii*, or searching for a flowering sakura tree to sit under for *hanami*. I liked the thoughtfulness and care with which everything is handled, from personal interactions to products and design and food. Look at the artistry of the varieties of *wagashi* confections, for instance. Even a centuries-old European thing, like espresso, they can take and re-design so that it is better. And there are enough espresso connoisseurs in Tokyo for there to be a market for it. There is so much class in Japan that the world outside the islands seems barbarous and crude in comparison.

As someone with no permanent home country, a foreigner everywhere, I became accustomed to having a shifting sense of identity, changing over time. It would in fact be quite bizarre to me to imagine a person so changeless over time that they spend their whole life always tethered to the same sense of cultural or national identity. Hilaria Baldwin was ridiculed by the press for identifying as Spanish, just because her origin is Boston. Gustave Flaubert hated being considered French; he loved the Orient, especially Egypt and considered himself a citizen of the world, not French. But very often language permanently fixes someone in their cultural identity and it is the single biggest obstacle to being culture fluid, since it is so hard to acquire. Luckily my school from the beginning was half English/half French in Geneva, both languages being native to me. Over different parts of my life I alternated between identifying as Swiss, French, English, European, or American. Maybe, I now realized, I am a little Japanese too.

On my second visit to Tokyo, (the last part of a larger trip going through Iberia and Moscow) I met a girl called Haruna in a bar. While Misako was a polished Ginza lady, Haruna was a pretty gyaru girl who hangs out in Shibuya 109. She had light brown colored hair, short denim shorts, and a white t-shirt which had the word "love" above an illustration of a stiletto-heel shoe. Consistent with the message on her shirt she had on white platform heels which made her legs look very long and thin.

Tokyo has a lot of diversity in clothing styles: the luxuriously elegant in Ginza and Omotesando, the kimonos in Asakusa, lolitas and loli-goths in Harajuku, manga styles in Akihabara, bohemians in Shimokitazawa, punks in Koenji, business in Shinjuku, and gyaru in Shibuya and Roppongi.

Talking with Haruna in a bar in Roppongi, I asked, "Are you hungry by any chance? I know a good *yakitori* close to here."

She said yes and we went there, ate Japanese oysters and sticks of barbeque, and then went to another bar. We were having such a good time she forgot what time it was, until she finally looked at her watch and became paralyzed with shock. "I missed the last train!"

The distance that she had to go would cost more than ¥15,000 in a taxi since the trains had stopped operating. Seeing she was stranded, I offered her to sleep in my hotel, where I had a bed large enough for two, without any improper implications. She agreed, and we have remained good friends since. The point is that a situation like this, with such relaxed and amiable relations wouldn't ever happen to me in America or Western Europe. So many things wouldn't happen there in an entire lifetime, for whatever reason, but do manage to happen in the short few days I am traveling somewhere on other continents.

I sent Haruna a letter once, via international air mail, applying to the paper a decorative *kawaii* cat stamp that I use on all of my letters. She actually replied, sending me a nice letter on beautiful Japanese stationary faintly decorated with sakuras, on which she drew in pencil a cute illustration of a cat.

It was so overwhelmingly sweet my eyes filled with tears when I opened the envelope. It remains to this day the only time in my life I ever received a personal letter, or any mail, from anyone besides family.

At the Wat Arun temple in Bangkok, I met Citra, an Indonesian model. Bangkok has one of the best architectures of any city worldwide. After watching her take a dozen selfies for a few minutes, I ventured to offer to take a shot for her. I directed her where to stand and how to pose and took the shot. It turned out to be one of the best photos I ever made. We talked and discovered that we both happened to be staying in the same hotel, the Shangri-La. We agreed to go back together and later go to dinner near the hotel but she wanted to take a taxi. I knew it would be madness to take a taxi through the crazy Bangkok traffic at this time of day. I wisely suggested to take a river boat instead, not a ferry but one of those small propeller boats criss-crossing the river.

We went to the riverbank and waved down a boatman, negotiating the price. (It was around 300 baht). Favorably, the hotel was directly situated on the river and had its own pier. The only confusing part was when the boat stopped midway, in the middle of the water, and the boatman said, "Okay, you get out here."

We were in the middle of the river.

I asked, "What, here?"

"Yes, here."

"What do you mean?"

His bad English made further inquires futile. We waited. Eventually, we saw another boat approaching from the south. Apparently, we would get out here to transfer to the other boat which would take us the rest of the way!

We went to Vertigo, which is at the 2nd highest open air rooftop bar in the world. (The 1st highest is also in Bangkok). The next day, I took her to the Sofitel pool party, which was an event happening only once a month. She fit in well there in a swimsuit and a transparent sarong tied around her waist. Citra was a contestant in the Miss Indonesia pageant a few years ago and was in the top 10. She was from the Sultanate of Yogyakarta in Central Java. Later, she went into acting and I started seeing her in various Indonesian movies on Netflix.

Meanwhile, did I ever encounter a Miss America contestant or even just any attractive girl on the river taxis between Manhattan and Brooklyn? Of course not.

Despite the considerably longer time I have spent in New York, living there and only taking short trips out, I've never had success with a girl like Citra there. The most significant progress in 10 years were the few dates in Summer 2020 already summarized in an earlier chapter. Unlike Nadia, I definitely don't want variety; I want stability, and dislike the burden of meeting new people. But stability is not a feature of a big wealthy city like New York, where there are so many options nobody is interested in commitment. As proof of this, compare the average age of marriage of the rural states in America like Iowa and the City.

Overnight trains in Eastern Europe are a great place to meet people. They have a restaurant car – you eat dinner, drink vodka, then go to sleep, the rocking movement of the train and soft noises very conducive for falling asleep. On a train journey from Riga to St. Petersburg, my cabin had two beds and my fellow traveler was a Russian called Donat. We went to the restaurant car, where he encountered a portly acquaintance, Yevgeny Konstantinovich, or Zhenya in short. He had a slight resemblance to Mikhail Krug, the chanson singer with Russian mafia ties. Zhenya pulled out a 750g bottle from his capacious jacket pocket, and he poured all of us another 100 grams, saying, "Vodka... vodka. Drink." I tried to resist, as Donat and I had already finished a bottle of wine. But it is futile to resist a Russian's offer of a toast. These perpetual offers, to have another vodka, are a constant danger in Russia, where they are not so much of an offer but a command, since it could be offensive to turn it down.

As the evening progressed the scene in the restaurant car became more and more unrestrained. A little further down the carriage a group of men wearing Adidas tracksuits were singing a bleary rendition of a Vladimir Visotsky song. Shouts and conversations were conducted across tables. Zhenya had collapsed at his table and his friends were asking Donat if he knew where he should be carried, since they didn't know where his cabin was. Donat didn't know either. Recruiting my help to assist in lifting his sizeable mass, we simply carried him to the nearest empty bed we could find.

When Donat and I retired to our cabin, he instantly passed out but I remained awake for another hour reading. At the Russian border the train slowed to a crawl, and finally stopped to allow guards to inspect the passengers. We were about to pass the Iron Curtain.

The door of our cabin opened and an attractive woman came in. "*Kontrol.*" She had a peaked officer's cap with border control FSB insignia, a leather jacket, and leather boots. It was past midnight – the incursion into my cabin by this severe woman in an officer's hat, who looked like a dominatrix, was intimidating, but also exciting. I showed her my passport, which had the necessary Russian visa pasted in from the consulate in Paris. The visa satisfied her. (Russia was the only one out of 80 countries where I needed a visa from a consulate in advance).

Donat must have known about the border procedures, since before passing out he had placed his Russian passport in between the fingers of his hand. The FSB lady took the passport from his hand, looked at it, put it back into his hand while he remained sleeping, and left.

Although much more sober than Russia, Iran was nevertheless one of the most interesting countries I've been. Since the 1979 revolution and the seizure of the US Embassy, relations have been hostile between Iran and the US but they didn't mind, at Imam Khomeini airport, that I was coming from New York, as long as I used a Swiss passport to get in. No questions were asked at all – even Canadian passport control officers sometimes inquire my reasons for entering Canada, but here they were not curious.

My hotel had a fancy, glitzy rooftop bar, girls coming in Louboutins, relatively short skirts (for Iran), and very risqué low-falling hijabs displaying a lot of hair. There was no alcohol though, only shisha. Iran would be a normal country, like Türkiye, if not for the dictatorship regime. When boarding the Doha-Tehran flight, zero women on the plane wore a hijab, only putting it on when disembarking.

At the airport I exchanged a $100 bill and got a giant stack of 50 and 100 thousand rial bills, each with Khomeini on it. Thanks to recently elevated economic sanctions, the rial had lost much of its value. Later I found some larger one million rial bills which lightened the load.

Dinner with a girl in Darband, including shisha, cost 1,100,000 rials. This was only $9. She lowered her hijab as much as she could but hijab laws were still strict in Iran. She had the most exquisitely beautiful winged eyeliner on her eyes. Niloofar told me how in the past, on three separate occasions, she had been arrested for improper hijab and taken to the police station, although released without any fines. It was not just for hair – one time it was for a skirt being too short.

She had a car and drove me to her parents' house in order to find alcohol. They had a secret stash of beer that they covertly obtained from the Italian embassy. Unfortunately, her mother came back while we were drinking. Nilu got in trouble for inviting me and I had to leave. We parted on the street, with her mother watching from the door of the house, and displeased that I had the audacity to kiss Nilu on the cheek when leaving, as I was accustomed to do. Apparently such a kiss is illegal here. Even just the fact of Nilu being on a date with me, a foreigner, someone she wasn't married to, would have been illegal several years prior when things were more conservative. Iran has made a lot of progress since the early days of the revolution, when anything a woman did:

wearing bright colors or mascara, or even just eating a banana in public, could have been construed to be overly provocative.

Even with my lapses in cultural awareness and faux pas, even with the rigors of the Islamic regime, I still thought it was easier to make progress and go on dates here than in New York.

The suddenness of my departure meant that I was without a taxi to get back to my hotel. There were no passing cars on this quiet residential street, but luckily I had a Persian version of Uber, which Nilu had helped me download earlier. It was all in unintelligible Persian script, but I could guess at what to click and use the map to indicate the approximate location of where I needed to go.

Most drivers didn't speak English but eventually, after several taxi rides, I found one with whom I negotiated to take me down south to the cities Qom and Isfahan on another day. Isfahan, the pinnacle of Persian architecture, with its opulent mosques, tiled façades, ancient bridges, evening passeggiatas, and lack of tourists, not to mention the cute flirtatious Persian girls riding bicycles around Naqsh-e Jahan Square, is one of those cities that enriches anyone who passes through – it is like adding a colorful treasure box to the collection of memories in one's mind.

Later, in Buenos Aires, I was walking in the Palermo Soho area during a massive rainstorm. I noticed a girl walking in the same direction, with long hair, tight jeans, and black high-heel shoes, getting wet because she didn't have an umbrella. I offered her mine.

She was very grateful. She didn't know English but made me understand that she was going to a party and invited me to come along. Her name was Claudia. The rain got harder, with thunder and lightning. It was such ridiculously crazy weather that it made us laugh.

At the house party, some of the people helped us translate but they were not totally fluent in English either. Suddenly a girl came running in, Claudia's friend, entirely wet from the rain, so wet as if she had fallen into a pool with her clothes. It was the kind of uninhibited environment in which she felt at ease taking off her pants and changing her chemise to a t-shirt she borrowed. She found a towel to dry her hair with and was trying to dry her pants. There was good music being played and I danced with Claudia and kissed her. I noticed people were kissing in various corners of the house, including two girls on the divan who were deeply immersed in each other.

This party was like a surreal dream where anything seemed possible. Does life have to be all gloom or is it possible for a glimpse of light somewhere at some point in all the darkness? Why shouldn't things be possible? A bunch of young people, all incredibly good-looking, are just having fun in the middle of the hot summer in Buenos Aires. And yet I had never experienced a salacious and liberal environment like this at any party in the US. In just a brief time in Argentina I found this but for some reason I have never found a party like this ever in New York.

It was getting late, and I was trying to ask Claudia to come back with me to my place.

The girl with no pants (I forgot her name) translated for us: "Claudia says, 'Let's go home to my place instead.'"

I said, "Tell her okay sure."

When we got ready to leave the girl said bye to Claudia, kissing her briefly on the lips. She also kissed me, and added, laughing, "Call me if you need help with the translation. But I'm sure you will be fine."

XVII
ROME

XVII – Rome

In August 2021 I went traveling through the Balkans, intending to go from there to meet Nadia in Rome in early September. I flew to Zagreb, then went to Sarajevo, Dubrovnik, Kotor, and Tirana. From there I boarded a ship crossing the Adriatic to Bari in Italy.

Somewhere between Montenegro and Albania, Nadia messaged me saying that her airline notified her that Italian entry requirements were changing. I looked it up and it was indeed true – in these times travel was precarious and even meticulous preparations to deal with corona travel restrictions could be moot if something changes suddenly.

Italy, without warning, decided to add a requirement to have a negative test for anyone who had been in the US recently, apparently determining that corona cases in the US were unacceptably high. Before this, only a vaccine card was sufficient to enter Italy.

Fortunately, during my planning I had already contemplated the possibility that things might change and one of the things I had given Nadia when I saw her in July was a negative test where I wrote the date to be two days before her flight in September. What seriously worried me though, was that she showed me that her vaccine card had gotten wet and the ink was smeared. In an authentic card, the ink wouldn't smear like it did on this printed one. There was no time to get a new one so I told her to go with this one.

When I passed border controls from Albania to Italy at the seaport, I had to fill in a form listing all the countries I had been in the last two weeks. I concealed having been in the US, since that would have now required a negative test, something I could not fabricate as I didn't have a computer with me. Nor did I consider actually searching for a clinic in Tirana, not only because it would have been a big hassle, but also so I wouldn't suffer the indignity of complying with this farce. My Swiss passport showed stamps for every border crossing starting from entering Croatia, but didn't show anything before that.

After the overnight ferry, I walked around the port of Bari in the morning, getting coffee in an espresso bar, "*Buon giorno... Un caffé per favore,*" putting a euro coin on the counter.

"*Prego.*"

After I finished: "*Ciao! grazie*".

"*Grazie. Ciao.*"

I had another espresso at the train station and took the 4 hour train to Roma Termini. Nadia's flight would get here early in the morning, so I was there the first night without her. The rooftop bar of the hotel overlooked Piazza Navona, right by the side of the cupola of Sant'Agnese cathedral towering overhead, and I could see the sun setting over St. Peter's Basilica in the distance. Sophia Loren's apartment, in her film with Marcello Mastroianni, *Yesterday, Today, and Tomorrow*, also overlooked the piazza, but from a different side. Nadia sent me a message saying she was able to check-in successfully with her tarnished vaccine card and fake test, which was a relief. It is great that the US made things so easy to fabricate. Almost every other country had QR codes on its tests, making them possible to verify online for authenticity. Europe had digital vaccine proof which had to be displayed on your phone and scanned. This couldn't be faked merely by printing a card at home and writing on it.

During another trip in early 2022, when flying from Azerbaijan to Qatar, I was informed at Baku airport that my vaccine card was no good. Qatar required that the latest dose be more recent than 9 months ago, and mine wasn't. On the spot, I took a pen and wrote in a third dose with a later date on my card, then went to a different clerk to successfully check-in.

* * *

In the morning, just as I finished coffee, Nadia arrived to the hotel – and I finally saw her again after a month and a half!

She had already drank a little bit – taking advantage of the unlimited alcohol on the flight she ordered some more in the morning as the plane was landing. Straight away we went to breakfast at the hotel. This would turn out to be the only breakfast she would make it to over the entire trip.

The breakfast room had a beautiful, sunny outdoor terrace overlooking the Egyptian obelisk in the piazza. We took pictures there, and for a better shot she got up and posed reclining on the narrow stone ledge, on the other side of which was a straight drop down to Piazza Navona some 40 meters down.

She updated her eyeliner and changed into a short skirt and sleeveless shirt and we left to walk around the city. We started by looking inside the Sant'Agnese church, then went west towards the Vatican.

Rome is one of those cities amazing to find oneself in for the first time, to walk around and get lost in, admiring the architecture, layers of centuries blended on top of each other. I had been a number of times to Rome, but for her it was all new. There's only once in life we can have that experience of exploring the Eternal City for the first time.

And there are many other compact cities where one can have that feeling of being the first day wandering in a place incredibly interesting, a place with both character and architecture: Lisbon, Cuzco, Saigon, for instance. I had Dubrovnik a week ago, which was new to me. And despite having been to so many cities, there are still a few more that interest me, to which I've never been, like Valletta and Samarqand.

It was incredibly hot, and on the way to the Vatican we stopped in the cool darkness of a tavern to have an aperol spritz. Getting to a bridge over the Tiber, we emerged from the narrow streets of the old town to a vista of the city, august and radiant under the bright azure, bristling with bell towers and cupolas, priests in black garb on the approach to the looming and ominous Castello Sant'Angelo.

We took pictures at the fountain in the middle of the Vatican square. But at St. Peter's Basilica neither of us were allowed in. The pope's guards objected to her lack of coverings over her arms and legs, and to my lack of covering on my mouth, since I had neglected to bring a facemask in my pocket for this eventuality.

In the vicinity north of the Vatican, we got a pizza at an outdoor restaurant and she also got a glass of tequila. A piece of prosciutto fell off a pizza slice that she picked up. I picked up the prosciutto and she lifted her mouth up and opened it so I could put it in. When we left she spotted an electric scooter parked on the street – one of those that is like a skateboard with a handlebar and can be rented online.

She said, "Let me see if the app for this works in Italy." It worked and the scooter became activated. "I see these outside my house all the time and I've always wanted to try it."

"You mean you've never done this? Why didn't you try in Miami?"

"I can try now. *Andiamo!*"

I got on behind her, but it was very difficult to hold on to her waist with on hand, while also holding the pizza box containing the rest of the pizza we were carrying back. She accelerated and braked abruptly, swerving around pedestrians and cars while riding over the Vittorio Emanuele II bridge. I also had to balance on just my right foot, as only one foot could fit on the back of the platform. We almost crashed into a Roman Catholic priest at the end of the bridge.

I decided to leave behind the pizza box on a window ledge since it was impossible to ride with it, and got on more securely behind her. We managed to go a considerable distance through the Roman traffic, although cobblestones on some streets were a dangerous obstacle. Near Piazza Venezia, police whistled at us, yelling something in Italian that I gathered to mean that two people were not allowed to ride together. We turned into a side street.

Naturally I was thinking of how similar this was to Audrey Hepburn and Gregory Peck on a motorbike in the 1953 *Roman Holiday*. Unfortunately the analogy was lost on her since she didn't see the film. She said she doesn't watch black & white movies.

The point where we got off happened to be close to the Pantheon, the 1,900 year old Roman temple. Nadia decided to try to get a bag of cocaine and said she would think about who to ask. I followed her through the square in front of the temple, until she noticed a man standing on a corner and approached him to ask. Surprisingly, the very first person she thought to ask actually had a small bag with him at that moment. After various hemming and hawing, the various small talk that traditionally constitutes the negotiations of a black market transaction, he let her have it, and even at a discount.

When we dressed for the evening, she put on a beautiful flared Alaïa skirt and Diego Dolcini high-heel sandals with white socks. We went to a cocktail bar overlooking the Colosseum just before sunset, placing the ancient structure against an orange sky. Then as night fell, back to the old town to an outdoor table at Per Me, a good Michelin star restaurant.
"*Buona sera,*" I greeted the hostess.
"*Buona sera signore.*"
We split a bottle of wine and dinner was great, as was the whole day up to now. We went back to the hotel, and I was infatuated with her, so beautiful and beguiling – I kissed her in the elevator, embracing her by the waist. In the bedroom, she said she's too tired. But ironically for being tired, she declared we need to go out again and have shots. She changed her high heels back into sneakers and we went out.

Because of corona, large nightclubs were closed in Italy but all bars were open. And hundreds of Italians were drinking on the streets as is the tradition in summer. Directly west of our hotel, near the 15th century Chiesa di Santa Maria della Pace, was one such place where a huge crowd of people were drinking outside. Nadia had two shots while I just had one. It was hard to keep up with her.

After that, she became noticeably unwell. We wandered towards the Piazza and she told me she needs to throw up. We found a suitable area; it was dark there and far from the crowd. She asked, "Can you help me? My fingers actually aren't long enough to reach the back of my throat."

I was confused, "How can that be? Have you never needed to induce yourself to throw up before?"

"Yes, I have, but I always used a toothbrush or some long object to do it."

So this was how I found myself, in an alley in Rome just off the Piazza Navona, with people walking by, putting my hand in a girl's throat, then pulling it out just in time to avoid a projectile of liquid emanating from her mouth.

It was actually kind of quaint; I empathized with her. It might have been caused the bad quality of the last shots that we took rather than the overall excess of alcohol. The thing that completely surprised me though, was what she said next, "I just lost all this alcohol; we have to go drink more now!"

So she dragged me through the crowd to several other bars by the side of the streets. At this point I got a message from Chiara, asking, "How is Rome! Is Nadia behaving?"

I wrote back laconically, "No, she is not."

Having her fill of more shots, Nadia declared that she cannot go to sleep without smoking weed. But Italians don't usually smoke so nobody had any. She went around to countless numbers of people in the crowd asking for it and talking on an overly-amicable basis with everyone. It was getting unpleasant. A group of shady Italian guys surrounded her. Another one come up to me and asked, "Is she your girlfriend?"

I said, "Yes."

"Get her away from here. It's becoming dangerous."

I did what I could, moving her along when she determined that nobody had any weed on them. Finally, after passing several streets, she saw people smoking and asked (insisted) to join them. She smoked half of their joint and was ready to go home at last. When she reached the bed she fell on it and immediately passed out. I had to remove her black Alaïa skirt and then lift her to be able to put her under the covers, again a scene reminiscent of *Roman Holiday*, when Gregory Peck has to reposition Audrey Hepburn, who plays the princess, on the bed after she passed out.

Lunch at Cantina e Cucina was the breakfast the next day. They had a fantastic prosciutto with mozzarella for only €9. It is too bad she could not drink coffee, because the strong Roman espresso would have benefited her a great deal. Instead, she combined cocaine with chianti to get into a decent mood. It seemed like she could no longer function without alcohol, needing it at the start of the day. She was not like this when we lived together at the very beginning in South Beach. After she drank a little, she was okay for a while, until a certain point in the evening when she had drank too much and was unmanageable.

Something else had changed, even from the first day when she got to Rome. She was already not as affectionate as she was before. She was not kissing or embracing of her own volition, but only responding if I did it. Thinking back to some moments in February or June I could tell from how she looked at me and interacted with me and longed for a kiss that she liked me then. That had faded in September.

While she paid for some things in the past, now she entirely stopped paying for anything, unless she was getting an extra drink by herself. She would become irritated much more often. When we like someone, we try to act in a way that makes them like us more, thus if some small thing displeases us, we don't express that displeasure. But now that her liking of me had diminished, she freely expressed any annoyance or irritation with me that she experienced.

But we were still getting along well, having good conversation, enjoying the things we were doing. We went to the Via dei Condotti, the Piazza di Spagna, and a few more churches, with her drinking along the way at random bars we encountered. We ended the night at a nice restaurant in a distant part of Trastevere, having pasta with seafood. Then a tequila bar, which impressed her with its variety of tequila, something hard to find in Italy. When we were trying to get back, it was late and there were no taxis anywhere. The ubers were all giving us estimates of 15-20 minutes to arrive.

She saw a Carabinieri car with the policemen standing outside it and said, "I'll get them to take us."

She walked up to the car, drawling out her words, indicating her extreme intoxication, "Can you take us to Piazza Navona...", and without waiting, opened the door of the back seat and went in. The carabinieri were confused. None of our English, French, or Arabic helped, as they only spoke Italian. I tried to get her to come out of the car but she persisted and remained inside. I was not that sober at this point either and I thought maybe she actually can convince them to take us.

The carabinieri were relatively patient with her. "*Questo non è un taxi*. No taxi, no taxi *signora*."

Eventually we got an uber.

XVIII
SAINT-TROPEZ TO BAGHDAD

XVIII – Saint-Tropez to Baghdad

The Côte d'Azur is a place that elevates one's spirit, not just with its natural beauty but with the concentration of stylish people who go there in part because of the concentration of people like themselves.

When we meet a friend in an elegant cocktail bar or rooftop bar where both the setting and the people are beautiful, the conversation, which may have been unmemorable if held in a drab pub, becomes more animated due to the atmosphere around us. The Côte d'Azur is an entire region with such an atmosphere, and the effect is lent to any activity – driving with the windows open, an al fresco lunch, or a swim in the azure off a boat.

The very names of the legendary places along the coast strike one with religious reverence: Cap d'Antibes, Cannes, Villefranche-sur-Mer, Cap-Ferrat, Èze, Monaco, Monte Carlo, Menton. All of these are in the vicinity of Nice. A few hours drive west, inaccessible by train, lies the best of all, Saint-Tropez, its remoteness supporting its exclusivity. Striking up a conversation with the people seated next to you in the garden of the Christian Dior restaurant you will discover a prince of Liechtenstein together with a competitive skier; at another table the daughter of the Hungarian ambassador to France and her husband, the general manager of the Cartier store in Paris, the two of them so well dressed one is incredulous how anyone can pull off such effortless style.

With Nadia, I rented a black BMW and we drove to Monaco-Ville, the oldest part of the principality on a hill overlooking the port. It is fun driving in Monaco, as long as one has GPS. It is a very dense city built into steep hills, with lots of efficient tunnels out of which one might emerge somewhere one didn't expect.

She couldn't drive because she had already drank a good amount on the flight from Rome in the morning. She thought there wouldn't be wine on the flight so she made sure to drink extra hard in the airport lounge before boarding, but the flight did indeed have more wine.

We had lunch, then drove down to Monte Carlo. On my last visit to Monaco, it took me a long time to find parking in a paid underground garage. But now, we easily found a spot right next to the casino. Inside, we heard the familiar rattle of chips being raked across the baize, the commentary of the croupiers, "*Trente-et-un. Rouge. Impaire et passe.*" Jackets are required and photographs are not allowed. Afterwards we had drinks at Buddhabar around the corner, where we encountered many Russians. For some reason, every casino in Europe, even going back to Baden-Baden in the 19th century, has attracted lots of tacky Russians, as evidenced in Turgenev and Dostoyevsky novels.

We got the car and took the A8 back to our hotel in Nice, which is a more lively place to stay, going to dinner at a seafood restaurant in the *vieille ville*. The next day we drove west.

Nadia asked, "Did you go here often from Geneva?"

"Sometimes, not every year. It's an all day drive to get here from Geneva. More often I went to Lyon – it's one of the best places to eat in Europe and it was just a 2 hour train ride."

"Switzerland doesn't have any really big cities right?"

"No, but Berne is very cool, for its size. That was also a 2 hour train ride, in the other direction going east. Also Paris was not that far – 3 hours on the express train."

Driving the BMW past the guards standing by its immense gates, we stopped to eat lunch at the Hôtel du Cap-Eden-Roc, the storied hotel famous from the novels of Fitzgerald and the runways of Lagerfeld. On a terrace overlooking the Mediterranean, we had octopus and langoustines with rosé from Provence, finishing by splitting a crème brûlée with espresso and kir blanc.

Cannes was after this, which we only saw from the car. And then instead of the highway we took the scenic route to Saint-Tropez, along the red cliffs of the Corniche de l'Estérel, listening to the Congolese rapper Maître Gims on French radio, songs which became permanently affixed, in my memory, to this drive. Whenever I heard them much later, they would call to mind specific snapshots from the drive: the red cliffs, the reflections of sunlight on the azure; looking over to see the jasmine-scented breeze streaming through Nadia's hair as she sat with crossed legs, in short skirt and dark sunglasses, smoking a vape.

Les Caves du Roy, the famous nightclub in Saint-Tropez, had already reopened after corona. Having some time before the wedding, we also went to cute restaurants in the *vieille ville*, chic fashion shops, and the Port of Saint-Tropez, the scene of so many classic films like those of Brigitte Bardot and Louis de Funès. Despite its reputation, the town is not very expensive, especially if compared to Switzerland. The only difficulty are hotels, which would be expensive if not reserved many months in advance.

Nadia did not want to make any long excursions – just walking around the port and *vieille ville* fatigued her – so I climbed up to the Citadelle alone, resorting to asking random strangers to take a photo of me at the vistas above the town.

One of my friends here for the wedding had come on a small yacht from Marseilles. We took a ride to Nikki Beach and around the waters close to Saint-Tropez. Even a jaded traveler such a myself was transfixed by the views as we left the port and rounded the peninsula.

Nadia in a teal swimsuit looked beautiful on the boat, by far the most beautiful person there, I noticed, as champagne was being poured (and sprayed) around. People were jumping off to swim in the warm sea. She said, "I'm going to jump in, but I can't swim. Can you catch me?"

I wasn't sure how that would work, but I said, "Okay."

Other people were entering the water from a low point of the boat. Instead of that, she found the highest possible place she could climb up to on the structure of the yacht, and jumped from there. She landed next to me, and it turned out that she wasn't joking – she actually wasn't able to swim. I had never had to rescue someone from the water before, and it was difficult, as she was pushing me down under the water and I could barely keep from being submerged and drowned. For a few seconds I was worried, but eventually I managed to reach the stair with her.

We went downstairs inside the yacht to change into dry clothes. Swimming off a boat in the gorgeous waters off Saint-Tropez, drinking champagne and kir royals in this atmosphere with Nadia, had sharpened my senses like a psychedelic. It was exhilarating being down there alone with her. We were still wet from the sea. She looked lovely. She took the bag of cocaine from her purse and scooped some up with one of her long nails, which were the ideal form for the purpose. "Want some?" she offered.

I kissed her instead. While the others were occupied above deck, we had an intimate moment in the washroom of the yacht, I lost in admiration of her tattoos and dark tan, her wet hair, feeling once again the transcendental, spiritual, and lustful connection, that I thought we were in danger of losing in the previous days, but which, when experienced again, cannot be doubted to be a bond with someone that is anything other than lifelong, so far does it transport one to a supernatural plane of reality that leaves one dazed and bewildered that such things are possible.

Through a failure of imagination, or not knowing because we simply cannot know unless we experience it personally and directly, we often fail to realize what life could be like. We endure life often because we think that this is how things are. Until something miraculous happens, a radical change, and we do not recognize the life we had before.

*   *   *

Disembarking from the yacht in the center of Saint-Tropez's picturesque port, we walked back to the hotel to get ready for the pre-wedding soirée being held at the Hôtel de Paris rooftop. Once again, Nadia was the most stunning, her elegance enhanced by thigh-high, high-heel black leather boots, indigo short skirt with pink accents, and short black motorcycle jacket (the same one she wore at Setai – hopefully the reader remembers). I wore a gray and blue plaid Versace jacket.

I saw Georges, my friend who was getting married, and embraced him, "*Bonsoir* Georges! *Félicitations!*"

"*Merci* Richard!"

I finally got to introduce Nadia to Georges, as well as to many of my old friends from both New York and Geneva. The soirée was followed up by many drinks at Caves du Roy until it closed.

The wedding the next day was black-tie, and while most men opted for a plain black dinner jacket, I chose one in a dark burgundy color with a black shawl lapel. The ceremony and dinner were held outdoors before sunset at the Château de la Messardière, on a hill overlooking the bay. Everything was perfect. There were colorful parrots in the trees. Nadia wore her Alaïa skirt which thankfully wasn't soiled with vomit in Rome, and her best shoes, 140mm black patent leather Louboutin Biancas. I caught myself thinking about what locations would I want to have a wedding in, perhaps in a year's time – foolish as such thoughts perhaps are, thinking about the prospect was pleasing.

Late at night after the dinner, when everyone was having drinks and standing around talking, with the stars overhead and the lights of the Port of Saint-Tropez in the distance, I happened to be in a conversation with Nadia and Severine, an old friend.

Severine asked Nadia, "So how long have you two been dating?"

Nadia replied, "Oh, we're not dating."

I stared at them, first one, then the other, but they were deep in conversation and took no notice of me. I looked all around me, my mouth agape, as if in search of someone who could come and explain this all to me. I no longer recognized where I was, my surroundings, what world I was in. My thinking process was fogged by wine and I didn't know whether I was in a bad dream. I had heard something spoken. What was spoken was something cataclysmic, and I could not understand why, something so colossal as that, was said so matter-of-factly, nonchalantly, as if it was any common unimportant utterance. This was effectively like a break-up, since we were, as I believed, in a relationship since three months ago in June. But the delivery of the news was such that it implied the relationship was not even worth calling one. The way in which she imparted the information seemed to imply – How could I even think it was possible for us to have long-term prospects? I wanted to pull her away to ask, but there was no opportunity. She was still in a conversation – one in which, in my state of shock, I no longer had the capability of hearing any words although it was happening right next to me – with Severine and another person who had also joined.

Many times in my life I tried to become acquainted with a girl only to have her tell me suddenly that she had met someone else and they were now dating, which meant they were in a committed relationship. Therefore she couldn't see me anymore. I met a girl in Taipei, Evelina, and wanted to see her again to try to continue the courtship. But Taipei is far, on the other side of the world, and the next time I could come there was 10 months later. We corresponded the whole time and I was looking forward to seeing her again. Three weeks before I was supposed to be there she was still excited to see me. One week later, though, she suddenly said that she met someone – they fell in love and were now dating and she couldn't see me. I had other reasons to be in Taipei as well – I hiked the famous Zhuilu Trail through the high mountains in the south of Taiwan, and later also visited Singapore. But I didn't see her; she couldn't even meet for coffee.

Another time Georges wanted to introduce me to a Parisian girl who was single and lived in New York, Yvette. Through our mutual friend Georges, we became acquainted online and based on what he told me, she was very interested in me and wanted to meet. But some travels and events delayed this meeting for a week and a half. When the day came, she had stopped replying. Georges later told me what he found out – that during that period of time (a week and a half), she met someone and they became engaged to be married.

What was astonishing in these and other cases was not that the girl found someone better, which is very easy to understand, but how quickly, how actually instantaneously, these people decided that they must be in a relationship forever, without any doubts.

Such instantaneous courtship has always eluded me. Even now, when I thought I had made it, after 7 months of knowing Nadia, after living together in Miami, traveling to Rome, Monte Carlo, and Saint-Tropez – still no – it only really lasted for a summer.

In retrospect, the things she said, which, at the time gave me comfort in our relationship, could have been interpreted differently. When I left her in Miami in June, coming back to New York, she said she had no intention of dating anyone else in Miami. But now I saw that meant nothing, as it actually implied nothing about us. At the time I also asked her if I could consider her a girlfriend. She said, "Yes, of course." This made me happy, incredulous in my good fortune throughout the entire summer, while I was away from her in New York. But what she said was actually ambiguous. What she might have meant was that I could feel free to consider her a girlfriend if I wanted, but she had no intention of considering herself that. It remains unknown if she never considered a relationship, or if perhaps she did at some point in the summer, but then changed her mind. I prefer to believe the latter. All in all, much of the misunderstanding that I had could be attributed to the abnormally poor communication that she maintained when we were apart.

At one point in August before the trip, she videocalled me from Miami, something she rarely did, in the early morning as I was waking up for work. She was very drunk – for her it was the end of a long night. She was laying and rolling around on the carpet, in exquisite makeup and earrings, complaining that some unknown people were inconsiderate to her. She asked if I wanted to get married. I thought she was joking. I said, "Yes, but I don't know if you want to."

She said, "I'm down."

I didn't attribute much meaning to this call and she later acted as if it never happened so I assume she entirely lost memory of it. But I took it as a favorable sign. Whether she was conscious of what she said or not, it was nevertheless the first time someone asked me that.

I spent many summers in a small village in the mountains not far from Geneva, in the area of Gruyères. Swiss people have the mountains in their blood – they cannot dwell long in the city before the yearning comes again to love the nature, mountains, trees, and cliffs that Switzerland is full of.

The village, with its centuries-old houses and mix of forests and green Alpine fields, was beautiful. I knew every tree there. Occasionally the rolling fields were punctuated by a solitary tree, seemingly eternal, stoically indifferent to the lives of men, a green dome of tremendous leafage, that I would climb on a windy day to listen to its movement.

But it was very conservative in the village – traumatically conservative. It seems to have regressed from the time in 1816 when Stendhal described Gruyères with the opposite characteristics.

In those years I thought that the chances of making progress getting acquainted with a girl were better in the village than in big city Geneva, and I was putting a lot of stake in that premise and coming back every summer. In the village everyone knew each other, and, from seeing the same people all the time, I formed bonds of friendship there that I could not achieve in the busy city. Years later, I realized that the very thing I thought made it easier to gain a girl's affection (the fact that everyone knows each other), actually made it harder. My friendships there would never translate into a summer fling because in the conservatism of a Swiss village where everyone knows each other, a girl could not do anything outside of the context of a formal courtship without ruining her reputation. Each time I thought the summer had such limitless possibilities, and each time I was mistaken.

There was a couple there: Jean-Luc and Veronique, who were officially 'dating' for a year and yet their so-called relationship was completely unconsummated. It was exasperating – I could not understand what they were doing and what it meant if they did not even have any real intimacy with each other. Since they were 'dating' I could not take Veronique out for tête-à-tête in a pub. She could only spend time with Jean-Luc. It was bewildering – two people came to the decision they liked each other, and that was it – they suddenly entered into a compact to be in an exclusive relationship forever. Meanwhile after all of my experiences with Nadia in five countries (I count the

Vatican as a country), I still saw I could not have what these two yokels in the Swiss village had.

Coincidentally, Severine who Nadia was talking to, was from that very same Swiss village. Georges had come with me to the village for portions of a few summers and we had some mutual friends from there. It was, many years ago, to Severine that I had complained about the rigid village social codes that forbid someone from even taking a girl out to a pub or café unless you were already 'dating'. Almost everyone was already paired off, which included the best ones, like Veronique and Sylvie. But there were still some others who were single. I asked Severine why any of them can't be dating me. She would laugh, as if it's so ridiculous that someone from Geneva, not living in the village year round, would ask, that it doesn't warrant an answer.

Years passed. While they all stayed in the village I went to business school in Paris, then moved to New York. I explored every region of the vast world while they barely went as far as Geneva. And I came with a stunningly beautiful girl to Georges' wedding. Only to have her say to Severine, "Oh, we're not dating."

There is a very powerful novella by Gérard de Nerval – *Sylvie.* Proust was heavily influenced by Nerval, taking the main theme of *À la recherche du temps perdu* from Nerval's ideas of time lost and regained. The first time I read it I was overwhelmed – I was stunned how closely it was expressive of the same emotions of revisiting the French village from one's past. I, as well, knew a "Sylvie" there and like in the novella she was inevitably unattainable and ultimately lost.

I sought to find something in upstate New York that would remind me of the setting of the village. And I found something – Mohonk Mountain House, an 1869 Victorian chateau in the Shawangunk range, had enough almost-European character to be close. The chateau is perched on a lake amidst white cliffs, its red turrets and spires set against the pale blue outlines of distant mountains. For a few years I was excited by it, exploring every meter of the network of forest trails and cliffs, going there for long periods every summer and sometimes in the other seasons as well. Although summer was best, the fall had colorful leaves, the spring had flowers, and in the winter, one could put on crampons and climb immense frozen waterfalls, exploring the caves that they would form with massive walls of ice. The magnetism of this land endeared itself to me like no other piece of nature in the Western Hemisphere. But this ended in significant disappointment as all my efforts over the course of many years to bring someone from New York there to share all that splendor failed.

But I have digressed too far and need to get back to Nadia. I finally managed to pull her away and ask her what she meant. She said, "I don't want to talk about this now."

Nevertheless I insisted and she said that she had "recently" (a year ago) gotten out of a relationship and doesn't want to be in another one right now.

I knew right away that these were meaningless phrases that were commonly used in order to be diplomatic. As when Queen Victoria would say, "How is the weather outside?" when she wanted to turn down a courtier's proposition and end the discussion. It has never happened that a girl has really liked someone, and has chosen to not be with them because the timing is bad, or because of some influence from a previous relationship, or something their mother said against the match. When they like someone none of these trivialities are relevant, and they want to join together as eagerly as Evelina, Yvette, and Veronique did.

I saw that it was over.

The rest of the time in France she was more irritable than before, and argumentative, especially when drinking too much, which happened every night now.

We flew back to New York together, but, like the last time when she stayed with me here, she spent the entire time away visiting other people, until she returned to Miami.

She left with a lot of things unresolved. But one thing was clear – my idea of spending a longer time in Miami next winter, first renting my previous apartment in South Beach, then staying another 3-4 weeks in her apartment would not work. She said her apartment was too small to have someone stay that long. I decided instead to go to Colombia after Miami and work remotely a few weeks from there.

When she was leaving for the airport she was in a rush and the time still available to talk to her kept narrowing until it narrowed to nothing. "When can you come back – October, maybe November?" I asked, a great hopeless How on earth can I keep you? crying out to her beneath my words.

I knew that good things cannot last. Still, it was somewhat hurriedly that fate stopped them.

The day after she left was abysmally desolate. When waking up that day, for the first few lucky seconds of consciousness I did not remember everything that happened. But then the flash of memory erupted suddenly in my mind – memory is horrible at times like this, when it brings one back to the living nightmare. Better never to wake at all.

*   *   *

When I looked at other people I felt as if, in comparison to me, they all had already lived a lifetime, and then had gone back in time with all their experience and wisdom to start again – so aptly and adroitly did they do everything, relative to me. I envied how successfully they could decide between choices, instinctively know exactly what they wanted to do, and master social situations. I, on the other hand, made so many brutal mistakes, made so many poor decisions, and took so long to gain experience in any skill or subject, that I perpetually felt behind everyone in life, as if on a derailed train, continuing to spin its metal wheels in the dust while others are on a glittering track.

I was coming to my company's office once a week. The mandatory return was being postponed to early 2022. I happened to tell someone in the office, Kate, about my difficulties in securing an apartment in Miami for the winter. Prices and demand had gone up significantly. Kate asked, "Do you know anyone there – a close friend or relative to stay with?"

To hear this question was heartbreaking, because I actually did know someone there. Someone who was the most intimate person in my whole life. I had to reply, "No."

I didn't necessarily think that everything was definitively over, since I recalled the story of Kitty Shcherbatskaya and Konstantin Levin in *Anna Karenina*. Kitty turned down Levin's proposal because she was infatuated with the charismatic rake Alexei Vronsky. Years later, they reunited and Levin saw that her refusal at the time, was not a refusal forever. Embarrassed as he was from the first refusal, he tried again.

*   *   *

One day I had a lengthy dream involving Nadia. In it I was picking up the trail of research started by Vladimir Solovyov, the great theologian and sophiologist. In the late 1800s, he had attempted to develop a theology based on Sophia, after having visions of her in London and in Egypt. Nobody knows exactly what Sophia is, however, even Solovyov, who was a sophiologist. I decided to go straight to the source: the Sophia church in Constantinople, and I somehow was there in the 6th century, when it had just been built, during the Byzantine Empire. The church was apparently a library as well. I was researching sophiology from an ancient, immense book, a book so large it was impossible to lift and there was a wheelbarrow next to me for the purpose of carting it. Suddenly a bell rang, which I knew indicated that the library was closed and the deadline for returning books was now over. They had fines for a late return of a book and apparently the larger the size of the book, the larger the fine. It was some absurd sum. I looked into my pocket, and saw that all I had were $2 bills. Interestingly, they had an illustration of Mohonk Mountain House on the back. When I tried to use one of them to pay the fine, the cloaked Roman legionary refused to take it, saying it was illegal to use or even to have any kind of foreign currency. (This probably came from my actual past experience in Syria, where restaurants would refuse to take dollars when I ran out of Syrian pounds. Due to capital controls, it was only possible to exchange money on the black market and it was so illegal for a business to accept any non-Syrian currency that they would rather forgive me the amount I owed rather than take a $5 bill). The dream turned into a nightmare of persecution. I could tell a whole range of legal proceedings were being amassed against me. Christopher Walken, who was apparently a close advisor to the Emperor Justinian, was telling me that this was a very serious matter: numerous laws had been violated, especially as they had found out what I had been researching. "I believe the word 'heresy' was spoken," he said. None of this was amusing. In the dream, this was my reality – what happened was an exceptionally grave matter for me with horrific consequences that would destroy my life. The scene changed, and I was suddenly with Walken on the coast of the Black Sea. He suggested that I go with him to Sofia, Bulgaria. Once we cross the border, the Romans would not pursue. Meanwhile he had transformed into a dark looking Greek or Turk. He declared that if he was driving such a far distance, he would need to be smoking a shisha pipe while doing so. He could not drive for so long without constantly smoking. To that end, he constructed a 'shisha-mobile', a vehicle with large tanks of water in transparent compartments all around the driver's seat. What resulted was that with all the water tanks, there was only enough room for one person in the car, so he went to Bulgaria by himself. I knew that the police were still actively pursuing me. I wandered the streets of Constantinople; apparently only by luck nobody apprehended me. Suddenly I was in a café, and Nadia was working there. I was a bit surprised she was there – why didn't she tell me she was in the 6th century? But I was very glad to be with her. We sat together on a divan seat along the edge of the wall, and with my hands on her waist I kissed her. The police were still around – in fact they had gotten into the café and were arguing, in a foreign language, with the portly Greek owner, about him harboring a fugitive. Also, *a large number of cats*, perhaps dozens, had run in through the open door. But, as is typical in dreams, despite all the commotion around me, the only thing I could think about was the lovely girl I was with and all the possibilities with her. Nothing else was a concern: the police, the legal issues, getting back to the 21st century, why Nadia was working in a café in 6th century Constantinople, or the vital questions of theology that I was investigating so recently. I was oblivious to everything since being with Nadia was the only thing that was relevant – the only thing that mattered to me in the whole world was the emotion I felt being near her and running my hand along her stocking-covered leg or through her hair. We kissed more, and, I woke up.

I awoke with a very sad feeling upon realizing this was only a dream. It felt so real, and I had so little time with her – why did it have to end so quickly? There was so much nonsense with the construction of the shisha-mobile and so little of the dream was spent with her! Now I was alone again.

But then I looked around me in the semi-darkness and saw that no, that wasn't the case – there she was, asleep. I was relieved. But where were we, exactly? It seemed like New York but I couldn't quite tell right away. She moved a bit, coming in contact with me – I was so content she was here – and then, I woke up again! It was a double dream; in reality I was indeed alone.

Dreams are real as long as they last. This latter one felt especially real since one doesn't expect to still be asleep after one wakes up.

What about life? The only difference is that it is longer than a dream. But is it always that much longer? All I had with her were a handful of moments...

*   *   *

Friends were no consolation to my loss. Helen and Steven said I was better off without Nadia. I showed them pictures from the trip and Helen said, "You actually look better than she does in this picture. Look, you had some good times with her and that's good, but now you have to move on because she's clearly unsuitable." They pointed out her poor background, lack of education and career, unhealthy lifestyle, and commitment issues. "You could do better."

This didn't help – apparently they had a much poorer grasp of reality than I had. I told them, "The truth is the complete opposite of what you are saying. The problem is rather that I'm not good enough for her."

In the meantime, she had entirely ceased communicating. In the past, seeing instagram videos where she appears tantalizingly beautiful and unbearably cute were good since I was expecting to see her soon and knew she had affection for me. But now seeing her all the time like that was painful. It also reminded me of how many other people she was spending time with, sparking jealousy of anyone who was granted such pleasure. I stopped looking at her instagram and began to distance myself from the thought of her.

* * *

Mainly I sought consolation from travel. I was suffocating in the vacuum of solitude that is New York and wanted to plunge into diverse and unpredictable climes, the more exotic the better, as I felt this would be better suited to make me forget everything about home.

I had a brief stop in Casablanca on the way to Addis Ababa. Casablanca was familiar to me, and I revisited the Hassan II mosque, but everyone I used to know in the city had left it during the pandemic because the restrictions had been too severe. I got to Ethiopia and wandered the unlit streets of Addis Ababa but could find nothing of interest, either because the city's nightlife had not yet recovered its energy post-pandemic or because it is only active on Fridays and Saturday and I was there on the wrong days. Although I inquired a few times, it was hard to get any information from people on the civil war developing in Tigray, probably due to government censorship on the conflict. It was enough to step a bit off the central streets to encounter the most abysmal poverty and squalor, even worse than I had seen in India and Nepal. However, it did not feel dangerous; less in fact than certain areas of the Bronx.

There was nothing to see in the city except two interesting Ethiopian churches. In the all the centuries of civilization there, and being the only black African country with its own native writing script (Amharic), they have not managed to build any interesting architecture except these two churches. Still, that is more than many other countries.

The coffee in Ethiopia impressed me. It was the birthplace of coffee, in the 15th century, and the traditions have developed a coffee culture perhaps second only to Italy.

Hotels in most parts of the world simply do not understand that I need a decent amount of coffee in the morning. They bring a miniscule cup of espresso, then disappear somewhere. I've already finished it in five seconds but am now obligated to wait for the return of the waiter to order more. They don't understand the concept of the triple espresso or quadruple espresso. To counter this I usually order two double espressos, as if an imaginary person will join me soon, and then drink both.

"Only dull people are brilliant at breakfast," Oscar Wilde explained.

In Ethiopia there were no problems – the coffee was sufficiently strong and plentiful.

Having extra time, I continued my search for Miami apartments and was able to secure the same one I had last time, but at a higher price. Due to advances in modern technology, although having nothing with me except my phone, I was able to negotiate the deal over an internet call in Addis Ababa, then print and sign the contract from my hotel in Istanbul, and then execute the Citibank wire transfer while in Baghdad.

As the journey progressed the thing I started to look forward to the most was reuniting with Gökçen in Istanbul, the beautiful svelte girl I had met in September 2020. I thought that we could pick up where we left off a year ago. She met me at a shisha lounge, and only then I discovered that she was already engaged. I looked at Istanbul tinder, but unfortunately, the world had returned to normal. There was never an easier time to get a date and become acquainted with new people than the corona pandemic. This was clearly the case in New York Summer 2020 and Miami Winter 2020-21 – I would never have met any of the girls I met if things were normal and they were busy with their thousands of options. Chaos, crisis, and societal upheaval shake things up and can present opportunities in unexpected ways. This was noted by Stalin, who built his plans of spreading communism throughout Europe and Asia through the chaos of the 2nd World War.

Corona was the biggest global calamity since WWII. But even during that war, there were many individual people who benefited enormously. For instance, American soldiers who found themselves in the occupied territory of Bavaria and ended up meeting and marrying beautiful Bavarian girls. How would they ever have met otherwise? The soldier might have been a farmboy from Iowa and the war gave him his only opportunity to leave the country and see something other than cornfields.

In Istanbul as well, 2020 was the best time for dating and Fall 2021 was no longer the same. As a result I found myself on the Soho House rooftop alone. The bar had relocated indoors because of the season, but it was a warm night and I wanted to see the sunset so I took my cup of straight Havana Club, with a piece of ice, up to the roof.

It was the most beautiful sunset I had ever seen.

It was a sight that brought me to tears, so heavily did it overwhelm my powers of admiration and oppress my spirit with acute *Sehnsucht* and with the fact that I was witnessing this spectacle alone.

A year ago I was in this exact spot with Gökçen. Nobody was here now – I was the only person on the rooftop.

There was a rainfall of roses in the western sky. I stood up from my chair in amazement to watch this. Everywhere rose petals drifted down, slowly and delicately, covering the gray dome of the Yavuz Selim Mosque and the waters of the Golden Horn. A million pink petals from celestial gardens collected over the quiet unknowing city, the radiance illuminating the entire sky.

I was the only person seeing this sight. I repeatedly looked around to check again – was there really nobody there? Did nobody else come up? Why was this sight wasted only on me? If any person had come up to the rooftop, it doesn't matter who, it would have heartened me so much to point out this miraculous sight and to share, with someone, the admiration of the sublimity. No, I was still alone.

Then it was over. The sun had vanished, and I watched the colors fade, feeling a sudden chill in the air. I was overcome with gloom.

I sipped my glass of rum and, wrapping my jacket more tightly against myself, pondered on metaphysics.

We all know those irritating people who describe themselves as happy, the ones who think the world is not really that bad, and all you need is a positive outlook and a lot of hard work. "Just change your outlook," they say.

This is hurtful. It implies that there must be something wrong with you and how much you've failed that the world appears bad to you.

One friend persisted in tell me this. I later found out she was seeing a psychologist, which is where she must have picked up these naïve platitudes that contradict reality. To think this way one must either be young, lacking much experience, or simply refuse to observe and understand the world, like a clerk working in a hospital on the frontlines of a war, who shuts his ears when doctors walk by discussing how many casualties occurred that day, as if to convince himself that there is no war and the explosions in the distance getting nearer and nearer are actually harmless thunder.

While our wellbeing is better served by finding contentment where we are and accepting our limitations, society criticizes us for trying to ignore the ladder of hierarchy. The structure of hierarchies, which was first studied by Laurence Peter in *The Peter Principle*, are everywhere in life, from economics to social relationships, and the pressure of practical society compels us to strive to get somewhere beyond our capabilities.

For instance, how many parents have prodded their unmarried sons or daughters with the constant question of why they are not married yet, setting them up on dates with the most unattractive of their acquaintances' children and then nagging for years about why they couldn't just get married already and be happy?

What they fail to understand is that desire and work alone is not enough. *Seinfeld* was an astute series about four people in New York, none of whom ever had a successful relationship. At one time Jerry Seinfeld pondered, "99% of people in New York are undateable. How do these people get together?!"

For a long time, we have been directed by materialistic society to wake early, work hard, save money, have children, and be happy, under the axiom that material progress and procreation brings happiness. Notwithstanding the possible contradiction between these things themselves, the command, "Be happy," – equating happiness with virtue – is dangerously incongruent with the reality of the world, and the desire and the striving of many people to follow this advice, has ironically led to much unhappiness when finally clashing with this contradiction.

That mankind is incapable of actualizing this – even in heaven, if it existed – is proved by the fact of boredom, (ranging from common *ennui* to the more sophisticated feeling of *noia* described by Giacomo Leopardi) since if existence were good in and of itself, boredom would not exist.

To seek happiness in the accomplishment of objectives or the satisfaction of desires is as naïve as to attempt to reach the horizon by walking straight ahead. The further one gets, the further the horizon recedes, since expectations grow with every success. This is a natural tendency – after the lovely tryst with Nadia on the yacht in the Mediterranean, did I not start thinking right away about locations where I might want to have a wedding? But the basis on which these thoughts took hold was entirely a fiction in my mind.

Another tendency is to at least expect to keep what we already have, but we can never even be sure of that! If some contentedness, or at least the alleviation of suffering, can be found in life, it is not the satisfaction of desires, but the gradual reduction of expectations that should be sought. This is nothing profound – one of the simplest things that can be learned from Buddhism – but I saw that I needed reminding of it.

In the initial stage of disappointment from losing Nadia, I felt as if adrift in a sea of misery without any shore in sight, a sea whose boundlessness is like the interminable amount of time the suffering must be endured – one doesn't know when, if ever, it will end. One despairs of ever reaching a port; adrift at sea without any ability to steer or to even know which direction one is going.

This was from losing hope – hope which she herself had given me when she showed me things I had never thought possible. I blamed various problems and faults of my own; sometimes I blamed some of her traits or various circumstances that I thought hindered our accord.

But in doing this I lost sight of the bigger picture. When I realized that hope was irrational in the first place, and accepted that somehow by chance I had some fun and that's all there is – there's nothing else to hope for or desire

– I reached a more comfortable stage: not adrift, but letting myself be indifferently carried by the current, without attributing any value to remaining life. What I've been lucky enough to achieve already with Nadia is enormous. Let others struggle; I have nowhere to rush – I have no goals. I felt better once I understood this. Despair was replaced by a more stable melancholy, which, if we are being realistic, is the best we can do.

To accept the evil of the world means to stop incessantly and automatically blaming our own limitations or finding fault with the shortcomings of others. What can we reasonably do to counteract such a setup of evil?

In the Old Testament, God creates the world in six days and goes so far as to actually applaud himself for it: "He saw everything that he made, and, behold, it was very good." The Catechism of the Catholic Church explains that God, infinitely perfect, in a plan of sheer goodness, through his agents Jesus Christ and the Holy Ghost, has gifted mankind a blessed life.

No, this is entirely unacceptable as a foundation of metaphysics. That mankind should be created and delivered into this world of pointless hard labor, desperate unemployment, loneliness, and illness, is our lot. That a young girl like Nadia should be almost blown apart by a Hezbollah bomb in West Beirut is also our lot. But that all this should be called "very good" and "blessed"? That is quite insulting.

Although the Old Testament viewpoint is popular among Americans with their culture of Protestant work ethic (hard work and materialism brings happiness), most other cultures have taken a more natural and realist viewpoint, from Buddhism to ancient Greek tragedies to

Victor Hugo's *Notre Dame de Paris* and *Les Travailleurs de la mer*. The world of Hugo is a world of exemplary romanticist individuals, ultimately all inevitably destroyed by the malevolent world around them. He pre-dated Kafka and Camus in depicting the absurdity of it all, and he is superior to them, as he shows that even exemplary individuals, pursuing rational values, are doomed and destroyed by the world, not just average individuals. This is consistent with Buddhism, according to which we are in *samsāra*, a world of inevitable suffering – only a rare few somehow escape the world into *nirvana*.

The life and death of Heinrich von Kleist, revealed through his numerous letters, is an interesting case of the trajectory of a man who in the beginning of his life was a strong proponent of a *Lebensplan*, or 'life plan', a strict framework of goals and planned accomplishments that would shape and direct one's life over the span of decades, until he suddenly realized the senselessness of it all – that nothing can actually be done; that there is a fatal mismatch between the way we are and the way the world is, and that trying to fix it, to find what we are lacking in order to fit into the world, is futile. Simply put, von Kleist had formed too many expectations. Instead of the *Lebensplan* he found greater meaningfulness in dying with his friend Henriette Vogel.

Many authors have expressed this sense of derailment. I recalled the famous first lines of Dante's *Inferno:*

> Midway upon the journey of our life
> I found myself within a forest dark,
> For the straightforward pathway had been lost

* * *

Most Americans I have known, actually declare that they are content with their jobs. They have no problem waking at ungodly hours like 5 or 6, before dawn, and commuting more than an hour, even cheerfully doing some work on the morning train. With their commitment to work and chores, they have more energy in the morning without any coffee, than I do with numerous espressos. When they were younger they were also content with studying all sorts of irrelevant subjects in schools, no matter how useless, pointless, or boring. I could never understand that kind of mentality, since I have always had a seething loathing for being coerced into doing work like a slave. Put someone with a different mentality, such as a philosopher or an artist, in an office job and see what happens. It was just 2½ years of loathsome office work that fueled Arthur Schopenhauer to construct the most pessimistic metaphysical philosophy Europe has ever seen. It was Franz Kafka's insurance office job that inspired his Kafkaesque hopelessness.

It is only by a rare stroke of luck that one can find a job that is reasonably tolerable, rather than a source of active suffering happening every day.

Sometimes I thought maybe I have a mental imbalance to have such a deep uncontrollable aversion to being forced to do work that I don't want to do, at school or in a job, while other people seem content with it. But I had to conclude that this is not the case, because logically it seems normal to detest nonsensical work and those people who are content with it are rather the ones who are abnormal.

Most work in a large organization is nonsensical. For instance, I write reports – they are the result of days of deep analysis and research. If they are not flawless in every way, in every inconsequential detail, criticism from management is severe. Revisions are made until the one or two people reading them are satisfied. They are then forwarded to another department, where their receipt is noted and they are sent to a third department, where their receipt is also noted and they are kept in storage. Nothing else is done with the report. When I ask the logic behind all this I am told, "It doesn't matter whether they do anything or not with them; that's their responsibility, not ours. We still have to send it to them."

Half the company is engaged in work like this, the other half in auditing and triple-checking the results of the other half. It is no different than the boulder that Sisyphus is condemned to roll to the top of a hill, watch it roll back down, and being again. Nothing is accomplished, nothing created or produced.

This may be a cause of great concern and dismay, such a wastage of time and effort, but on the other hand, I realize that it is actually a great thing that the company is filled with so much nonsensical work. Because it provides me a salary. But that doesn't make the work itself less loathsome.

I'm reminded of the journalist who was interviewing one of the leaders of the Syrian Interim Government. Having covered numerous topics about the problems and conflicting factions in Syria, the journalist asked a silly question, "So, what's the solution?"

The reply was, "Maybe no solution."

How naïve to think a 'solution' exists for every issue. *Maybe no solution.* It is the same for life. When you examine the predominating, inestimable, and boundless evil of the world, you are forced to conclude that there is of course no remedy. The remedy would be a total annihilation of the world. In other words – in order for evil and the need for it to disappear, the universe itself must disappear.

*   *   *

From Istanbul I flew to Baghdad. Only recently did Iraq become open to visitors without a visa. Before this, Westerners only went there on military-related business. They did require a negative corona test though. Instead of fabricating my usual one from New York, I showed one from a clinic in Kiev, thinking that it's more plausible to say that I had been in nearby Kiev in the last 72 hours rather than New York. I happened to have a template from someone else's test in Kiev and simply changed the name and dates. They barely glanced at it on arrival in Baghdad airport. I immediately noticed that Iraqis don't like masks. None of the staff and police at the airport were wearing one, which was unusual for airports worldwide at this time. I suppose they have greater problems in their country than worrying about these useless pieces of fabric.

I went to the old town – there was nothing but dusty, crumbling and rubbish-filled streets. One mosque looked interesting, with a colorful Persian-looking dome and minaret, but it was closed. In a narrow alley next to the mosque, a man was driving a horse cart laden with boxes. I walked to the end of a dingy, sand-covered alley towards the river, seeing a statue of someone with his arm raised who I thought was Saddam Hussein. It was actually Al-Mutanabbi, the 10th century poet. Meanwhile a military Chinook helicopter flew in an arc overhead and I heard automatic rifle fire from somewhere across the river.

Besides the old town, the giant green onion domes of the Martyr monument are the only thing to see in Baghdad. But when I got there in a taxi, the gates were closed. At first

I thought I couldn't get in, but I noticed a watchtower with some army people. I waved to them and they descended and slid open the iron gate a bit to question what I wanted.

"I want to see that," I said, pointing to the green dome.

They were surprised I was there, but let me in.

After 40 years of war and recently being the world capital for terrorism, security was tight everywhere. My hotel, the ziggurat-shaped Babylon Rotana, was like a fortress, with multiple checkpoints to get in and armored trucks with machine guns stationed outside.

Alcohol is legal in Iraq, but people rarely drink and most restaurants did not have wine. There were no wine stores either. I was staying in the best hotel in the city and was shocked to discover that the stylish hotel restaurant, in an outdoor garden, did not have wine. The concierge didn't know any restaurants nearby that had it. I found one online and went there to hunt down some wine. I had to walk two kilometers at night through obscure Baghdadi streets to find it, since taxis were difficult to order. But I got there – it was a riverfront rooftop restaurant with Arabic music, where I ate grilled fish caught from the Tigris, and bought enough wine to take back to the hotel with me. Nobody spoke English anywhere, but everyone was friendly and tried to help. I engaged a driver passing by to take me back to the hotel for a few dinars. Now I could enjoy a shisha in the hotel garden, also with a cup of wine. There were many beautiful Iraqi girls, as the restaurant in this hotel was a gathering place for Baghdad's upper class, but they were unapproachable. There was no bar scene. Also, oddly there was no tinder. In Tehran and Jeddah, where there are no bars at all, people rely heavily on tinder to meet people. In Baghdad there was neither option.

Having nothing to do the next day, I went to the sauna in the hotel, where I met a naked Australian man here on some kind of business. He persisted in avoiding the subject of what business exactly. He asked me what I was doing here.

I said, "I don't know. Traveling, chilling."

"Where are you going after this?"

"Back to New York."

"I haven't been back to Australia since corona. I was able to leave, but I can't go back unless I want to do quarantine in a government-run facility. And I'd have to pay for it. No thanks!"

"Australia is crazy."

"Still, it's not the worst place. I was in Afghanistan this past August, during the Taliban takeover of Kabul. It was truly a depressing scene. People were desperate to get out. They would leave everything they have, all their possessions, just to be able to get out, but they couldn't."

"Why did this happen, in your opinion?"

"It was preventable. It is entirely an error on the part of the US – to leave suddenly, knowing that the Afghan army can't defend the cities. The Afghans, the ANSF, they were depending on logistical and air support from the US – things like reconnaissance technology. They were shocked when all this was abruptly withdrawn. The people here, in Iraq, are on edge. They see what happened there, and they're worried that the US withdrawal here will allow the Islamists in the north to come back. I just got back from Mosul. It is unstable... Although whatever happens up north, I don't think they will ever take Baghdad itself – it's too well defended. But we could see terrorist bombings in the city again. ISIS in Afghanistan is also building strength

– they could soon have the capability to strike targets all over this area."

"I ran into Bill Burns at the Harvard Club in New York, before he was the CIA director," I said. "I had some questions for him about Iran, cause I was about to go there. We also talked about Iraq. His opinion was that overthrowing Hussein was a net negative for the region."

"Yeah, it's hard to say. Maybe it's not his removal but a mishandling of things afterwards. Iraq is such a messed up place. Hey, wasn't Burns the US Ambassador to Russia?"

"He was."

"He certainly failed to rein in Putin then. There was Georgia, then Syria, then Crimea and Donetsk. Putin believes no one will stop him. The US is weak now. Watch out for Russia. Mark my words – they are on the verge of launching a full-scale invasion of Ukraine."

I was surprised that someone would make such a prediction. Even the following February, when I saw that Putin was amassing troops along the border I thought it was just a bluff.

"I've been to Ukraine," I said. "It's too big – it would be impossible to hold."

"He doesn't need to hold it, just to change the government in Kiev and to annex and fortify the eastern and southern Russian half – from Donetsk to Odessa."

"What would that accomplish? I mean, what is his personal incentive to do this?"

"Who knows? What's the incentive for half the things happening in Baghdad?"

I had gone from Saint-Tropez to Baghdad, from the best place to the worst place. In a way this was a metaphor for my life.

XIX
0

XIX – Omicron

In November, in the final days before winter in Miami I could barely sit still from the excitement. I recognized that the feeling was similar to the one I experienced as a student in Geneva when the endless hateful school year was over and I was once again returning to my familiar village to spend the summer in the nature of the Swiss Alps. In those years, I would start counting down the days when there were 100 left to go; my happiness increased proportionately as the number of days of hard toil that remained decreased and decreased. On the day of finally getting to the village, I would almost want to jump out of the car my parents were driving before it reached our house on the far end of a grassy field. It would be impossible to restrain my agitation and to start the summer by patiently carrying luggage and groceries from the car to the house – no, I vanished into the forest, seeing my familiar trees again, breathing the sweet and sultry scent of the woods that I had not felt for so long I had forgotten what it feels like, falling blissfully onto the grass, clutching it with my hands, looking up into the sky, into the azure of endless possibility of a brand new summer.

The winter of 2021-22 everyone wanted to be in Miami. Demand shot up so much for Miami Art Basel weekend that prices in the 1 Hotel escalated to $3800 per night. That amount is 16x greater than the effective daily price I was paying for my apartment, even though it was in the same space as the hotel.

Not long before I left, the news media became fixated on a new corona variant that was discovered in South

Africa. They called it Omicron. Countries were already starting to restrict travel from southern Africa to the rest of the world, erroneously thinking that would contain it. Right away, based on the level of panic and hype of the news coverage I recognized that this would be a problem. The news were not focusing on the scientific analysis already done in South Africa that determined that Omicron was much milder than previous variants and thus not a significant danger. Instead they were emphasizing how it is resistant to vaccines and much more contagious.

We can only hypothesize on their motives, but it was the media's coverage of Omicron that most clearly made visible that their agenda was to spread as much fear and panic as possible, regardless of what was actually going on. The pandemic was coming to an end – restrictions everywhere were gradually being lifted in late 2021 – but now there was something new to latch onto, and everyone who wanted to continue the pandemic, found a way to do so via this variant. What actually happened was that Omicron was so mild it may have been a benefit, as it improved herd immunity against the earlier more severe variants. The danger of Omicron was a media propaganda hoax.

Earlier in the year, while talking with Chiara, I made the prediction that as the pandemic naturally fades, they are going to have to invent something new that threatens us in order to keep the controls going.

I was going to Miami, where I knew none of this would matter. Regardless of what was happening elsewhere, I knew I would be safe from the medical fascists in Miami. People there had already stopped caring about corona a year ago. But there was no telling what the fascists worldwide would do in response, and I was concerned of the risks to other travel, such as Rio de Janeiro during Carnaval 2022. (And it did end up happening that Rio Carnaval was postponed due to Omicron, from February to April, and I had to change my flights).

In the fall of 2021, schools reopened to all students in New York. This was already a year after Florida successfully reopened schools. And in Sweden they never closed in the first place.

But the schools reopened with a major caveat – mandatory masks. It grieved me to see children in schools forced by their slavemasters to abide by this nonsensical monstrosity of a rule, not being able to breathe or speak normally for an entire school day. What kind of parents would permit this torture to happen to their kids?

The year and a half of closures set back kids' learning, increased their fattening, and the whole bizarre situation of uncertainty, isolation, propaganda, and fearmongering sharply increased diagnoses of anxiety and depression.

And for what? It was completely futile.

* * *

I did not anticipate the array of emotions I would feel coming back to the same apartment in Miami after a year. In the days leading up to the journey the only anticipation was excitement and thoughts of how much I will enjoy another winter there. I wasn't thinking about Nadia, except in the sense that the memory of what happened with her imparted an optimism that maybe, in the sultry and fashionable setting of Miami, similar things could happen with someone else. (In fact, even before I came I already had a date set for the second day with a girl I knew from before, Petra from Czechia who lived in Design District).

Getting to the familiar driveway of my building on 23rd street, seeing the familiar elevators and carpeted hallways, sparked many memories of good times here.

But when I entered the apartment, it was a more melancholy feeling, since predominating among my other impressions, were a flood of memories of Nadia – I recalled that this glass cabinet was where she would leave her sunglasses; over there was the place she typically sat when doing something on her laptop. I stepped outside to admire the glorious view over the beach, and in my mind, saw how she one time precariously sat on the edge of the balcony railing, with her legs over the edge, to take a photo.

At the same time, the memories seemed as though they were unfathomably far away, from another era of time, given how much had changed. She seemed almost a different person now; I myself had changed and was a different person, not to mention that the entire world was different. That particular period in Miami, at the peak of the pandemic, was a bizarre and beautiful island in the sea of time.

Sometimes memory would lie in ambush. The first time I visited the beach bar this winter it did not produce any strong emotions. I was glad to be there again, and told this to the barkeep, but that was it. Then, on a visit another day, they had fired up the barbeque grill. A certain odd kind of woodsmoke was emanating from the grill – when I inhaled it, I was immediately struck by a flashback of memory to an exact moment 303 days ago in this spot, when I was looking at Nadia's eyes while she rubbed her nose with her hand and talked about a metal concert she had once gone to. I stopped in my tracks and hung on to the involuntary memory until it faded.

Days fall down like sheets of paper, gathering up in a haphazard pile on the ground of our memory, and like those papers they bury in their midst the oldest, the first to accumulate. But a sudden wind can ruffle this pile. Nothing other than a simple woodsmoke scent was able to recover what I had forgotten, regaining a moment in time that had been lost.

Fond as the recollection was, for it brought to mind how beautifully, how enchantingly her eyes appeared as she looked at me, I recognized that this was a distant and remote past and the need now was to focus on the present. And there were many things going on, in the first days I was back in Miami. Chiara, Helen, Steven, Petra, and others were around. Alexys set up an art gallery where I met the artist Zachary Knudson and was introduced to his unique style of glass mirror art.

Sometimes, after having dinner in the southern part of South Beach and riding my bike back north, I would continue a little further along the beachside path to check out the scene at the beach bar. If it was empty I would retire home. One day, it looked very lively and I decided to stop by for a drink. I parked the bike at the lot on 24th street and walked in to have a seat at the bar.

While drinking a cup of rosé, I noticed a beautiful girl with light brown hair sitting at a table under the trees with her family – I assumed it was her parents and a younger sister. They looked slightly foreign-looking. I paid no more attention to her, paid my bill, and left to go home. The nearest washroom to the beach bar is at a considerable distance, at the top of a set of stairs and across a courtyard. It happened to be on my way home. When I was heading towards my apartment, by chance I saw her exiting the washroom to go back downstairs. We made eye contact and she smiled back. She had green eyes and denim shorts, and was tall with wedge-heel sandals.

I asked, "Hey, where are you from?"

"I'm from Brazil! What about you?"

"Oh I live right here," and I pointed up at the building we were standing next to. "Where in Brazil?"

"Rio de Janeiro."

"Ah cool; I'm actually planning to go back there in February. Are you having dinner down there?" We moved towards the edge of the terrace, next to a tuft of red salvias bordered with heliotrope, where we could stand looking over the palm trees of the beach bar, with the ocean visible in the distance.

"Yes, I'm with my family."

"What are you doing later? Any plans?"

In a rare stroke of luck, she actually didn't have any plans, didn't know anyone in the city, and was in fact looking for something to do on the island but didn't know what to do alone. Her family was staying in a hotel on the mainland. We were talking with the easy familiarity of old acquaintances, even though we had just met this moment. I suggested to have a drink at the rooftop bar after she finished. From where we were standing, we could see the palm trees at the roof which I indicated. We exchanged numbers.

I went home, and later met Verônica (that was her name) in the 1 Hotel lobby and we went to the roof. "What did you tell them you were doing?" I asked.

"I told them I just now found out a college friend was here and that she'll come to meet me at the 1 Hotel. Then after they left I texted you."

She was in her last year at Universidade Federal do Rio de Janeiro (UFRJ), and was in Miami for the first time.

We had sake at the rooftop, while I got some ceviche, then I showed her my apartment balcony view and we had more wine. People always struggle with a legitimate reason to invite a girl to their home for the first time. When one has a view, the justification is always ready and available – that you want to show her the view.

When I was in Ethiopia I bought a pack of cigarettes, with Amharic writing on the box, even though I don't smoke, just because the price was so low: $1. But for a long time I was struggling to get rid of them. She helped me do that by smoking all the remaining ones.

The extreme surprise that I felt on getting a kiss from her when she was leaving showed me, when I reflected, how demoralized I had become since Nadia, despite the upturn of being in Miami now. And the trip to Africa and the Middle East didn't help, especially Baghdad where my only social interaction was with the naked Australian man.

The next day she went with her family to the beach and immediately after that came to see me and we talked on the balcony again, this time with the daytime view. Her skin was scented by sea salt and suntan.

"How do you like the beach here?" I asked.

"It is okay," she said, shrugging. I saw she was not impressed. She continued, "In Ipanema or Leblon, there is just so much more life on the beach. There are many many people, everyone is drinking, chilling, having fun. Here it seems little reserved."

"I know what you mean. Rio has the best beaches in America. One time I climbed the Dois Irmãos mountain, the one that's at the end of Leblon. You know it?"

"Yeah, I've been there too."

"It's beautiful isn't it? – When you stand there at the edge – the whole length of Ipanema below you... It was a very hot day. When I came down – those motorcycle taxis that you need to get in and out of the favela near the mountain, I asked them to take me all the way to the beach and I went to swim in Leblon right after the mountain."

"That's the best thing to do after you're hiking the mountain." She pulled on my shirt to pull me closer to her. I was wearing a shirt that had snaps instead of buttons, and she undid one, then another.

"And they have caipirinhas on the beach. It's almost impossible to get a good caipirinha in the US."

"I know," she laughed. "I tried."

She had already pulled open the last snap, so I saw it was time to kiss her, while also unfastening the buttons on her shirt.

Although she was only here a temporary time, the affection I got from Verônica was an immense relief and recovery from the feelings I had of being demoralized. It was very significant to meet her and I felt good again for the first time since Saint-Tropez. But she was gone, and as the days passed, each day making it one less day that I have in Miami before I have to leave, I had to reassess what was going on.

By now, I had seen enough to make it plainly clear that the scene was much worse than it was last winter, when it was the peak of the pandemic. Verônica was a really lucky coincidence of being in the right place at the right time, but aside from this, there was nothing in Miami even close to how it was a year ago. Everywhere the trend was repeated. The dating scene during corona everywhere was astonishing – so many girls wanted to go out; it was the period of time when I met Nadia in Miami and many others. It is a certain fact that I would never have had a chance to become acquainted with such an amazing girl in normal times. Like the French Revolution, the crisis overturned society, making previously unthinkable things happen. When things returned to normal, the potential for dates fell back to the minimum. I had two dates with Petra and it didn't work out. There was nobody else.

In addition, all the places that I liked in Miami the previous winter were not as fun now. Last year I didn't need to ride past the beach bar to see if it was lively or not because it was always good, always full of interesting people. Now it was empty most of the time. In the previous winter less venues were open and their hours were abbreviated, concentrating people. It was possible to run into acquaintances in Mila or at the 1 Hotel rooftop. This winter, everything was open again in Miami, including all the big clubs all night, diluting people across the whole city. And the quality of people was down, since everyone across the country was traveling again. In short, things had returned to normal. The peculiar little island in time that we lived on during the pandemic was over.

I was trying to see Nadia again for old times' sake, since we were in fact in the same city, albeit she was on the mainland and I was on the island. We agreed to meet at Setai one day, but she canceled at the last minute.

She couldn't decide on any alternative day so I called her. She was having various problems. She was low on money and doing various odd jobs like getting paid along with four other girls to attend a party on a yacht. Some of the other jobs she was taking made it seem like she was moving disturbingly close to the direction of an actual courtesan. I offered to visit her downtown but she said she'll come to the island and promised to definitely make it next time. We agreed to a Tuesday after work.

She was supposed to let me know exactly what time when it was Tuesday. But I end work at 5:00 and already it was 4:00 and there was no reply from her. I kept waiting. I had freed up my schedule, wasn't going to dinner, and was just sitting at home waiting. Finally, at 6:00 she texted me saying she just woke up and was too hung over to do anything. This response summed up the degeneration of her daily life and her disregard for me. I was fed up and resolved to stop thinking about her.

As in the previous year, Christmas passed unnoticed in Miami, so I had the good fortune now to miss two Christmases in a row. The primary justification for the holiday is to provide some kind of bright and festive mitigant to the winter gloom. The decorations, lights, and trees are nice to have in say, New York where they are needed and do mitigate slightly the dark oppression of winter. But on a tropical island, there is no gloom, so there is no need for Christmas.

On New Year Eve, I went to the beach along Ocean Drive where people were on the sand and in the water watching fireworks being shot just off the coast when it became midnight – like they do in Rio de Janeiro.

By chance, I reconnected with Zeynep, having not had contact with her since she left New York to go back to Izmir in Summer 2020. She told me she was moving back to New York in a few days. I said I was spending the winter in Miami and suggested to her to come down and stay with me. I offered to buy her flights.

When she came to Miami and I saw her again I was immediately glad I came up with this idea. She looked stunning, even better than before. Her fashion sense had improved, never without stilettos at night. When her long brown hair was wet in the pool, her face seemed extremely familiar – later I realized that was because of her exact resemblance to Mia Sara from *Ferris Bueller's Day Off*.

However, prior to this I didn't know her that well, and I soon found out that her appearance was her only positive attribute. She would constantly interrupt my work, even though I told her in advance that I would be working on the weekdays and only have the entire day off Saturday and Sunday. She didn't like any of the food I had in my refrigerator, and demanded we go out for lunch, not able to go by herself because she was helpless on her own – even getting lost within the hotel – not to mention that her bank debit card had just now suddenly stopped working for some reason, and she "forgot" to bring any cash for the trip. She treated my apartment like a hotel, wearing shoes inside after I asked her not to, and using each towel only one time, ending up accumulating a giant pile of towels in the corner that needed to be washed later. I showed her around town in the evenings and on the weekend, taking her to the best places. Recently, I had discovered Gitano in the Mid-Beach Faena District, which has both a restaurant and a rooftop bar, and I took her there. But she was disrespectful of my costs, ordering things she didn't need. She ordered a cocktail and only took one sip, intending to leave it, even though it cost $22. The most important problem though, was that it was boring with her. There was no interesting conversation. It was tedium.

When I mentioned my former girlfriend, she was displeased that I still interacted with her and apparently had some liking for her. In my ignorance, I had thought that to speak well of a former girlfriend would be a positive thing, but I overdid it, leading Zeynep to believe that I was still harboring too much affinity for someone else.

Her annoyance increased when she saw messages from Nadia lighting up on my phone, showing up as Nadia ♥. The actual text of the message was not displayed in the notification, but it showed who it was from and my contact entry for her had a pink heart icon after her name.

In any case, we were not going to get along, which I already suspected back in March 2020 when we had disagreements over corona, but I wanted to give it another try. After she left I had to spend half a day cleaning up after her.

* * *

Especially starting in January 2022, every weekend someone I knew was visiting Miami. Carlos came, along with some of his friends from Santiago, and we had drinks at the Gitano rooftop. It was a chilly night and I was wearing a leather motorcycle jacket with a black turtleneck pullover. They called me the "Swiss James Dean".

I told them the story of holding on to Nadia on a scooter in Rome, balancing a pizza box and being yelled at by the Italian police.

Carlos was excited, "You should write a book about that!"

"No, it's impossible," I said. "I don't have time."

"Think about it. She has character. I don't know about how well your actual relations will go, but one thing is certain – this girl, she is a gift to an author. She is so unique she belongs in literature... You could call it *Love in the Time of Corona* – like the cholera book!"

XX
NYMPHETAMINE

XX – Nymphetamine

I had not thought about seeing her for some time, but just at this moment, Nadia said she was having a New Years dinner with a few people in Brickell and invited me to join. I was running late – the driver had taken the Venetian Causeway and the drawbridge was being raised. I had no conception of what would happen in my mind seeing her again. Four months had passed. Seeing photographs, both old and new, and various random communication had an effect on me, but a manageable one. I thought that since I experienced no serious emotions when looking at her photographs, the same would occur when seeing her in person. This was not the case. Neither photograph nor memory could adequately prepare me for the experience of seeing her beauty in reality, when, on that January day I approached a group of people standing by the bar in Novikov and saw her turn and recognize me.

We kissed on the cheek and went to the table, where I sat by her side on a divan.

Since we were with others, I could not ask her about anything personal, any of the score of questions I had about how she was doing. It wouldn't have been appropriate to touch her hair, or her hand. Sometimes she said something directly to me, turning towards me, and I got another beautiful glimpse of her face.

She was wearing a form-fitting soft pink cashmere pullover. Absence, as well as the lack of communication, gradually made me forget, but seeing her again immediately made me enamored with her. There was a group of people though, interfering with us.

I wanted to embrace her.

After the dinner, everyone went to her apartment for more drinks, but thankfully they soon left and I finally got to be alone with her. She explained how she recently had a bad episode due to xanax and decided to stop taking it entirely. This led to some withdrawal symptoms and also a higher frequency of anxiety, which she alleviated by drinking heavily. From a combination of mental and physical reasons, she could barely move out of bed for many days, even struggling to walk her dog. She described how she had to take the freight elevator and use a back door of her building when walking Argo in order to avoid any possible encounter with people, which she couldn't handle.

I asked, "If it's that bad, how are you able to cope with anything? Your job for instance? You work in nightlife; it requires a heavy amount of social interaction."

"Lots of tequila," was what she said.

Her real character, in the absence of alcohol, was actually somewhat introverted, and even a bit shy and demure, especially if compared with Miami nightlife girls. When she drank a lot, she became very sociable, talkative, and assertive. She might hit you playfully like a cat; she might jump off the highest railing of a boat like she did in France.

I told her about my trip to Addis Ababa and my struggles to find alcohol in Baghdad. She turned on a movie and asked if I wanted to stay for a while. She fed me some kind of pill.

"What is this?" I asked.

"It's a very very rare magic pill!"

I was skeptical.

"Trust me," she said.

She had two of them and took one herself, so I followed. I later found out this was a blend of THC and cocaine, balancing each other, plus maybe some psychedelic.

We sat on her divan, but she kept a space between us. The effects of the drugs kicking in, the feeling was that of an intense, limitless happiness, the source of which was merely the proximity with her – the fact that she was right there near me. I could see waves of electromagnetism pulsating between us and binding me to her. I felt like the whole of reality was materialized in these magnetic waves, as if all of life was implicit in them, as if being with her was the one and only reality, the only meaningful one. Sometimes, she gave me an excuse to touch her – for instance she showed me a new tattoo on her arm and this enabled an opportunity to physically touch her arm. A contact like this with her was electrifying.

I desperately wanted to pull her to sit more closely and to lean on me so I could put my arm around her. Such a thing would have overwhelmed my soul. In fact, I almost feared it. Why? As I analyze it in retrospect, the slight worry I felt at her moving closer and making too much contact with me, was of dissolving under a pressure of reality greater than my mind could handle, and of not being able to let her go.

The moment of parting was a bittersweet moment, since I could finally embrace her, but at the same time I was leaving her. She was like an addiction rekindled, causing withdrawal symptoms for a long time after leaving.

* * *

Seeing how completely normal life in Miami had become this winter, one could easily forget that we were 'in a pandemic' and many people in other places worldwide were still concerned about corona. Only by turning on BBC could someone be reminded, with reporters talking about case numbers in Brazil, Russia, or elsewhere with grave seriousness while video footage showed a multitude of people in masks.

But no country in the world was as paranoid and terrified of corona as China, the place where it originated. At this moment, while in Miami nobody remembered what corona was or what a mask was, in China one could see squads of medical workers and riot police in fully-enclosed hazmat suits marching through cities, performing mass testing or enforcing quarantines of entire apartment blocks.

When I was in business school in Paris, people discussed the merits of working in various places where they were offered jobs, usually dismissing the political environment and focusing on the money. "Why do I care about the political system there? As long as I stay out of politics, and make enough money, it won't affect me!"

So some of my fellow students went to Moscow, where they ended up in a place crippled by economic sanctions, with flights nearly cut off, and the threat of arrest for saying the wrong thing about Ukraine. Some went to Qatar, where they faced mandatory facemasks outdoors for many months with heavy fines for non-compliance. Others ended up in Shanghai, where it was alright until 2020, when it became *1984*.

China applied lockdowns selectively, only for specific regions where cases were found. When Omicron cases were discovered in Shanghai (98% of cases were asymptomatic), the city of 25 million was kept literally imprisoned under house arrest for 2 months. A Chinese lockdown is not like a French or Italian one, where people were at least allowed to shop for food sometimes. Nobody was allowed out of their homes. An army of 11,000 workers delivered food in hazmat suits.

Of course there was a struggle for everyone to have enough food. People bartered for it within their apartment buildings, sometimes able to find what they needed.

Occasionally, if a cluster of corona cases was identified, there would be a surprise mass deportation. Buses would come to an apartment building and forcibly transport residents to immense quarantine gulags, where people were held in small cells in isolation for a period of time, hazmat-suited workers walking around distributing food rations like in prison cells.

Some smaller cities, like Yuzhou, were locked down after the discovery of just 3 asymptomatic cases.

At times without a lockdown it was still tense, with masks, frequent testing, and contact tracing. BBC showed video footage of a crowd of people overpowering guards and escaping from one of the doors of a Shanghai Ikea, where authorities were trying to barricade them in to quarantine them because one person inside the store was a close contact of another person who tested positive. It was bad to be a 'close contact' of a positive case. All these people would get a change of their permission status on their phone, requiring them to drop what they're doing and immediately isolate themselves at home.

Earthquake rescue workers were unable to get to the site of a urgent disaster to do their job until testing negative for corona.

China decided that nothing is worse than the risk of getting corona. This is despite the example, right next door, of Japan, which had no mandatory shutdown at any point and things were fine, with one of the world's lowest fatality statistics. The low fatality rate might be a factor of genetics, with East Asian people having more natural immunity to this category of viruses than Europe and America. Perhaps another factor is less kissing. A group of French or a group of Brazilians cannot part with each other until each person has kissed each other person twice on the cheek. In Geneva it's even more – they go for the triple kiss. Meanwhile Japanese like to do a slight bow at a distance and rarely even shake hands.

China's approach, the opposite of Japan, its totalitarian biomedical enslavement of society, was something more absurd than the nightmares of Kafka and Orwell put together. One thing that must have been extra painful for the people enduring it was the humiliation and indignity of all of it – the shame of being treated like an enslaved convict or an animal, to be stripped of one's dignity as a human being. Being subjected to forcible imprisonment by some obtuse minor bureaucrat, one's apartment building encircled by a barrier, not able to get out, not knowing how long this will last. And for what? For no reason. The danger was fake; it was invented, the people made to believe it was a black death when it was merely an abnormally severe cold. In Japan next door people were living normally.

China scared the world so much through its overreaction that foreign companies have started to pull their operations out – nobody trusts the country anymore to risk living there.

Globally, most countries' reactions to corona were consistent with their past tendencies, but some were a surprise. China was already known to be a dictatorship, so its approach was not very surprising. France and Lebanon had ongoing rebellions they needed to control, so their eagerness to lock down was understandable. But Belarus was surprising – the least free country in Europe, a backwards dictatorship – was one of the only ones that denied the risk of corona. When I was in Minsk before the pandemic it felt like a relic of the Soviet Union. I visited the Stalin Line, a museum of WWII fortifications where, since it was the Belarusian independence day, a display of nationalistic military strength was exhibited, with tanks showing their agility in rolling over cars and blowing up targets. Many of the spectators were waving red USSR flags. But, surprisingly, given that it is essentially a smaller version of Russia, and that in Russia at this time lockdowns were being enforced, the fact that Belarus went the other way and had the wisdom to keep life mostly normal during corona, without much restrictions, is very commendable.

The US, Switzerland, and Japan were consistent with their values and they were relatively more free than countries in their region – nothing very startling here. But Australia was a surprise. I did not expect that a country with such notable traditions of individualism and economic freedom would break the record of having the longest lockdown in the world – 262 days in Melbourne.

The Novak Djokovic story sums up how twisted Australia had become. Djokovic, the world's #1 ranked tennis player, was going to Australia to compete in the games. He obtained an exemption from Australia's vaccination requirement on the grounds that he already had corona and developed immunity from that. When he arrived in Australia the exemption was overruled and he was detained in a quarantine facility under extremely poor conditions. His lawyers fought the decision and he won in court and was allowed to stay.

However, public opinion was against him. 71% of polled Australians wanted him to be deported. The Australian Minister of Immigration intervened and revoked Djokovic's visa, on the basis that the government has the right to selectively deny someone a visa if they are deemed to be a threat to the public interest. Djokovic was deported and couldn't compete in the Australian Open.

Clearly, vaccines are a benefit to most people, as they do help to slightly improve immunity to corona, but are not necessary for all. Djokovic was right that judging the benefit was his call to make, not the state's. Why was he forcibly deported from Australia? Not because he was hurting anyone. Because his thinking was too contrary to the collective group-think.

* * *

After Miami I decided I would go south, and work remotely for three weeks from Medellín, where I had some friends. And I came up with the idea of spending a few days to chill in Cartagena on the way to Medellín.

I knew that Verônica could not visit me in Colombia because she was busy with college. Also it was very far from the south of Brazil and would require two airport transfers, in both São Paulo and Bogotá, to get to either Medellín or Cartagena. I could have offered to Chiara or another friend to come with me to Cartagena but there was in fact nobody I more wanted to come than Nadia. So I asked her, although conscious of the fact that it was a long-shot. Clearly we got along in an cordial way, but there was no attraction from her side – she didn't think it worthwhile to see me in 5 months except one time, nor to communicate at all – so why would she agree to drop everything, including her job which is on the weekend, and go to South America with me? But to my surprise, she agreed.

Still incredulous of this as we met in her apartment, she washed away any of my tenseness with multiple offers of tequila shots. We had more in the MIA airport lounge, and more on the plane, a tiny Avianca jet where we had seats 1A and 1B. Everything had changed – seeing her again that day had been enough to elevate my soul. The gaze in her eyes cleared away the dark shroud of melancholy enveloping me, like when we go outdoors on the first bright day of spring and are bewildered by the freedom of the air, being able to walk without the winter's dark and cold oppression. There had been barely any affection when we met earlier in Miami – now our closeness and contact increased more and more as we sat next to each other on the plane, no armrest between us. In one moment she even kissed me.

Do not ask me about what relationships and flings she might have had in the months past; nobody is ever aware of the true multitude of secrets that govern a woman's decisions and affinities. Not thinking of the past or the future, I was content in this moment, of feeling warmth from her, of being able to kiss her in the midst of an intimate conversation.

In addition to drinking wine, of course kissing was another reason why it was essential to remain without masks on the plane.

For some of the flight I was reading Marquez's *Love in the Time of Cholera*, coincidentally also set in Cartagena, but in the 19th century. Some of the events take place against the background of intermittent cholera epidemics, which one of the main characters, a doctor and epidemiologist, tries to curtail. Similar to how it was during the coronavirus pandemic, some of the methods thought effective against cholera were actually meaningless – for instance, the garrison fortress fired a cannon once every quarter hour because it was thought gunpowder purifies the atmosphere.

When we landed and were waiting to have our passports checked, next to us was a frightened-looking girl whose face was barely visible because of her glasses and N95 mask. Nadia and I, of course did not have any masks because it was extremely rare that someone in an airport terminal would ask for it. Even when Nadia wore a mask, her's was made of a mesh fabric that was completely unobstructive to breathing. From a distance, it looked like a real cloth mask.

I told the girl that it wasn't necessary for her to continue wearing this mask in the airport. She was surprised. She rather questioned why we weren't wearing one.

Nadia said, "They're going to tell you to take it off anyway, when they stamp your passport."

"So I'll do it at the last moment, when I reach there."

"Aren't you coming from Miami too?" Nadia asked. She was right to be confused – something wasn't adding up.

"Yes, but I only transferred in Miami. I'm coming from Germany."

That explained it. Germany was one of the countries with strict mask mandates and a corona-believing population. For some states in Germany, a cloth mask mandate wasn't enough and they required people to wear more obstructive N95 masks. The effect was the same as the firing of cannons in 19th century Cartagena. The virus didn't care about masks – it came and went in a series of waves. When a wave came in Spring 2021, it was identical in magnitude in Bavaria, with an N95 mandate and shutdowns, as in bordering Switzerland, which was relatively free. I was in Switzerland skiing during that time and masks (or scarves) were only asked for occasionally, on trains and cable cars.

It turned out that this, in the end of January 2022, was her first trip out of Germany since corona began. We told her about Miami and she couldn't imagine how free people were living there all this time.

*   *   *

Cartagena de Indias is the most beautiful city in the Caribbean region. One can wander its streets for hours amidst ancient churches, pink and red bougainvillea spilling out over balconies, and glimpse the sea from the top of the old stone walls surrounding the town. The sun is scorching, 32° every day, but it is not unpleasantly hot, since it's not humid in the winter.

The city is so old there was nothing on the Atlantic coast of the US when it was founded. Boston was settled 100 years later. When all of America, from California to Peru, was under the Spanish crown, Cartagena was its main port. Once or twice a year, heavily armed convoys of Spanish galleons would sail from the West Indies to Spain. They would store their silver and gold and spices in Cartagena until the journey.

At the time Charles V was the Emperor of both Spain and Austria, Henry VIII had just married Anne Boleyn in London, Ivan the Terrible was trying to form a tsardom out of the Duchy of Moscow, and Roxelana was Queen in Constantinople. Perpetually, England and Spain were at war, and at one point Francis Drake, with 30 ships, briefly managed to capture Cartagena from Spain.

Despite its history, Cartagena is not like a museum city overcrowded with tourists. Most visitors are Colombian from other parts of the country. It retains the authenticity of a seaport city, especially in the grittier Getsemani area. Prostitutes stand around the main square next to the clocktower, and the streets are filled with drug smugglers offering their products. Police only care about collecting bribes.

When we got to the city it was already night, so we went straight to El Baluarte, one of the bars on top of the fortified wall, then the rooftop at Mar y Zielo to eat, then Alquimico, the famous cocktail bar. It was my third time in this city and the best places to go had not changed. It felt amazing to be back in these familiar places again with someone I adored as much as Nadia.

When we returned to the hotel, we sat on the bed drinking wine and talked about I don't know what until 5:00. She was beautiful – hair in a ponytail, sitting up on the bed just wearing panties and a long sleeved short pullover. Her hourglass waist (with a navel piercing) and slender legs were very tanned.

We did not do anything more than kiss, but sharing a bed with her was a sweetness, being such a contrast from the days in which she could not even find time to see me in Miami and I thought I completely lost her as a friend. When I woke up, and felt a contact with her, having discovered that in the midst of the repositionings throughout her sleep she had happened to move closer and her arm was laying on top of my arm under the cover, I was happy.

In the morning we saw that the windows opened directly onto the cupolas of the San Pedro church, with the triangular Plaza de la Aduana below. The pure bright yellow of the building across the street contrasted with the blue of the sky, drowsy sounds of horse carriages and bells reaching our floor. In the Sophia hotel, one of the advantages was the ability to take breakfast at any time. There was a menu, you could order from it once per day, and it didn't matter at what time. Normally, hotels only allow breakfast up to a certain deadline, and if you want to partake, you must suffer the hardships of setting an alarm and rushing downstairs at an excruciatingly early hour, in a stupor of reawakening. Why is this the norm? More hotels should emulate the breakfast concept that was so convenient here.

Nadia got sangria with breakfast and then more sangria and we carried it up with us to the rooftop pool. She was drinking constantly now at this period of time, right from the start of the day. She claimed that she needed it, which must be true, but it's unfortunate to be so reliant on it. And there's no way to stop.

One of my friends from Medellín was in town, Sean, and we met up with him at Café del Mar. Sean was originally from British Columbia, but relocated to Colombia. At the same time, Nadia's friend from Bogotá, Angelina, was also here for the weekend and joined us. We drank more and walked around the town. Nadia was in short black shorts, making her legs appear long even in shoes that were almost flat. Her hair was long and straight, and colored slightly lighter brown than before. She spread so much tantalizing energy from her presence I thought –

How could anyone be without her? It was a pleasure to look into her blue eyes; seeing them would lighten any room.

I do not like drinking during the day, only at night, but all three of them were greatly in favor of it and I kept up. Nadia had already acquired a small bottle of aguardiente and was carrying it with her. Angelina had a bag of cocaine, which she opened to take some while we were in a taxi, Nadia at the same time taking sips of aguardiente. The driver didn't care.

Despite Angelina and Sean living in the country, they generally relied on me to figure out the geography of the city and where to go. I recommended to get dinner at Niku, a discretely elegant Japanese-Peruvian place with a dark open-air interior courtyard filled with trees. Later, it was Sean who found out about a new nightclub that just opened, Seven in Getsemani, and we went there. Sean got a bottle of Havana Club and we drank some in the club's rooftop where a DJ was spinning house.

At some point in Cartagena she was finalizing plans with some wealthy benefactor in Los Angeles to get flights to go visit him after she is back in Miami. She was unashamed of this and even described how prosperous of a garage he had, where she could choose among many interesting cars to drive. This disappointed and disgusted me. I understood why she so often happened to be in California, where she knew a lot of wealthy people. It perturbed me that she was already, just after seeing me, already making plans to go visit someone in Los Angeles. I cautiously inquired what her thoughts on getting married were, but unfortunately her point of view was still the same as it was in France. She had a desire for constant variety, rendering her incapable of not getting bored in a relationship that requires commitment and exclusivity. This was the opposite of me, since I valued stability far more than variety. I found out that even when she was in her last long-term relationship, before I met her, and living together with a guy in New York, she still did things like leave for a week to travel to Dubai at the invitation of some patron who gave her gifts. She told me that she could only be convinced to get married if it secured a reasonably wealthy and comfortable lifestyle. It is not because she was spoiled or materialistic and couldn't survive without wealth. I saw how she took trips by herself to London, Berlin, and other places, staying in the cheapest of hostels, and was content with that. It is rather because she did not want to permanently withdraw herself from the freedom of her single life, unless the offer secured her exceptionally well economically.

When I first met her in Miami, I recognized that it would be difficult to keep the attention of such an attractive girl with so many connections and acquaintances. I kept trying though, because I thought there was progress and she made me think that the chance existed.

She told me stories about her life I didn't know, like how bad the Houston suburbs were. It was a place of tedium where young people had absolutely nothing to do, so everyone did drugs. The crowd she was in turned to progressively stronger items; they would have crazy sprees. Many people she knew had died from drug-related causes, for instance overdosing, driving, or drowning. Sensing it was an abyss, she got out of there, collecting all her belongings into a car and moving to Las Vegas, where she got a job as a bartender. She continued talking, about traveling more than once across the country with no money sleeping in a car, being arrested for various things and mistreated by the police. Listening to this I thought, is this real, or did she just come out of the crazy world of a Dostoyevsky novel? I was amazed she survived through all this (not to mention her earlier, even worse troubles in the Beirut wars) to be so beautiful and gracious.

* * *

The weekend was over; she went north to Miami, I went south to Medellín. We parted affectionately at the airport with embracing and kissing. I was missing her terribly right after.

It's worth mentioning again, that if not for the corona pandemic, I would not have had a chance to become acquainted with her at all. In normal times I would not have been in Miami for the winter, and she would not have needed to stay with me as she did in January 2021. It would be an incorrect and irrational way of thinking to find fault in anything about her, since it was exactly the way she was that led to us to being right for each other to become acquainted at that moment. If she was in any way different she would not be available or amenable when we met.

Now that I know her, could I wish that she could change? Of course. Undoubtedly, if she met someone she really liked then she would compromise on everything – she would forget about variety, and she would even agree to try to reduce her drinking. If she met someone she really liked. That's not me.

In Medellín I stayed at the Charlee hotel, working on work for the company from a desk in the room. It was a good place to be since it has the best rooftop bar in the city, and lots of good restaurants within walking distance. I didn't rent a motorcycle like last time, as I mostly stayed in the Poblado area, except for one time when I rode the cable cars to the favellas. Nightlife was in full swing after the pandemic and the streets were full of people. The disadvantage is that almost nobody speaks English in Colombia.

I prepared myself for the eventual return to New York, where I did not want to go. The only positive was that the winter was almost over, and only a small portion of it would have to be endured there until the spring came. And then what? Walk and bike in Central Park, which I have grown tired of? Bike down the island to go to dinner alone in the Village after work? Drift along and see what happens? We are all drifting, on some haphazard balsa wood contraptions to keep afloat. Some people's contraptions are bigger and more sturdy, but they will sink anyway. It's a matter of time. Feverishly, everyone is engaged in relentless effort, working every day, in the struggle to keep them afloat. Why keep them afloat?

Why work? What for? What do you gain?

This is a serious question. Tell me, if you know something about the world that Tolstoy, Schopenhauer, von Kleist, and Baudelaire have overlooked.

In one of Chekhov's plays, Irina laments, "There will come a time when everyone knows what all this is for, all this suffering, when there will be no mysteries. But in the meantime life goes on... We must work, work and nothing else."

123 years later this time that Irina mentions hasn't come yet.

* * *

Charles Baudelaire was very emotionally affected by the dismal winter rain in Paris; his poetry is saturated with the imagery of the heavy sky pouring out upon the sad world a black daylight more gloomy than nights. At length, he compared the immense streaks of cold rain to the bars of a vast prison: *Quand la pluie étalant ses immenses traînées / D'une vaste prison imite les barreaux.*

Later he would observe the rainwater in the gutters, carrying away the remnants of the night before, the torn up pieces of a rejected love letter, a discarded flower, all the melancholy of living in a bleak and pitiless city.

Ernest Hemingway, who lived in Paris in the 1920s, also wrote often about the gloom of the winter rain. But what do Baudelaire and Hemingway know of rain? They have not seen the kind of rain that I have seen. In New York in the winter it rains harder, more often, and with colder temperatures and stronger wind than in Paris.

When there is a rainstorm and the temperature is around 0° it is so cold that gloves and hat are necessary – otherwise one's hands and ears will begin to hurt; and at the same time one also has to confront with one's umbrella the overwhelming downpour of hard rain and wind. This is very typical in New York. But a more amusing rain is the one that comes after a snowfall. This creates massive puddles, lakes of icy slush that are impossible to walk through, at every street intersection. You could also have freezing rain creating a slippery layer of ice over the snow as you walk, fighting with your umbrella as it inverts against the wind. I am curious to see what kind of poetry Baudelaire would compose about that if he saw it.

Of course, climate is a marginal element in life – a winter could be completely ignored and unnoticed if one has someone to tightly press against and embrace, if one has warm feelings and affection.

For many of us though, there is rather coldness in totality – coldness in the environment and coldness in affections.

Baudelaire's existence was characterized by constant discontent, an acute *Weltschmerz*. He had a desire, a yearning, one could even say a suffocating anxiety, to get away from everything, to go somewhere else, "Anywhere! anywhere! so long as it is out of the world." *N'importe où! n'importe où! pourvu que ce soit hors de ce monde!*

> Take me away, carriage! Carry me off, frigate!
> Far, far away! Here the mud is made with our tears!
> *Emporte-moi wagon! enlève-moi, frégate!*
> *Loin! loin! ici la boue est faite de nos pleurs!*

Baudelaire's restlessness made me think of something I had read in Dostoyevsky's prison memoirs. This is a book that I have opened up again and again over the years. Sometimes it would give me comfort, to see how the mighty author was coping with his own lot of hard-labor and loneliness, when afflicted by those things myself. In one part he describes convicts escaping from a Siberian labor camp, even though they are aware that there is nowhere they could possibly go. They are deep in Siberia; it is thousands of kilometers to the nearest city. The only way they could theoretically make it is by murdering someone and stealing their passport, but even that doesn't guarantee they won't be found. Practically everyone who escapes is eventually caught and sent back. Yet they continue escaping.

When the convicts were interrogated as to why they escaped, many of them repeated the same thing: they wanted to *change their lot*.

> Any fugitive envisages the possibility, not so much of gaining complete freedom – he knows this to be almost unattainable – as of landing in a different institution, being sent off to a settlement, or standing trial again for a new crime committed in his wanderings – in short of going no matter where, so long as it is not back to the old place which has grown so tiresome to him, not back to his former prison.

When life is too intolerable or unbearable, under whatever constraints and burdens that make each of our own lives a prison, the impulse of getting away grows and one thinks of *changing one's lot*, even if it is totally unknown if one will be worse off. I recognize that this was the primary motivation for me in the past, when I went from Paris to New York more than 10 years ago, without a clue as to whether it would improve my life or not. I did not benefit from the change. Now I decided that it is unendurable to be here any more, and to try to move to London.

One could also end life entirely – that would undoubtedly make one better off, but it is final and irreversible and thus we hesitate. Eventually logic and rationality should prevail, the more our unlikely remote chances for something good happening diminish and diminish. In the meantime we could seek to change our lot in some way.

But how far can one travel? Is anywhere far enough to effectively change one's lot? One of the draws of travel is the desire to see if there is a place that is different from the purgatory we know. I've been everywhere – there is no such place. I traveled east, continually going further and further east until ending up back in New York. In fact I did this on three occasions, circumnavigating the globe like Francis Drake. But the human condition is the same everywhere.

The English reading public usually demands some kind of dramatic ending to a plot. But I'm not going to give them that, as it would be inconsistent. Of course, what I would like to have happen is to discover, against all probability or plausibility, that the entire Earth is a hollow sphere filled to the brim with fine grain black gunpowder, and to hold a match to it and blow it all up in a giant puff of white smoke. Pufff. Nothing is left except a puff of smoke particles traveling throughout the galaxy. But that would be a happy ending, and we won't have a happy ending to this story. I already mentioned, did I not?, that everything would be downhill after the first sentence of this book. The story merely fades away, like a lost love, like misguided hopes, like futile plans, like life.

Map of Manhattan

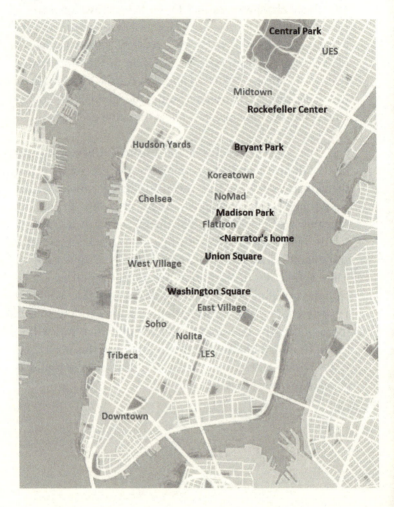

327

Map of Miami

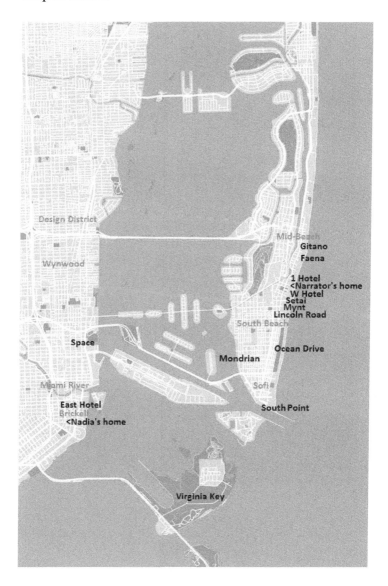

About the author

Ron Cogan is a New Yorker who has also lived in Milan and Miami and has origins in Rīga, Latvia. He works in banking.
< https://www.linkedin.com/in/roncogan1 >

The photos opposite were taken on the Miami River in December 2020, Stockholm in July 2020, and San Francisco in May 2021. The photo above is from Cartagena in January 2022.

Island in the Sea of Time, the author's second novel, was written in New York (along with a small portion in Cape Town) over the period of August 2022 to May 2023.

Made in United States
North Haven, CT
05 June 2023